Secrets of Peaceful River Valley

A Ponte Vedra Series

Suzanne Sinclair

For more information, email hello@SuzanneSinclairAuthor.com.

ISBN: 979-8-89694-144-6 - Ebook

ISBN: 979-8-89694-145-3 - Paperback

Dedication

To my Mom and Dad, now one in heaven,

Every memory we shared is a treasure I hold dear, a comfort in the void your absence has left. I miss you each and every day, with a longing that words can scarcely capture.

This book is a tribute to you both. Mom, your endless support and the encouragement to write were the kindling for this flame. Oh, how my heart aches for you to be here, turning these pages, your laughter filling the room like sunlight. Dad, your teachings on resilience, work ethic, and the faith you nurtured within me—these are the lights that guide my path. You both remain my greatest sources of strength and inspiration.

With every piece of advice you gave, with each cherished memory, I feel you both beside me. I pray this book honors the profound legacy you've gifted me.

Until the day we reunite.

Saved by Grace,

Your ever-faithful daughter xoxo

Chapter ONE

If comfort food were a human being, it would be personified in my Aunt Dottie and not just because she would arrive, annually, with her box of doughnuts for comfort on this melancholy day. Her hugs were like a warm apple pie enveloping me—comforting, loving, nourishing. Aunt Dottie was the only living relative I knew on my dad's side, and I needed her hugs like a sugar addiction.

She also had the most warped, inappropriate sense of humor. When mom and dad died, she went with me to the funeral home for arrangements and caskets. Amidst solemnity, Aunt Dottie, unsatisfied with the casket prices, let out a series of cusses, gasps, and eye rolls, sending the mortician away. I was mortified, but it got wilder. Aunt Dottie proceeded to climb into one of the coffins on a stand in the 'quiet room', by tipping over a box of urns and using it as a stepladder.

"Get in Kyra. Seeing these things are so expensive, maybe we can see if two would fit in one box. Then we only need to pay for one."

"Aunt Dottie, no. Shhhhh... what are you doing?" I looked around quickly to confirm we were alone. I protested, but it was no use... seeing that old woman hoisting a leg into a coffin in her stretchy leggings and big sweatshirt as she tumbled into the plush white satin lining was enough to make me double over, instinctively folding my arms into my stomach and silent laughing. I tried to breathe in, but I was laughing too hard. The physical reaction of trying to contain my laughter while also not making a peep of noise resulted in my infamous nose snort.

"What do you mean, shhh? I am being quiet, ain't I?" Aunt Dottie giggled and her upper body vibrated up and down as she tried to contain her laughter. "Get in here next to me Kyra girl... I'll move over some." She felt around for the satin pillow underneath her. "There's only one pillow. They will have to share. Unless we sneak one in from home. Oh, I bet Ken would like that old plaid gold and avocado green pillow from the recliner."

I tried to contain it, but I just couldn't. I stood at the open casket looking down at my Aunt Dottie scooting over, as she smiled up at me. I cried and laughed and cried some more. She was the best memory maker. She invoked feelings in me of warm apple pie on an autumn day. Those memories flooded back into my mind as if they just happened yesterday. But it wasn't yesterday... it was twenty years ago. Twenty years without mom and dad. Enough time had passed that my grief was significantly less. Within the first decade, we transitioned from grieving to celebrating the life and legacy of Kenneth and Katherine. The grief may be less, today, but their memory lives on in my mind. Like watching a time lapsed camera, my grief transitioned from melancholy to pushing through and ultimately embracing the future.

I waited on the front porch swing for Aunt Dottie and enjoyed the quiet solitude only found before sunup. Peaceful River Valley, in May, was the most beautiful time of year. I watched darkness in the sky begin to ombre into lighter shades of blue. I was admiring my lovely May flowers, blooming in an array of happy spring colors as they danced in the zephyr. They lined both sides of the driveway, giving life to the dull gray pavers.

Using the tip of my toes, I reached for the porch and pushed off, causing my swing to rock me gently back and forth. I sipped my coffee, enjoying the calm, until I felt a hot flash begin. I sighed. The hot flash and night sweats that started in my forties were all too familiar. I woke in a pool of my own sweat this morning in a sixty-eight-degree room. I needed a mattress made of ice. God certainly has a sense of humor when it comes to middle-aged women, as sweat dripped from my eyebrow directly into my coffee mug. Well... a little salt in life was hardly something to cry about.

"Good morning, Kyra," said Mr. Packer.

I waved, put down my coffee, picked up the pan with the quiche in it and began walking over to Mr. Packer next door. As I traversed the sidewalk, I noticed two plastic bags at the end of my driveway. I picked up *The Ponte Vedra Parrot* in its plastic bag on the left. *The Parrot,* our weekly paper, was filled with local advertisements and stories. This little newspaper showed up magically every week on my driveway. Today, I had two *Ponte Vedra Parrots.* The second one had to be Mr. and Mrs. Packer's. Halfway up the driveway, Mr. Packer was stepping off his porch in his shorts and a wide-open button-down Hawaiian shirt with a thick cigar hanging out of his mouth. Not smelling the aroma of cigar smoke in the air, I assumed the cigar was not lit. Mr. Packer seemed to be just chewing at the end of it. I was sure Mrs. Packer imposed rules against such lit devices in her lovely home. "Happy Friday, Mr. Packer. I got your paper for you."

"Oh, is it Friday? Thank you, Kyra girl, thank you," Mr. Packer said, standing upright and immensely proud of his grey chest hair atop his firm beer belly. He was not shy and not closing his shirt. "The pill box tells me what day it is now, KayKay."

"Yes, of course. How is Mrs. Packer?" I asked while trying to divert my eyes to the ground where I noticed open-toed shower shoes. The neighborhood gray and white cat rubbed up against his ankle. Without missing a beat, and seeming not to mind the cat, Mr. Packer opened his paper.

"Ethie is good, real good. Oh, we both loved the apple-cranberry cobbler you made us. I ate the whole thing, I think. Ethie barely got a bite. When are you going to open a bakery or restaurant of your own, Kyra girl? Those wholesome treats you make are way better than those grocery store boxed pile of fake treats."

"Oh, Mr. Packer, you are shinin' me on now," I beamed, loving the compliment. "I love it, sir. I'll take it. I'll bake you something again real soon. I'll holler over to Mrs. Packer to get your requests."

"I'll never get in the way of you making me a baked good, Kyra girl. Mrs. Packer is a wonderful cook, but she doesn't bake those treats like you do. Don't suppose you would tell me how you get them to taste so good?"

"Tallow, Mr. Packer. I put it in almost everything. I never use anything but wholesome butter, tallow, or bacon fat. Just like my Grandma used to bake."

"Genius," Mr. Packer said as he folded his paper and placed it under his arm. He took the large rectangular dish from me.

"This one is a quiche. Sausage, cheddar, and potato quiche. This time, I added a spice called Everything Bagel to remind you of those bagels you loved before Mrs. Packer took your carbs away. Sorry about that, Mr. Packer," my eyes instinctively looked up at Mr. Packer while I tilted my head down. My face contorted into an apology, like a puppy dog who wanted forgiveness.

Mr. Packer's face turned sullen, and the corners of his mouth turned down for the first time in the conversation. "No crust on this quiche?" His lips smacked together, making a slightly childlike yummy sound as he lifted the pan above his head to see the underside of the glass dish.

"No sir," I shook my head side to side. "I had strict instructions. No bread or pasta. I don't want Mrs. Packer mad at me now," I stated confidently.

Mr. Packer looked bewildered suddenly. "Kyra. Answer me this. What time do you get up on Friday morning to prepare, bake, and deliver a casserole out here every dan gum week for us by 6 am?"

"Three. Sometimes four. Can't sleep. Wish I could. I like the quiet of the morning before everyone is up or before I start work."

"Well, your meals were wonderful while Ethie was ill. I do really appreciate it, now. But you don't have to keep cooking for us now that she is back to health."

"Is the food going to waste or are you eatin' it up?"

"I'm eating every morsel." Mr. Packer bent down towards me like I was his granddaughter getting a lollipop. I knew he loved the dishes and didn't want them to stop.

"Oh Lordy... here comes your aunt," he said.

I turned and made my way back towards my driveway as I slightly waved my hand at Mr. Packer. I noticed Aunt Dottie pulling up in her golf cart. She was dangerously close to the curb... yep, she went up the curb, drove over my grass, over my flowers, and back onto the driveway.

"When they gonna take away her license, KayKay?" Mr. Packer shouted, watching my eighty-plus-year-old aunt try to get out of the golf cart as gracefully as Inspector Jacques Clouseau.

"Oh my... no. Ain't no one gonna take away her keys," I confessed and walked back home.

"Don't strain anything, Aunt Dottie," I said as I walked towards my driveway. Aunt Dottie grabbed doughnuts from the back seat and limped towards me, waving. It was perhaps the only weight training she had done in a long while, but I was sure relieved to see her. I needed a hug that only a mom type could give.

"Hello, dear. Are you putting on weight?"

"Ouch, Aunt Dottie. Be gentle with me, I'm fragile today," I said as I grabbed the doughnuts from her hands.

She wrapped a comforting arm around my waist as we walked to the front door. "I know you are, dear. Keep your wits about you," Aunt Dottie said.

"I'm trying."

"I know. Death anniversaries are morbid times. Let's celebrate the life they led," Aunt Dottie squeezed me.

I wiped the corners of my tear-filled eyes, one at a time, as I transferred the doughnuts from one hand to another. I felt a hot flash coming on. As we made our way through the front door, I was thankful for Aunt Dottie's hugs, doughnuts... and air conditioning.

I sighed and swallowed my emotions hard, like I was choking back a chunk of gristle. "Yes. I'm a pillar of strength today... for the family," I stated with confident resolve.

"You have always been here for them, Kyra. You don't need to remain the matriarch. They are adults now. You raised them right. You're done," Aunt Dottie said.

"The boys, maybe. But Kat still seems unfocused, lost and fragile," I protested.

Aunt Dottie poured herself coffee. I deposited the doughnuts on the island and pulled a glass serving tray from the pantry. Aunt Dottie silently watched me as I took to task. I arranged all the doughnuts in a half circle, according to the decoration. First the plain doughnuts, followed by the cream-filled and jelly-filled leaning upon the plain doughnuts. I meticulously arranged the icing types perfectly up against the plain and filled doughnuts, avoiding damage to the icing, and starting to fill in the circle. I could feel Aunt Dottie's stare as I worked quickly through the box. I reserved the center for the bear claw and cinnamon rolls. Lastly, the decorated topping doughnuts completed the circle, just barely touching, so as not to disturb their decoration.

"Lovely," I said as I finished. I looked up to find Aunt Dottie raising her eyebrows at me with her stare.

"What?" I shrugged, grabbing napkins.

"What was wrong with leaving them in the box?" Aunt Dottie questioned with a smirk.

"Just making them pretty," I said looking away as if my obnoxious need to make everything in my world aesthetically pleasing was a sin.

"My darling, Kyra." Aunt Dottie hugged me and there it was... the feeling of warm apple pie. Aunt Dottie continued as I sank into her embrace, as if I relished the comfort of a time-tested chair. "Kat is fine. She is an attorney now and almost the age you were when they died. It's you who needs to move on and stop arranging doughnuts for them as if they can't help themselves."

"Can you be an attorney without a job as an attorney? No, she is a wandering genius with no law career. She is lost. Lost but adorable. So, yes... she does still need my guidance."

"She took the bar and passed... so quickly. I can't imagine what it must be like to be that smart and still stay sane," Aunt Dottie half laughed and shook her head.

"But she has not even looked for a job." I studied the tray and consulted the doughnut oracle for the morning's biggest decision.

"She is just taking some time. She will figure it out." I carefully studied the tray, feeling Aunt Dottie's intense scrutiny on my back, a silent pressure in the still air of the room. "Oh Kyra, your parents would be so proud, my dear. You have done a spectacular job with them. Let's focus on you now for the next 20 years," as she stood beside me and brushed wisps of hair out of my eyes.

I cut the cinnamon doughnut in half, dipped it in my coffee, and enjoyed the sugar dissipating on my tongue. My eyes instinctively closed and rolled back in the enjoyment of the rare sinful treat as I tried to ignore Aunt Dottie.

"Kyra, honey, are you listening to me?" I braced myself, the smell of her lavender perfume heavy in the air, as I faced Aunt Dottie, knowing a lecture was imminent. "Quit playin' pack mule. It's high time you go build the life you've been too busy to dream up." Aunt Dottie held my shoulders tight as she reached up to kiss my forehead.

"Nah... I'm good," I said with a mouth full of doughnut.

Chapter TWO

Twenty years ago, mom and dad died together, leaving me as the caretaker for my twin brothers, Ken Jr. and Killian, and a very small child, Katherine Anne Teresa. I was catapulted into a single mother role in my late twenties. Thankfully, I had a stable job that allowed me to keep a roof over their heads. I could not bear to deposit them into the world of someone else to raise. I had to man-up, so to speak. It was important that we stay together. No doubt I would raise them, as Ken and Katherine would have raised them. My sole purpose was to provide and feed them with love, good food, laughter, education, and churchin'. This weekend, the twentieth anniversary of their death, would be difficult. But we had one another and we could get through it. I would be strong for them this weekend, I told myself. We would survive this anniversary as we had all the others.

I gazed into the picture frame of mom and dad on my fireplace mantel in the living room. I kissed my fingers and placed them gently on the center of the frame. "Miss you every day, Mom and Dad," I whispered softly to the picture and then prayed for strength for this upcoming weekend.

At that moment, Aunt Dottie returned from waking sleeping beauty. My little sister, Katherine Anne Teresa or Kat for short, said "Morning," as she poured herself a cup of coffee and added a swirl of honey.

"Morning, sleepy head. Thanks for taking the day off with me. We can go to the beach and grocery shop for dinner this evening. We can even go for a bike ride to the Palm Valley bridge," I added as I sat in the chair in the living room.

Aunt Dottie and Kat both grabbed doughnuts and their coffee, slowly making their way towards the living room. Kat was looking outside towards the courtyard. "No, not this year."

"No, as in no bike ride to the bridge this year?" I glanced over at Aunt Dottie who was swinging her legs up onto the couch and now reaching for her coffee on the coffee table a mile away. I leaned forward and handed it to her. She blew me a kiss and smiled.

"Correct. I do not want to go for a bike ride this year to the spot where Mom and Dad died. I think we should put that annual ritual to bed," Kat said nonchalantly as she sat in the chair across from me.

"I'm surprised."

"I know you are. It's okay. Thanks for asking, though," Kat said quietly.

We all sat sipping our coffee, listening to the peaceful piano songs from the morning playlist. I remembered twenty years earlier, when Kat asked me to take her to the place where Mom and Dad died.

We both stood at the construction cones on the west bank of the intra-coastal waterway, known as "The Canal" to the locals. The Palm Valley bridge was a drawbridge back then with road made of brick. The same brick at the entrance of The Ranch, the subdivision in which we live. Peaceful River Valley was steeped in such amazing history. The bridge was renovated and now soars sixty-five feet into the air with smooth concrete.

We sat that evening at the construction cones and fixated on *the spot*. I recall Kat in pig tails holding her stuffed little white lamb. The very first stuffed animal Mom & Dad gave her as a baby. It was a musical wind-up lamb that played "Mary Had a Little Lamb." It was in her crib and bed with her throughout childhood. She had the lamb, that first time we sat by the canal. She wound it up and played that song a dozen times while she sat on my lap holding the lamb, looking out at the spot.

When the music played the last time, Kat asked "What happens now?"

"I guess we will be sad now," I said as I cradled her in my arms as she sat on my knees. "We will be sad because they are no longer with us every day, here on this Earth. But we will never forget them. They are part of our souls. We come from them, and souls don't forget their origin."

"Will you stay with me, KayKay?" Kat said, using my only nickname, a nickname provided by her because she could not say Kyra.

The Ring chime announced the front door opening and jarred me back to present day reality. We all turned to see Jess, my closest and dearest best friend, walking towards the coffee and doughnuts. Her sun-bleached chestnut hair was cascading down her shoulders in freshly washed soft tendrils. Her upturned brilliant blue eyes looked directly at me. "King family... why is your door unlocked at seven in the morning for every ruffian to walk in and steal all y'all?"

"Hi Jess." I blurted out with a laugh. "Ruffians? In Peaceful River Valley? Doesn't happen." Jess made me laugh even on a sorrowful day as today. Jess and I had been best friends since growing up together in Palm Valley, on the other side of the canal. We did everything together from activities like shopping and running to more strenuous activities like surfing and kayaking. I've always considered shopping an activity if you do it right and fully commit to it. We did less surfing now in our fifties and more pickleball. But every Saturday morning, we still kayaked together. "Come on in here and take a load off," I said.

"Yeah, come on into the living room with your doughnut on the only day of the year we are allowed to eat doughnuts or eat anything at all in the living room," Kat teased.

"Now, now. Kyra runs a very organized and tidy home. Unlike the tornado of a space, I like to call home. We all have different styles," Aunt Dottie shrugged and grinned as she continued to sip her coffee.

"Thanks, I'd love to eat in the living room. But I have to get to work," said Jess as she tore into a doughnut and left the remainder on the glass tray. She headed toward me, and I could feel the emotion overwhelming me. We hugged. She squeezed me tight and whispered "I got you" into my ear.

Those were the same words she said to me twenty years ago when I told her my parents died and crumbled into a limp, bawling bag of bones. We'd been best friends since the age of six and had seen all the trauma, happiness, sadness, joy, pain, and torment in one another's lives. We knew each other's buttons and how to press them. She knew the names of all the skeletons in my closet, and I knew hers.

"I wish you could stay, but I know how much you love your work." I squeezed Jess harder. "We will see you tonight for the life celebration, right?"

"Yes, absolutely. Be here around six-ish." Jess pulled away and winked at me. She diverted back towards the doughnuts, held her latest selection into the air, and headed towards the front door. "Good-bye King family."

When I sat back down, Kat stood up and said, "I'll go get ready. Can we go into town center and grab a croissant sandwich before we head to the beach?"

"Yes, of course," I said as Kat was already exiting the room down the gallery hall towards her room. Turning to Aunt Dottie, who was now lounging on the sofa reading her digital book, I asked, "You look comfy, Aunt Dottie. Are you coming with us to the beach?"

"That depends, dear. Is there sand there?"

I burst out laughing. "Yes, afraid so."

"Then no, thank you. I wanted to start the Italian gravy and meatballs this morning."

"That sounds wonderful. Everything you need is in the fridge. I'll pull out the spices for you and leave a chunk of parm cheese on the island with the grater."

"Thanks. I'll be done and have the kitchen clean before you all get back," she blew me a kiss and went back to her reading.

A phone was ringing, as if it was muffled by cushions. I walked to the chair where Kat was sitting. Her phone was buried between the cushion and the chair arm. By the time I fished it out from the chair cushion, it stopped ringing. I started walking towards the kitchen island and yelled down the hallway to Kat's bedroom. "Kat, your phone is ringing." I placed Kat's phone on the island, and she appeared from her room.

"I forgot my phone," Kat grabbed the phone and flipped it to recent calls.

"Who's calling you so early, this morning?" Aunt Dottie asked.

"I don't know, actually. The same number has been calling, multiple times this week," Kat emphasized the word multiple and included a head jab that made me smile. "It's not spam."

"What's the area code?" I asked.

"904. No messages. I'm not sure I want to call back, if they don't leave a message. I wish they would just leave a message," Kat said with another head jab.

"Well, if you call back, you will be able to find out who it was that called, right? It still works like that, no?" Aunt Dottie said in a questioning tone followed by a belly laugh.

"Ha..." I snickered. "Kat only wants to text on the phone. I'm not sure if she knows that we all used to talk to one another, on phones attached to the wall, for hours back in the days of my youth. Kat, did you try texting the number?"

"No, I've not texted it. What would I say? Stop calling me, psycho?" Kat said instinctively, making us both smile.

"I feel like we are trying to solve a little mystery, like Nancy Drew," Aunt Dottie said as we both nodded to one another.

"Who?" Kat said.

A smirk played on my lips as I watched Kat, trying to discern if her reply was meant to be humorous. Nope, she was stone cold serious. "Oh no, Kat, really?" I rolled my eyes and turned on my heels, leaving the room to prepare for my relaxing beach excursion.

Chapter THREE

I hopped in the Moke and turned the key, threw the shifter into reverse, and released the emergency brake. Backing out of the garage, I did a quick k-turn and parked in the driveway, waiting for Kat. The Moke was a type of electric golf cart that had an iconic design meant to turn heads. In Peaceful River Valley, most everyone had a golf cart or Tesla or both. EV charging was plentiful in town center, as were the golf cart parking spots. Often, the traffic was worse on the golf cart paths than the streets.

Kat bounced out the front door in a white see-thru, knee-length cover up with a black bikini bottom and long sleeve rash guard. Her beach ensemble was topped off with a huge floppy straw hat, humongous beach umbrella, and a towel that was three times the size of her. Her beach bag, made of straw, was enormous. It barely fit on the floorboards of the back seat. She wrestled it onto the floor.

"Ready" I said to Kat?

"Let's roll." Kat slapped her hands on her bare legs.

"Ever wonder why there are no golf courses here given the disproportionate number of golf carts?"

Kat was adding sunglasses to her face, as she gently avoided the white zinc on her nose. "Huh. I never thought of that."

"Ironic, right," I said as I threw the shifter to drive and slammed on the go pedal and sped out the driveway.

We live in a palm tree paradise. My little subdivision is called The Ranch. The Ranch is one of many subdivisions in our community which is called Peaceful River Valley, in the town of Ponte Vedra, Florida. The Ranch is a small, secluded neighborhood, eight minutes exactly to Mickler Beach in the east and four minutes to Town Center west of us, where Kat was desperate for her croissant sandwich. I selected this little community because it was quaint, idyllic, and nestled between one hundred-year-old mossy oaks and palm tree preserves.

"Dunkin or Panera," I inquired?

"Dunkin," Kat said with her nose in her phone and her left hand scrolling frantically.

I didn't mind Kat not talking to me. I could enjoy our ride and view the neighborhood decorations. Summer was upon us and Memorial Day in Peaceful River Valley meant the American flag gloriously displayed on almost every house on the block. Traditional style porches displayed half-moon pleated heritage flags. White rocking chairs adorned with red, white, and blue pillows. Tin planters bursting with big blue hydrangeas, white wildflowers, and red carnations. The occasional smaller yard flag that simply says, 'God Bless the USA'.

As I neared the entrance to The Ranch, I slowed my speed and came upon the dreaded golf cart traffic for bus departure. A boy on an EV scooter whooshed by me rushing to the bus stop with a dog eagerly chasing after him. Friday morning was more social than any other day of the week because it seemed every parent that could work from home on Friday, did work from home. Naturally, they took the kids to the bus stop in their golf cart. Golf carts were parked on both sides of the street as I navigated carefully between them with my senses on high alert, just waiting for a little kiddo or dog to dart out into the street. The entrance was buzzing with younger kiddos chaotically running around, while older kids were standing silently, scrolling on their phones, occasionally glaring at the parents. One cart contained the family dog strapped into the front seat harness as the cart went whizzing by quickly towards the drop off point as we pulled over to the right allowing an oncoming cart to get through the cart chaos. It was an unusual sight to witness... golf cart traffic... and only in Peaceful River Valley. Past the long lineup of parked golf carts, several parents were drinking coffee, chatting in small groups. *Was that woman still in pajamas?* I thought to myself as I did a double take. *That's really happening, huh?* Covid really changed attire. I waved to the neighbors at the bus stop as I inched the Moke closer to the entrance of our community. Lucy, our neighborhood social director, was dressed in jean shorts, t-shirt, and flip flops. Waving to her, she yelled into the air, "Remember book club Monday night, Kyra."

"Oh! Thanks, Lucy," I faked a smile. Dang, I forgot. I picked the book for this month, I gotta finish it. Lucy was the social activity coordinator of all the ladies in The Ranch. She organized our social calendars and kept the activities flowing with fun all month, every month. Book club, Bunko, Halloween cul-de-sac parties, holiday Christmas cookie exchanges, and even squirt gunning the kids when they got off the bus at the end of the school year. Lucy elevated us from living in a community to being a community.

"Did you read the book yet, Kat?" I asked as I turned out of The Ranch, leaving the bedlam behind us and heading west to Town Center.

Not even looking up Kat replied "Ahh... nope."

I made the 'Oh' face and asked, "Are ya gonna?"

"Sure. You selected it this month, right? Some military CIA mystery? It sounded interesting."

"I'm interested...what are you doing on your phone?" I asked.

"I'm stalking an influencer and watching her videos to get ideas on what she is posting and why it is getting traction and interactions."

"Kat, I wish you would spend half as much time focusing on getting into a law firm as you do trying to become an influencer. I don't understand why you have never had a job. I had six jobs at the time I was your age."

I paused and glanced over at her engaged with her phone and said with genuine concern. "Are you addicted to your phone?"

"I know you don't understand. You're old," she sniped.

"What? I am not old." I said in shock. "I'm old-ish... in a really hip... cool, kinda way," I replied with botched confidence and a bruised ego.

"What if I want to be an influencer instead of pursue some stuffy career in law?"

"Oh. Wow. That's not at all what you wanted to do three years ago or even seven years ago. Your entire education for the past decade has prepared you for a career in law. Why would you want to give it up now after you passed the bar?"

"I don't know," Kat said quietly with her head down looking at her fidgeting fingers rotating the phone like a Rubix Cube. "I like making podcasts and being creative. That is what I know right now," she said, as if making up her mind right then and there.

"Are we picking up inside or the drive-thru?" I asked, focusing on breakfast. I drove off the golf cart path at the traffic light and pulled into the parking lot.

"Drive-thru," Kat said, putting down her phone.

I sat quietly while we waited in the drive-thru line. My mind raced to discover a successful strategy to convince Kat of her path towards law. Why go through the grueling work of seven long years of school? Three years of which were all night studying and memorizing, to only then quit after taking and passing the bar? She just studied law for fun, I guess. I felt a hot flash coming on.

I pulled up to the window and gave our name to the attendee and started my battery-operated fan. A fan is a necessity in Florda for women of a certain age. I enjoyed the cool wind on my face. *I'm not old.* "Kat, I understand wanting to have a career that inspires your creative juices."

"You do?" Kat questioned.

"Yeah. I was close to leaving my corporate job once for something that fit my creativity better," I confessed.

"Really? You wanted to do something different than what you do right now? I can't imagine that. You're so good at telling people what to do all the time."

Laughing, I placed my hand on her hand. "I only boss you around."

"Seriously, if there was a female Dilbert character, you'd be her," she teased.

I smiled, secretly thinking, yes, the world of technology is very much like the Dilbert cartoon.

"I'm just sassin' you. But I really do want to know. What did you want to do?" Kat inquired looking at me over her sunglasses.

"Cook and bake and teach others how," I said with a smile. "Kyra's Kitchen or Kyra's Creations is what I would call it. I'd only serve the foods we love and use real wholesome ingredients from local farms."

"Well, that fits. You kinda do that now except you don't get paid for it." Kat winked at me and looked back at her phone.

I sighed and peered off into the lineup of tall, elegant palm trees that lined the main road. I've worked as a Geek Nanny for twenty-five years, but it was a career I was pushed into due to circumstances. Otherwise known as a Project Manager in the Technology industry, a Geek Nanny was my self-imposed euphemism for wrangling tech nerds and engineering geniuses with the patience of a saint. I structured and meticulously planned their existences to achieve corporate objectives and execute high value technology projects. Usually, when I introduce myself to people and provide my thirty-second elevator pitch, I get a lot of blank stares and eye blinking. I work remotely. I appear on camera... from the neck up. I'm literally a talking head. I know this career would have been unfathomable for my mother and father, had they lived longer. Dad worked in the construction industry all his life, which is fairly an 'in person' career. He was happy to put me through college where I majored in nothing related to what I do today.

I was jarred back to my reality when the bag of food was thrust out towards me and dangled. I passed the bag to Kat, who was still stuck to her phone. To reveal even greater distance between the generational reality, dad's youngest daughter, my sister Kat who I raised, has never held a job in her brief existence. She claims she is an influencer. Somehow, she receives money from online supporters and advertisers. Kat also works from our home. When she gives me her thirty second elevator pitch... I blink. I am shocked that people pay her to do... whatever it is she does. It does not seem like a real job. But she is her own boss and works for no one. This I envy.

"Speaking of food... what are you cooking us tonight?" Kat asked as if she sensed me staring at her and knew I dreamt of another life... one in which I cooked for a living.

"To be determined. I must plan both tonight's meal and Sunday Supper at the beach. Any requests?" I chirped as I pulled the Moke out of the drive thru line and almost hit a young woman who popped out from behind the building.

"Hey Kat," the woman, who was dressed shabbily from head to toe, knew my sister. That didn't fit.

"Hey Emi... you need anything?" Kat asked.

"No, I'm good today. Thanks," the woman waved and continued walking, tucking strands of her unwashed hair behind her ear that was littered with piercings. She had several tattoos on her forearm of her right arm in the shape of colorful flowers.

"Kat, that girl looks positively homeless. How would you know her?" I asked genuinely concerned about the woman's health and well-being.

"Well... she is homeless. Her name is Emily. She seems totally fine living in the homeless camp in the preserve." Kat removed her croissant snack from the bag and started munching.

"What? What do you mean? Is that a euphemism I'm too old to understand?"

"Ha... no, not this time. She lives with all the homeless people in the preserve." Kat said while chewing.

"There is a homeless group of people living in Peaceful River Valley... in the swampy preserve?" I was absolutely shocked at how anyone could live amongst the wildlife in the preserve. We have mosquitoes big enough to carry off small animals.

"Yep. I interviewed a bunch of them for a podcast a couple weeks ago. Do you ever listen to my content?" Kat muttered as she chewed sending a sideways glare at me that made me feel so guilty.

"Fascinating, Kat. Does Emily have a last name? Does she have parents there too?"

"Oh you always ask so many questions. You should have been a reporter."

I sighed and took a mental note to pay more attention to Kat's side hustle and cook once a month to bring a home cooked meal to the PRV homeless. Heading east, we returned to the golf cart path and set out towards the bright sun to enjoy Mickler's Beach over the bridge, in Ponte Vedra Beach.

Chapter *FOUR*

P eaceful River Valley, at one time, was a swampy stretch of land between US 1 and the canal. The Palm Valley bridge, over the canal,
transported happy people to the pristine beaches of Ponte Vedra. However,
the bridge over the canal held a traumatic historic event for my family. Tra-
versing the bridge to the beach was never a happy event. As we approached,
Kat stopped eating and I held my breath, as the Moke motored up to the
top of the bridge, allowing us to see clear up and down the intra-coastal
waterway. Early morning boaters, a few people kayaking, canoeing, and
fishing below us completely unaware of our pain. Me holding my breath
and saying a silent prayer for the heavenly souls of our parents who perished
twenty years ago, right here on the west banks of the canal.

I blew out my lungs. Kat looked over and asked "Did you say a prayer?"

"Yes, did you?"

"I said hello to their spirits," Kat said as the Moke cruised away from the
west side of the bridge. She started eating again and turned on the radio.

I whizzed by, keeping both hands on the wheel but still saying "Good
Morning" to the occasional runner or dog walker on the golf cart path from
Peaceful River Valley to Mickler Beach. I was in route to my happy place
and with the tunes rocking, I could allow my mind to calm and seek peace

as I enjoyed the ride. The path was shaded by two-hundred-year-old oak trees with moss streaming down and dancing in the breeze. The eastern sun was gently starting to gleam through the oaks and palm trees leaving the faintest tiger print patterns on the path in front of me.

I could feel happiness and sunshine, breathing into my lungs as the sorrow and bitterness breathed out with every closer inch to the beach. Wafts of coconut oil lotion with the perfect blend of seaweed and salt filled my nasal passages. The scent of Ponte Vedra Beach compelled me to be one with it.

The dunes were in sight. I crossed over A1A with a quick hard right into the Mickler Beach parking area. I popped out of the Moke and kicked off my flip-flops when I reached the sand. Friday morning beach time was bliss, especially in May, when the weather was absolute perfection. I climbed up the stairs to the long, sandy boardwalk and over the dunes. The boards creaked under my feet and alternated with the singing of the seagulls over my head, combining into a delightful melody.

The sun was up, but only barely. Beach walkers, surfers, and loungers were already scattered from north to south. Kat dragged her apparently heavy beach bag behind her while the humongous umbrella teetered on her shoulder.

"Where are you sitting, KayKay?" Kat asked.

I pointed to a vacant spot just above the wet sand. Kat followed. I spread out my towel. The beach chair creaked open while unfolding it and sand fell out. Making myself completely at home on the beach, I sat back, relishing the heat of the morning sun on my skin. My body relaxed hearing each wave lap up onto the shore. I felt absolute peace, with complete and utter solitude. Hard to believe, on a historic day like today, I could feel such peace, but I could and I did. Paradise.

Peace only lasted a minute, as Kat struggled with the umbrella. I stood up and dug out the hole for her while she spread out the six-foot square towel. I thrusted the umbrella, firmly in the hole I dug and once secure in the sand, I cranked it open. "Voila!"

"Thanks, KayKay." Kat plopped down on the towel under the umbrella, making certain not a single portion of her skin was exposed to the sun.

"I appreciate you coming with me today, Kat. I know you don't care for the sun or the beach."

"I don't mind it. It's lovely this time of year, really. I have my camera and equipment with me so I can shoot some photos and videos. That's always great content." Kat picked up the floppy brim of her straw hat and glanced over in my direction.

"I enjoy these moments, just the two of us. Just sisters enjoying the beach life," I said, wishing I did not need to be Kat's mother-type. What would it be like to just be her sister and have fun with her? Was she past the age of youth and innocence? Instead of guarding and protecting her, could I now have a friendship with her? How does one move from mother to sister? There is no instruction manual for that phase in life, but there should be. I started to ask, "Do you ever."

"Do I ever what?" Kat asked as she covered her legs with another towel.

"Never mind," I smiled at her, then placed my head on the chair pillow and sank back into the peace of the beach.

When I woke up from my little nap, Kat was gone. I looked up and down the beach. I spotted her big floppy hat in the distance. She was shooting photos of a dog in the water with a stick. I guess it was time for me to get to work, too. I had meals to plan for the weekend and still needed to find several recipes and create the shopping lists.

Comfort food was on the menu for the night's celebration of life. Aunt Dottie was making the meatballs and the Italian gravy. I could probably do a tray of baked ziti, roasted garlic bread, and pasta fagioli soup. Dessert would need to be something easy like tiramisù. Well... that is a perfect comfort food menu for a sorrowful bunch.

Now, what shall I concoct for the family Sunday Supper, I wondered. Aunt Dottie, of course, would be in attendance. Kat, was a dependable attendee because she lived with me. No move out date was in sight for Kat, to my dismay. I expected her to be in attendance each and every Sunday. Now, will those boys attend?

I quickly grabbed my phone and found my twins text group. "Sunday Supper, 3 pm. Both yes?" Suddenly, I heard Kat's phone ring. She was rarely without her phone, but there it was, protruding out from under her towel. My phone dinged twice.

"Confirmed," came the reply from Ken Jr.

Killian replied, "Wouldn't miss it."

When the twins were younger, they came to Sunday Supper for free food. Then there was a period of missing family Sunday Supper, as they got older, started dating more, and working longer hours. I had to establish rules. They could live their lives all other days and nights. Sunday night was reserved for a mandatory fun night with the family. I wanted mom and dad's children to stay close, connected, and if only once per week... remember what it was like to be a family.

Scrolling through recipes, I gravitated toward something on the light side and spring infused. I flipped through endless recipes on my tablet, finally deciding on scallops with spring pea pesto sauce as an appetizer. Typical spinach and strawberry salad with a feta and raspberry vinaigrette. For the main course, I decided to serve roasted chicken with a garlicky chard. I'd top it off with a dessert like strawberry shortcake, fresh whipped cream, and homemade bourbon vanilla ice cream. Sounded satisfying and would be a challenge to create. I loved a food challenge.

My little sun-filled world in my beach chair went dark as Kat appeared in front of me blocking out all my sun. "Are you almost done relaxing? I got useful content, and I want to get out of the sun now," she stated as she held out her hand for me to get up off my chair and go.

"So pushy. You're not the boss of me," I teased her but then took her hand. She pulled me up, and once I was standing in front of her, she pulled on my swimsuit top string, examining the change in skin color.

"Look at you. Tan as can be. You are not even burning a little. I'm slathered with sun block from head to toe and I'm still burning," she huffed and examined her arms and legs, which were a little pink.

"How did you get sun burn on your forearms... under a long sleeve rash guard?" I asked.

"I'm not sure. I used 30-block," Kat said as she collected her belongings.

"You got Mom's fair skin and light strawberry blonde hair. The rest of us have Dad's skin color." A chirp from an incoming text on Kat's phone interrupted us. "Oh, I almost forgot to tell you... you missed a call." I packed up my few items and was ready to go while Kat was still looking at her phone.

"Ready to go when you are, little Kit Kat," I said, using her childhood nickname.

"Ugh, I don't recognize this number. They didn't leave a message. Stalk-er," Kat said, examining her call log. "Have you finished the menu for Sunday?"

We started our way up the beach and onto the boardwalk over the dunes. "Yes, I've finished the menu and both Kenny and Killian are joining us, so I think we should have supper and then play a few games before you all need to retreat to prepare for Monday. I'll oversee supper; you be in charge of games. Okay?"

"Sure, sounds good," Kat said hopping into the Moke.

"Collaboration. Excellent," I winked at Kat.

"Or did you just Jedi mind trick me," Kat asked with a smile.

"You might never know." I said and eased the Moke out of the sandy beach parking lot. We left Mickler Beach behind us and started our quick trip back to Peaceful River Valley, albeit with sand on our toes. Kat and I were in sync, enjoying each other's company as we reveled in what seemed like the epitome of a perfect morning at the beach. Maybe we were ready to move back to a sisterly relationship rather than pseudo-mother / daughter relationship. I couldn't be certain, but I was hopeful.

We rounded the Mickler circle in Palm Valley. "Kat, do you ever go past our old home or Grandma and Grandpa's old land in Palm Valley?"

Kat looked down the road, "No, it's too depressing. I can't believe they built an entire subdivision on our family land. It's sad."

"At least they kept the old oak trees out front," I said nostalgically. "It's hard to believe that we owned acres and raised cattle here not too long ago. Do you remember that old story about how the cattle would walk off every day at the same time. Turns out they were down at the beach in the water. Then they would go back home to the King plains to eat their hay."

"Yep," Kat continued. "But I like Pop-Pop's tales from his trips to the churches all over North and Central Florida."

"The palm stories," I said nodding my head.

"Yes. When grandma and pop-pop would harvest all the palms off the land and sell them to the nearby Churches for Palm Sunday. Grandpa driving all over north Florida either on a horse hauling a bed of palms or in that old run-down Ford pickup truck. Then coming home with a big wad a cash and we would all get new shoes from his haul."

"Cash was it back in those days. No credit cards or PayPal," I jested.

Kat added, "Nor Bitcoin. Aunt Dottie says that they were in the hooch business too," Kat laughed and held onto her hat as she looked over at me. "Do you believe those stories?"

"True and yes, I do. The best hooch in all of Palm Valley. Almost one hundred years ago, this area was famous for its moonshine. Something to do with the use of the Datil pepper that grows here," I said loudly as I picked up speed over the bridge.

We both went quiet again going back over the bridge. I was intentionally looking towards Kat and north on the intra-coastal waterway. Putting the event of twenty years ago behind me both physically and mentally. Not wanting this banter to end with Kat, I said "Kat, why do you think everyone who doesn't leave a message is a stalker?"

"Ugh, you're such a Boomer."

My eyes nearly popped out of my head. "What? I am not a Boomer. Well... I'm almost a Boomer. It depends on which chart you believe. I'm Generation X," I quipped proudly.

"Whatever," Kat said softly but with pronounced mouth movements as she glared at me from over her sunglasses and pushed them back up her nose.

"Oh no. Just when I thought we were getting along so well," I teased her. "Plus... I'm pretty sure both Boomers and Gen X'ers leave messages."

We made it to the west side of the canal when I could feel the pressure change. I was suddenly aware of the slightest humidity, which is odd for May. Our idyllic atmosphere took an unexpected turn as we pulled into The Ranch. A palpable unease settled over me, and the weather seemed to mirror my internal turmoil. A dark cloud cast a shadow over us. One raindrop. Two raindrops. The sun was gone. Then, a tropical downpour drenching us in our topless Moke. I turned on the windshield wipers. I heard Kat's phone ringing again. As she grabbed it from her bag, it slipped from her wet hands onto the floor of the Moke. The phone continued to ring as we both stared at it on the floor mat. She grabbed it too late. The phone stopped ringing.

The race to cover the last two blocks to the house and dive into the garage was futile. We both emerged soaked from the topless vehicle. Kat was laughing, pulling off the soaked straw hat and squeezing the water out of her gorgeous locks.

"I didn't recognize the phone number, again," she said as she grabbed for a towel on the garage shelf. "But it looks like they left a message this time." An incoming text message beeped on Kat's phone. "Oh, a text message from the same number."

I simply nodded and entered the laundry room for a towel. I entered the house and shivered from the cold air conditioning pouring out of the mudroom. When I returned to the kitchen, I noticed Aunt Dottie was gone, but there was a large Dutch oven simmering on the stove. Kat was sitting at the island.

"Kyra?" Kat's voice sounded perplexed.

"Yes, Kat?" I asked slowly. When I heard no answer, I stopped stirring the gravy and retrieved the oregano and salt from the spice cabinet. I turned to the island where Kat was sitting. She was, unsurprisingly, looking down at her phone. I shook my head and made my way to the fridge for ice water and said again, "Yes, Kat?"

She looked up at me with the same sad look of disbelief as the day I told her there was no Santa Claus. "This text message is from someone named Mac. He says he didn't want to leave a message. He wanted to talk in person. He says he's a relative."

"Wow, really? A relative?" In disbelief, I made my way behind Kat to review the text on her phone.

The text reads "Hello Katherine-Anne. This is Mac, a relative. We don't know one another but I left a voice mail. Did you listen to it yet? I would like to speak with you personally."

"Well, this is exciting. Way better than a stalker," Kat chirped, smiling.

"Haha. Let's listen to the message together," I said. "That ancestry website was a great Christmas gift last year. I'm glad I thought of it for you," I beamed with pride.

"Wait, this is fascinating. It looks like ancestry did contact me. This email says that they discovered kin of 25% from my DNA test that I contributed." Kat paused and re-read. "Kin of 25%". What does that mean, KayKay?"

"You have 50% DNA match with Mom and 50% with Dad. That makes up 100% Kat," bopping her nose with my finger. "25% would be two generations back, if I recall my biology correctly. Perhaps a cousin we never knew about. This is exciting," I bellowed. "I want to hear the message," I said eagerly as I went to the stove to stir the sauce and add more spices.

Kat set the phone on the island, hit the play button, and then speaker. A deep, strong voice said "Hello Katherine-Anne. My name is Mac, and I got your contact information from Ancestry.com. According to our DNA tests, we're related. This says that you are the sister of my mother. That makes you, my aunt. So... it's nice to meet you, Aunt Katherine-Anne. I know this may be a shock. I really wanted to speak with you on the phone rather than leave an impersonal message. If you would like, call me back. I would like to get to know you and meet in person, if you are open to the idea. My mother... your sister... is also anxious to meet you."

Chapter FIVE

"What the actual fudge, Kyra?" Kat burst out loud and looked up at me waiting for a response. When it was apparent I was not going to answer, Kat popped up off the stool and began to pace. "Maybe he's a crazy person. A crazy person has my number." I was staring at Kat as she paused for a moment. "Although he didn't sound crazy." Kat paced back and forth in front of the kitchen island as she continued her diatribe. "He actually sounded sweet on the phone. Like a very sweet, crazy person." Her tone fluctuated wildly with her emotions as she tried to make sense of the caller. "Kyra? Kyra, are you okay? You look pale," She walked toward me as if to catch me.

What was happening? Stepping backwards, I was lightheaded. I had to sit down. Kat was already proactively pulling out the dining chair. I slowly sat down, clutching my ice water to my chest. My mouth was open. My eyes were unconsciously blinking ferociously with my dismay.

"Wha... what did he say? His... his... his mother is your sister?" I was surprised to find the water glass still firmly in my hand as I was numb all over. "No. How could this be?"

Kat had her hand on my back to steady me as I sat. "What? Why would he think that his mother is our sister?" Kat questioned.

My mind was blank, as if my brain suddenly stopped working. I felt utterly speechless. A sister? No, couldn't be. "Kat, this is all very strange," I said as my previous excitement turned to fear of the unknown.

"Mom had another baby?" Kat looked at me with wonder "Do you think that happened before she met Dad?"

"Absolutely not. Mom met Dad in her teens. There was only one man in her life and that was Dad."

"You don't think there is even a chance?" Kat probed.

"Yes, there is always a probability. But, no. I'm telling you... Mom was a young girl when she fell in love with Dad."

"Maybe a secret love she didn't tell anyone about?" Kat continued on.

"Your email didn't say anything about the relation, right? The email just said you have a relative." The words came out of my mouth so calm... much calmer than the words sounded in my head.

Kat sat down at the dining room table next to me. She flipped back to her email. I peeked over her shoulder but couldn't see a thing without my reading glasses. "No. The email says nothing about the relation of the match. But, Kyra... this must be a mistake, right?"

Kat looked into my eyes for answers. I had none. "A mistake? Maybe. I don't know, Kat. It sounds crazy."

Kat continued to look at me, searching my face for answers. "They mixed up our DNA. This is all a misunderstanding. I should email Ancestry.com," Kat said in denial.

"He seemed interested in talking to you. I think we should calm down and give Mac a call back. He could be as confused as we are right now," I said trying to hide my fear.

"We should call him back, yes," Kat parroted, as she continued reviewing her ancestry.com account and the emails about the found DNA match.

"His name is Mac, but I didn't hear a last name. " I drifted to the living room bookcase in a daze. I found the photo album with our family tree in it.

"Are we estranged from any relatives?" Kat asked as I opened the photo album on the dining room table.

"Well, maybe. Dad's side of the family was all Palm Valley. But Mom... her family heritage was a little more of a mystery. She didn't talk to her family after she married Dad," I glanced at each page of the King family tree looking for a clue.

"Probably from Mom's side of the family? We know all these people," Kat said flipping her wrist at the album and pushing it back over to me.

"Wait, hold the phone. He said his mother was our sister and that you were a match to him at 25%. Do you know what that means?" I questioned Kat in a panic.

"I am 100% certain I don't know what that means, Kyra. I didn't take any biology." Kat confessed.

"It means that his mother is also 50% DNA from Mom and 50% DNA from Dad. Just like you. Just like me." Taking in the weight of my own statement, I sat down again next to Kat.

"She is our biological full sister?" Kat asked looking at me for answers.

"Whoa. Maybe we should call Aunt Dottie," I said as I grabbed the hair on both sides of my head, outstretched my elbows, and looked at Kat with wild bewilderment.

"And ask her what exactly? Why didn't you tell us we had a sister we never knew existed?" Kat sniped.

"Yes, exactly." I said as I threw my hands up into the air in exaggerated solidarity. "She must spill the beans. She was always so secretive. I know she knows more than she lets on," I said to Kat, pointing my finger at the family tree album and breathing faster and deeper with an anger that I suddenly became aware of and never knew existed inside me.

We sat for several minutes in the quiet. I tried to calm my mind and body down from the disbelief of this jarring news. I silently thought through all the possible scenarios of what to do from here. My mind drifted to what this news meant to our family, both living and dead. Suddenly, Kat stood up abruptly and looked directly at me. Her intensity meant she had a monumental idea. But then she just pulled a doughnut off the pile and tore it in half and handed it to me with a napkin. I nodded in gratitude. We continued our silence while we nibbled on our treats.

Kat pushed the remaining doughnut into her mouth. "I think you were right initially. We should just call him," Kat garbled with her mouth full of doughnut.

"Don't you think we should calm down first? This information has me reeling with doubt," I said with hesitation.

"I am calm. That doughnut was just what I needed to refocus and gain clarity," Kat smirked.

She was breaking down the armor of doubt around me with her adorable quips. I straightened up in my chair, ready to discuss options. "I am curious if he has any information about how his mother could possibly be our sister."

"I'm skeptical," Kat said as she shook her head and positioned her phone between us both.

"Be kind," I said putting my hand on her hand and squeezing it tenderly. "But inquisitive," I felt a burst of excitement along with a good amount of fear.

"I'll put him on speaker phone," Kat said as she pressed call on his number. The phone ringing was like a gong in my head.

"Hello, Katherine-Anne. It's so wonderful to hear back from you. I know this must be a shock," Mac said in the most genuinely pleasant voice.

"Yes, hello... er, um... Mac. It is quite a shock. I have you on speaker phone. I hope you don't mind. My older sister Kyra is also on the line with us," Kat said, introducing me.

"Hello, Mac. I guess I'm your aunt... Kyra," I said. "And yes, we are in shock here."

"Yes, I'm sure you are, and I was too when I first heard the news," Mac confessed.

"Yes, it is a perplexing situation for us to find we have a relative out there. A relative we don't know about. The world of technology is fascinating, and it seems we are a product of advanced science," I added awkwardly, in an overly formal fashion.

I found Kat looking at me with a slight head tilt and squinted eyes that exposed those ever so small lines on her forehead above the nose. She whispered "Stop" to me as if I was not speaking English.

"Mac, we are a little overwhelmed here," Kat said slowly for affect.

"I bet. I was always hoping I would find relatives out there when I joined the site. But when the paperwork came back that revealed I had an aunt... well... I just couldn't believe the news. My mom has a sister, a sister she did not know about. Apparently two sisters," Mac said in an excited tone.

"And two brothers, too," I chimed in.

"Yes, Kenneth Jr and Killian," Kat added.

Clearly, Mac had contemplated and processed this information a little longer than us, as he genuinely seemed giddy with the discovery. "Mac, this is Kyra again. Your Mom, she was shocked to hear this news, too? Shocked to hear that she has a sister?"

"Yes, ma'am she sure was, but now she's tickled about it," Mac said with a slight Southern accent.

Kat shifted in her seat and directly asked without hesitation, "Does she know how this happened?"

Mac cleared his throat. "Um... ma'am?"

"Well... what Kat means, Mac, is that we are a family of four. I'm the oldest. Then we have twin boys ten years younger than me. Then Kat... I mean Katherine-Anne... is twenty years younger than me. Our parents are no longer with us. But they were together since they were teenagers," I said trailing off leaving the rest to the imagination.

Kat interrupted Mac as he was starting to speak. "You see, it is impossible for your mom to be our sister. We think this is all a big misunderstanding."

I rolled my eyes at the sharpness of Kat's tone and hoped he would not hang up. "Mac, it sounded like you were about to say something, please continue."

The line was quiet. Mac broke the silence. "I absolutely understand your reservations. We felt the same. I've been piecing together the puzzle. My Mom was born in 1967. Her DNA is a 50% match to Katherine-Anne's DNA."

"Which makes your mom her full sister by the same parents," both Mac and I said at the same time. I smiled at Kat, who was looking at me with a puss on her face. She simply mouthed Wow to me silently.

"Exactly," Mac said.

I tried to calm my tone as much as possible. "Well, Mac, we don't know how this happened. Our parents never told us about a previous baby, and they certainly would have raised her had they known she existed. So, we are curious to find out more about your mother and what she may know about our parents. Would you be interested in meeting and discussing it with us?" I said out of curiosity.

Kat slammed down on the mute button on the phone. "What are you crazy? We don't know this guy. He might be a psycho. What do you think he wants from us or from this exchange?"

"I completely understand your hesitancy, Katherine-Anne. Also, I'm a fairly normal guy." We heard Mac's voice say gently as we both looked down at the buttons finding the phone not muted. Kat dropped her head in her hands in embarrassment and turned and walked out of the kitchen. Mac continued "Which you can see when we meet. Can I bring my Mom?"

I watched Kat walk down the hall to her room and close the door behind her. "Mac, what's your mom's name?"

"Perdita," he said in delight. I could tell he said it with a smile. "Perdita."

Chapter SIX

I made a protein shake after my shower and sat at the kitchen island with my mobile phone, trying to reach Aunt Dottie one more time. Secrets are Aunt Dottie's specialty. She whips out the most elusive facts about the history of people, places, and things at the most inopportune times and mostly when she's had a hot toddy.

She once hollered, *'If you'd had a real Florida cracker upbringing like me—born and bred in the backwoods with gators for neighbors—you'd know how to snag one in the swamp without breakin' a sweat,'* right in the face of a St. Johns County Sheriff's deputy who'd nabbed us. We were tooling around in the Moke, off-road, headlights off, spotlight blazing, creeping toward a pond at dusk like a couple of deranged fireflies. His head was shaking and spouted out an angry *'Ma'am, what in the hell?'* as he slapped cuffs on me—my first rodeo, though Aunt Dottie didn't even flinch. We were cackling like hyenas in the squad car's backseat, tears streaming, so I never got around to asking if she'd worn the county's finest bracelets before that day. She just winked at the Sheriff—who lit up like she was his long-lost prom date—and poof, we were free faster than you can say 'gator bait.' I'm pretty sure she dropped that cracker line to bamboozle the deputy, but with

Aunt Dottie, who knows? That woman's got more secrets than a swamp's got skeeters.

Aunt Dottie was the oldest surviving King family member. She was Dad's older sister and the most secretive woman in the family. Aunt Dottie was the first person on my list to interrogate given she was the only one remaining to ask. Aunt Dottie was tight-lipped about her life, including her many husbands. But she was first to laugh, love, and provide the right smattering of empathy when truly needed. She was a complex woman, loved dearly by all who met her. "*Please pick up,*" I whispered as I made yet another attempt to phone her.

"Hello?" Aunt Dottie said as if she did not know it was me calling her.

"Hello, Aunt Dottie. I need to talk to you. Do you want me to come pick you up now?" I asked eagerly.

"Pick me up? Where we going?"

"Aunt Dottie," I gasped. "I'm coming to pick you up to bring you here for the weekend," I said looking at the gravy still simmering on the stove.

"Oh, no. Did I forget to call you? I will be over later. I'm going to chair yoga now. I need to keep limber for the hot men folk."

"I don't need to know that, Aunt Dottie," I said, now imagining my eighty-plus-year- old aunt flirting like a minx at the old age home. "Okay, I'll go to the Publix on my own. I'll be back in an hour. Get here as soon as you can, please. I have something sensitive to discuss with you."

"More sensitive than chair yoga? I'll see you in a little bit, dear. Have Advil and an ice pack ready for me."

"Aunt Dottie, please message me when you are leaving. I can always have Ken or Killian pick you up," I pleaded, thinking of all the harm she could do to pedestrians along the golf cart path.

"Oh, girl, you need to stop treating me like I'm too old to drive. I've not hit anything, not once yet this week," Aunt Dottie stressed with a belly laugh.

"Goodbye my fully competent and lovely aunt," I hung up and set my recycle bags out to go to the Publix.

I placed them on the island and tried to stretch my mind around the fact that Mom and Dad had a child before me. What happened to Perdita? Where did she go? How do you lose a baby? But poor Mom. Just thinking of my mom losing a child or giving up a child made me physically ill. I sighed with sympathy. My shoulders collapsed and I began to boo-hoo, as I buried my head in the pile of recycle bags on the island. I stood back up and used one of the canvas handles to dab the tears streaming down my face. As I stood at the island, I was overwhelmed at the loss of my parents and the strain of finding a sister.

Mom, we were so close. Why didn't you say something to me? I said to myself, wiping the tears from my confused face with the back of my hand. What happened that day in 1967?

I had to get it together. In a few short hours, there would be a gathering here to celebrate the life of Kenneth Sr and Katherine King. I needed to be prepared. But my body told me to sob into my recycle bags and let it out.

Chapter SEVEN

I woke up in the fetal position on top of my bed comforter. Crumpled tissues surrounded me in small piles, evidence of my emotional release that was absolutely necessary after years of suppression and resisting against it as it bubbled up within me year after year. I suddenly wondered what time it was, as the sun streamed through my window. I watched the waves move in the pool from the force of the bubbler on the tanning shelf. It could only mean early afternoon. I dragged my emotional bag of bones out of the bed in search of my phone which was the only remaining clock in the house.

My phone was where I left it, next to the recycle bags on the kitchen island. The house was so quiet. Where was Kat? Was she overwhelmed with emotion like me? I checked my face in the mirror on the mudroom wall. Pulling on my lower eye bags, I sighed. I looked like I had been crying snot bubbles for an hour, just lovely. At least I had color in my face. I headed back to the kitchen to grab the bags and run to Publix. The life celebration was only a few hours away and I still had time to shop and make an appetizer for the family.

I was quickly distracted by the folded note with my name on it standing up on the dining room table. I picked it up and opened the peach stationery. How unusual for Kat to leave a note. Usually, she texted me with her comings and goings. Wait a second... I recognized this peach paper. This was written on Mom's peach stationery. Where did she get this from, I wondered?

Kyra-

Changed my mind. Decided to ride my bike to the bridge.

-Luvu, Kat

Ugh, I wished she left a time on the note. I checked my phone and texted Kat to see if she was still at the bridge. My next text was to Aunt Dottie. Her chair yoga was taking longer than anticipated and I was eager to speak to her about Perdita and 1967. After fifteen minutes, when no one texted me back, I decided to abandon the idea of more food and preparation for tonight and hopped on my bike to join Kat.

I found her on the west bank of the canal, under the Palm Valley bridge. I quietly put my kickstand down and walked the gravel area until we were shoulder to shoulder looking east. We both stood at the Peaceful River Valley kayak launch fixated on *the spot*. The spot was across the intra-coastal waterway on the east bank. Twenty years ago, Mom and Dad perished in that very spot. Today, it was a boat ramp. But, twenty years ago, it was a grassy knoll of an embankment nowhere near a road. We lost everything in that spot, with little explanation as to what happened or why. Kat looked over to me with weepy eyes and placed her head on my shoulder. I wrapped my arms around her and held her while she cried. I inhaled in, deeply wishing I could extract all her pain and suffering with my embrace.

After a few minutes of sobbing, Kat pulled a pack of tissues from her pocket and gently extracted one tissue from the pack and handed it to me. She pulled another tissue and meticulously closed the pack and returned it to her jean pocket. She sat up and cleaned up her face as I blotted the corners of my eyes. I sighed heavily. Today's pain felt different from all the other years we sat here and cried.

"One just assumes after your parents kick the bucket, no other sibs enter your life," I said to Kat, hoping to ease the tension.

A nose snort came from Kat as she lifted her head off my shoulder. "Funny, but not funny, KayKay," Kat wiped tears away as she grinned.

"We come here every year on their death anniversary. We stand in this very spot and look over to where the car was found, at the exact time of their death," Kat peered across the canal, not taking her eyes off the spot.

"The first year you asked me to bring you here. Do you remember why you asked me to come here?" I cleverly questioned her, but already knew the answer.

"I wanted to see their spirits," Kat said with the softest grin at the memory.

"Well, you were six. It seemed reasonable at the time." I smirked as I flashed back to Kat in pigtails holding her little white stuffed animal lamb on the west bank. She held that lamb on her lap and played 'Mary had a Little Lamb' a dozen times while she sat on my lap wrapped in my arms. Both of us looking out at the spot.

"It feels different this year... being here where they died. Now, there is a bigger question. A bigger mystery out there," Kat said wisely.

"I know exactly what you mean."

"You do?" Kat's voice hitched with surprise, her gaze locking onto mine, fierce and flickering, as if she could burn through to the truth.

"Absolutely. First, they die in a shroud of mystery. Second, we now have another mystery around a lost sister. A family mystery mom and dad created. This year is different. Our family will never be the same again, twice in my lifetime," I said slightly perturbed, as if my parents did this with intent. They, of course, did not.

I was willing to accept, not knowing why Dad drove the car screeching to the right from Roscoe Road that day, landing submerged in the canal upside down. But I didn't feel ready or willing to accept another mystery about them.

An older sister? How? Why was she lost from our loving family?

Then as if Kat was reading my mind, she said "But, what do you think happened back then, Kyra?"

I looked over at my younger sister as she paused, drew in a whimpering deep breath, and continued softly. "What happened to Mom and Dad in 1967 to lose a child?"

I studied my beautiful little sister. The sun was low in the sky, and it highlighted her freckles on her fair Irish skin. I moved the long strands of soft strawberry blonde hair out of the way of her eyes. "I don't know what happened Kat. But I feel compelled to find out."

The more Kat aged, the more she looked exactly like Mom. I could see she was ensnared in a distant memory; her eyes, motionless and fixated on the east bank of the canal. Her body was perfectly still, appearing to be stuck in a trance.

"We will find out, Kat," I said, willing her to snap out of it. I was not confident that we would find out, but I needed her to believe and have hope that an answer was in our future. The only person that might know something was our very secretive Aunt Dottie. I could look for Mom's estranged relatives and ask questions. I could also research local records but that seemed like a long shot.

Imagining Mom and Dad giving up their child was unthinkable. It would never happen. I could feel the passion boiling within me to solve the mystery. I needed to know what happened. I needed to know what happened in 1967 to Katherine King and how Perdita was lost.

I let out a deep sigh. "Kat, what I do know is that they died too young and apparently with a lot of secrets. Living in the '50s and '60s, well... it was a very different era, but I knew Mom and Dad. The parents I knew could never give up a child, not for any reason."

Kat broke her silence and turned from the spot, her composure a thin veil over the dry tears that streaked her cheeks. She locked her gaze on mine and said, low but unyielding, "We need to meet her... she's family." Kat slapped her leg as she bit her bottom lip. "I'm ready to go when you are. These mosquitoes and no-see-ums are starting to bite."

We walked to our bikes, and once my kickstand was up, I looked over at Kat with complete resolve. I was determined to uncover the nefarious secrets that laid in the past lives of Ken and Katherine King. "Kat, it seems like a daunting task but I must find out what happened. Why and how Perdita was lost is now my new mission in life. Kat..." I locked on Kat's eyes and urged, "Will you help me?"

"Absolutely." Kat said with a quick smile, swatting a mosquito on her neck.

The sun was lowering in the sky and the Florida wildlife was taking over as dusk neared. The crickets and frogs chattered around us. I waved away no-see-ums in front of my face and smacked my neck, shoulders, and arms. "Yeah, let's go before we're carried off by mosquitoes."

Chapter EIGHT

K at and I returned home from the canal just before six. I quickly ordered pizzas for us all. Kat hopped in my car to pick them up while I dashed to the kitchen to make homemade garlic bread and reheat the Italian gravy and meatballs. This was the least amount of prep I've ever done for a family gathering but the news of a new found sister threw me off my culinary game.

Normally, our life celebrations smack of our Sunday night family suppers. We resembled the Norman Rockwell paintings admired in *The Saturday Evening Post* of the mid 19thcentury. I prepared a homemade meal with love. Ken began with grace. We shared our lives both the good and the not-so-good moments of the week. On Sunday nights, we played games like Yahtzee, Gin-Rummy, Uno, and Monopoly. Each year at the celebration of life, we reminisced about our times with Mom and Dad. It was an event that reminded us of how precious our time together was to us. Our time together was precious, but would the supper conversation be more controversial and lively than the 2020 election?

Boop-Boop. The security system dinged, alerting an open door. Ken and Killian walked through the front door and strolled into the kitchen in their work clothes. My identical twin brothers did not normally dress alike, but that day they were wearing matching blue jeans, and navy-blue polo shirts with a logo on the left breast of *King Construction* with a crown on top of a saw and hammer. Identical twins with Dad's dark black hair, blue eyes, and square masculine chin. They looked indistinguishable except for Killian's scar on his chin. A reminder of my very poor babysitting skills at the age of sixteen.

"Hey KayKay," Ken Jr. said as he kissed the top of my head, towering over me.

"Hey Sis," Killian said with grocery bags in both his hands. He placed them on the kitchen island and came over to hug me. "What can I do to help, you?"

"I would love some help. Boil the water and get the spaghetti in to cook for 8 minutes."

"You got it," Killian went directly to work in the kitchen while I placed the garlic bread in the oven.

I stood back to take another look at Ken Jr and Killian. "Hey there. Was the matching outfit an accident?" I cajoled.

"Of course. It happens more times than you would think," Ken Jr. said to me as he turned to the buffet in the dining room where the fancy drinking glasses were stored.

To my surprise, Aunt Dottie slowly followed behind them. "Aunt Dottie! You were supposed to call me back. How did you get here?" I questioned as I kissed her on the cheek and pulled her near for a much-needed hug.

"I caught a ride with the twins. They picked me up after work," Aunt Dottie said, squeezing me tight.

"It was easier for us to pick her up at the old folks home, than interrupt you and your preparations," Ken said as I watched him zip along the perimeter of the kitchen, stopping at the freezer, adding large ice cubes to several snifters. Effortlessly, he glided back towards the buffet and poured four glasses of scotch.

"Old folks' home... hooey? That's an understatement. We like to refer to it as God's Waiting Room," Aunt Dottie smiled. She headed towards the kitchen island, where Killian was waiting for the water to boil. I unloaded the grocery bags for Killian. Mostly alcohol and bags of mixed nuts.

"Aunt Dottie, I have some fresh honey for you and your friends at the old folks... er... um... The Starling," Killian said as he left the stove and joined Aunt Dottie at the kitchen island.

"That is thoughtful, Killian. Aunt Dottie and her friends have tea each afternoon, after naps," I said finding the honey in the bag and handing it to Aunt Dottie. I was happy to see the twins doing more for our oldest living relative.

"Those bees are keeping busy and producing more and more. We will need to sell the overstock at the Farmer's Market if the hive continues like this," Killian took the mason jar of golden honey from Aunt Dottie and placed in on the kitchen island as Aunt Dottie was climbing up on the counter stool in the most concerning and graceless manner. My eyes grew wider, as my concern became overwhelming. Watching the stunts of Aunt Dottie attempting to climb on the counter stool could give me a nervous breakdown. Killian stood behind her, ready to catch her or give her a boost up onto the stool, if needed. Finally, she scooted her little butt into the seat and slid closer to the island, reaching for the bowl of nuts. Smiling wide she admired Ken sliding in front of her a beautiful double pour of scotch.

"Thank you, barkeep," Aunt Dottie said. "You boys are angels! One with honey, and one with liquor. Not much more an old woman could ask for here. They look quite the same color... actually," she said as she put a hand on each one and drew them closer to one another admiring the rich burnt caramel color of them both.

Aunt Dottie raised it up to her narrow little lips and sipped slowly. "Mmmm... yes."

Ken added, "Better than that old illegal hooch you and Daddy drank in your Palm Valley moonshine days," resulting in a round of laughter from all of us.

I smelled something burning and at that very moment Aunt Dottie said, "KayKay, are you burning something?"

I fumbled the grocery bags to the floor and bolted to the stove, where Killian—bless his clueless soul—had jammed a full bundle of spaghetti into a sauce pan the size of a teacup. Half the noodles jutted out like a bad hairpiece, browning and blackening as the flame licked them on high. I snatched the pan with my pink flamingo pot holder, only to slosh a tidal wave of water right into the fire. Whoosh—a fireball erupted, and suddenly my bell sleeve was auditioning for the role of human torch. "Not good! NOT GOOD!" I hollered, flapping my arm like a deranged bird.

Ken barreled in behind me, fumbling for the stove knob while I - flailed like a gator in a whirlpool- dropped the saucepan in the sink with my left hand, cranked the faucet with my right, and shoved my flaming bell sleeve under the stream in one glorious panic move. A sizzle hissed out, then—"Jesus, Mary, and Joseph!" Ken bellowed, smacking my arm with flamingo dish towels like a man possessed. One caught fire mid-swat, naturally, and he chucked it into the sink with a yelp. The water snuffed the flames, leaving us staring at the soggy wreckage.

My heart was beating out of my chest and I wanted to clobber Killian with the saucepan, but I miraculously was not even scorched from the fire. I was looking at my smoldering bell sleeve of my blouse when I heard suppressed laughter from Killian and Aunt Dottie at the kitchen island. I turned around... and they were both red in the face, eyes closed so tight that tears rolled down their faces and laughing so hard I thought they would pull a muscle. It made me chuckle seeing them laughing so hard but I tried to conceal it as Ken stepped between us.

"Go change. I'll put a real pot of pasta on for us," Ken Jr said as he handed me burnt bits of my belle sleeve that had landed in the sink and were now soaking wet. Then he placed his hand on my back and patted me a few times like a baseball starting pitcher being sent to the dugout.

I stared down Aunt Dottie and Killian as they continued roaring like hyenas. "I'm fine, by the way, in case you were at all concerned." Chuckling harder as I finished my sentence, the sleeve was wet and disintegrating in my hand as I touched it. "Man, I just bought this blouse, Killian."

"I'll buy you a new one. No, really… you're on fire in it." Killian shouted out while Aunt Dottie burst out laughing.

Well, it would just figure… that I would light myself on fire today of all days. When I returned to the kitchen, in my less flammable shirt, Aunt Dottie and Killian were smirking at me but containing themselves. Ken Jr. was straining the pasta as I congratulated myself for not just blurting out the news of our newfound sister. I held my tongue. Kat needed to be the one to tell the story, and she was not back yet with the pizzas. I finished plating the spaghetti for Ken, combining it with a touch of Aunt Dottie's sauce. I lined up the prepared food on the island, then strolled over to sit at the dining room table. I hoped it would encourage others to wrap up the greetings and sit down.

Aunt Dottie nodded at Ken and looked over at me on the dining room chair. "Boys, how's business?" Aunt Dottie asked, now trying to get off the counter stool without tipping it over.

"Business is great, Aunt Dottie. We got the contract in Peaceful River Valley. Only took fifteen years to get on the list of builders here," Killian said sarcastically with an eye roll. "Looks like we have approval to build 20 houses in West End," Killian said proudly.

"Oh, your father would be so proud, Killian. You boys have done so well with Kenneth's business. Really, extraordinary work. Well done!" Aunt Dottie lifted her glass to the sky saluting the accomplishments of the twins in the past twenty years. "Growing Kenneth's one-man show, yet thriving business, into a three-county construction company. Extraordinary accomplishment, boys… truly." Aunt Dottie clinked her glass with both Ken and Killian. "Y'all should make Parade of Homes for certain with your designs," Aunt Dottie said with regal triumph and appreciation.

Boop-Boop. The Ring security system dinged, alerting an open door. Jess entered the room from the front of the house. I was trying to get up off the dining room chair. "No, no. Sit. Stay right there," she said to me while waving her hand to sit back down. "You are going to get some royal highness treatment today, bestie," Jess poetically stated as she neared me for a hug where I sat.

"Thanks for coming tonight. I really need you here tonight," I gushed as she hugged me.

"Of course. I'm right here. Whatever you need," Jess examined my face and looked me in the eyes. "What's wrong? You look like you have something to say."

I diverted my eyes, and grabbed my drink on the table. Dang it, Jess can always see right through to my soul. "Thanks, Jess. I need some more water, that's all," I sheepishly offered, trying desperately to hide my news that was both exciting and alarming all at the same time.

"What's that smell? Did you burn something?" Jess asked as she relieved me of my empty water glass and headed to the refrigerator for a refill and a glass of her own. This, of course, started a second round of laughter from Aunt Dottie and Killian as Ken Jr. explained the fire story to Jess. They were all here, my support network, except for Kat.

Jess returned to me with a cold glass of water and sat next to me. "A lot of excitement today. Do you need me to do anything to help or is everything done for dinner?" Jess asked.

"Oh, I need to get the garlic bread out of the oven," I said trying to get up when Jess set her hand on my shoulder, indicating that she would retrieve the garlic bread.

Jess headed to the oven. "What's for dinner tonight to go with this garlic bread?"

Killian was helping Aunt Dottie off the counter stool as I nervously watched, waiting for a spill. She hobbled to the dining room chair with her arm wrapped in Killian's. "Spaghetti with Aunt Dottie's Italian gravy and meatballs... or pizza," I said with disappointment as I thought back to how my day started with such a fabulous beach trip to plan the menu.

"Where is Kat, then? Anyone seen or heard from her?" Aunt Dottie said, approaching the dining table with her cocktail.

Ken immediately grabbed his phone. "I'll message her. I'll get her here," he said with a firm yet empathetic voice.

"No, she is out getting pizza. We were out all afternoon and not certain we would have dinner ready on time. She should be back soon," I said impatiently.

"I'll get her ETA," Ken said.

Ken had been the man of the house since sixteen. Twenty years ago, he went from a teenage boy to a man overnight. He had been our protector ever since. Both for me and for Kat. Every boy Kat went out with met Ken and Killian first. Ken, keeping intimidation high, would leave a baseball bat at the front door when a boy would call for Kat. He would let the boy in and grab the bat. Using the bat to pound on the floor for effect. *Where you two going?* Thwack on the floor. *What time will you be home now?* Thwack, thwack on the floor. I couldn't help but laugh. Kat was his favorite, for sure.

We all treated Kat like she would break. She was five when Mom and Dad died and of course felt abandoned. She had extra attention from all of us, at all times of her entire life. We just about never left her side. She was sheltered. Kat was not a gregarious child. When it came time for her to go away to college, she couldn't do it. She didn't want to leave home. She commuted daily to classes and events. She kept to herself in college and earned straight A's, which landed her a partial scholarship to law school.

"She just pulled into The Ranch," Ken said looking at the reply from Kat. He got up and went to help her with the pizza boxes. Ken was doing what he did best in life... protect and help the women he loved. I loved him for it.

"Since Kat's here now, why don't you all get your plates filled. Buffet style tonight, folks. Plates are on the island. You have your choice of pizza or spaghetti," I nervously tried to corral the family knowing the big news was about to bang like a gong in all our heads.

Kat entered with Ken, and he placed the pizza on the kitchen island. Kat stood next to me, grabbing a plate and loading it with pizza. "Did you tell them yet," she whispered to me?

"No, not yet. I wanted to wait for you to do it," I whispered as I plated antipasto and one slice of pepperoni pizza for Aunt Dottie.

Once the entire gang was around the table, Killian started the night off with prayer. "We gather today not just to feast on this spread but to celebrate the joy of togetherness, the laughter of friends, and the love of family. Bless this food, let it not only nourish our bodies but fill our hearts with the same warmth that Ken and Katherine shared with us. May their memory be as savory as this meal and may our stories of them be as endless as the refills we hope for. Here's to Ken, to Katherine, our Heavenly mother and father. Amen."

Killian then raised his glass, adding, "Let the life remembrance of Ken and Katherine begin, with a toast that would make them smile from the heavens."

"Here, here," Jess agreed while toasting to Killian's glass. "Who is starting the stories tonight?"

I quickly announced, "Tonight Kat will begin the stories. She has some news to share. I suggest we all sit down." When I sat down, I sipped my Scotch and watched the boys dig into the meat extravaganza pizza slices. While Jess used a spoon and a fork to twirl her spaghetti into a wad of yumminess, Kat stood up over her half-eaten cheese pizza slice.

"Are you not eating, Sis?" Killian said to me when he noticed I was having a liquid dinner.

"Mmm... I've got a spicy Hawaiian pizza waiting for me. But I don't want to choke as Kat relays her tale of extreme surprise," I said.

Killian laughed, "It can't be that bad. Kat... lay it on us, dude."

Kat announced, "I'll get directly to the point. We have a sister. An older sister. Her name is Perdita."

The room erupted in "What?" from everyone except Aunt Dottie chocked on her antipasto, huffed, and launched out a half-eaten black olive across the table. Handing her a glass of water, she coughed a few more unidentifiable items out of her mouth. I sighed and tapped Aunt Dottie on the back as she tried to sip her water and cough at the same time.

Kat was direct. She also seemed genuinely happy. I was mesmerized by her enthusiasm, as she continued. "Yes, a sister. Her son, Mac, is on Ances try.com. That's the website Kyra got me a membership to for Christmas."

"Best coupon ever used." I said still patting Aunt Dottie on the back.

Kat looked over at Aunt Dottie to explain. "Mac was alerted that our DNA matched. His mother then joined and provided her DNA. In the system, Perdita and I were matched at 50%, which Kyra explained to me, means his mother is our biological sister. We have a sister we never knew about. As scary as that is to say out loud, I've had some time to think about it this afternoon, and I think it is wonderful news."

Well, the day was getting more perplexing as it continued. Kat had moved quickly from disbelief to enthralled.

"I, for one, am still in disbelief, and I've had this news all day," I said in contrary.

Jess squeezed my hand and searched my face. "Oh my gosh... how?" Jess whispered.

"This is insane," Ken and Killian said in unison.

"Astonishing," I mumbled while examining the surprised faces of my family.

Killian placed his arms on the table and sat forward "We have another sister? What is her name? When was she born?"

"1967, which makes her the eldest King sibling. I've looked her up online, and she owns a beach house right here in Ponte Vedra Beach. She is an attorney and a widow," Kat said, looking over at me while she sat down.

Ken's mouth was wide open. "You looked her up? What does she look like?"

"Bogus! She's lived here in Ponte Vedra Beach all this time and we never knew her or run into her?" Killian stated without using his favorite expression of *Dude*.

Killian calmly stated That seems unlikely."

"No, I think she lived in several places. She has a law practice in Jacksonville Beach and it appears to also have offices in Pennsylvania. If we did bump into her in Ponte Vedra Beach, it would have been like meeting a ghost. She look just like Mom." Kat, the stalker, explained to us all.

"She looks just like Mom? You saw a photo of her?" I asked quickly.

"I've looked her up on social media. Look at this photo. Doesn't she look just like mom?" Kat said gleefully while showing her phone to Ken, Killian, and then Jess. I stood up behind Jess and looked at the photo. A woman in a suit stood in front of a judge's bench. She was fair skinned, like Mom. She had Mom's long strawberry blonde hair with heavy streaks of grey in the front. The room fell quiet.

All eyes were now on Aunt Dottie who was picking up her half-eaten olive from the table and putting it back in her mouth. She stopped chewing, and said, "What? Why are you all looking at me?"

Ken jumped in quickly "You must know something about this, Aunt Dottie. Could this be true? How could Mom and Dad have another child, and we not know about it? What happened?"

"Before you say anything, Aunt Dottie, we love you very much. We would never criticize you for holding on to Mom's secret and keeping it so close to your heart," I said tenderly as I sat back down next to her and motioned to Kat to show Aunt Dottie the photo of Perdita.

Aunt Dottie examined the photo on Kat's phone with her mouth gaping open. She touched the screen with her index finger and muttered a few indiscernible words. She swallowed hard, looking around the table at all her nieces and nephews one by one. Finally an impatient huff and her face contorted into a look of confusion with the smallest wrinkle across her forehead. "No, this is completely shocking news to me. I don't know anything. How do we know this is really Ken and Katherine's child?"

I was not certain Aunt Dottie was telling the truth. Before I could answer, Kat chimed in gleefully with 100% certainty. "Yes, 50% matches my DNA. I have the DNA results from the website. We have a sister. It's amazing." Kat was nodding and smiling holding the phone with the photo of Perdita in front of Aunt Dottie.

Aunt Dottie blinked to focus on the photo. She held Kat's wrist further out away from her face so she could see the photo clearly with her old eyes. Aunt Dottie's face was frozen in disbelief. I expected, now, she would fess up about the entire situation.

Aunt Dottie was wide eyed. She was mesmerized by the photo. The screen wallpaper popped up and the photo disappeared. "What did you say was her name?" Aunt Dottie said softly.

"Perdita," Kat said.

"Mom & Dad would never give up their own child. This is a mistake. It must be," I said and then abruptly stopped. My outburst shocked everyone including me. Jess leaning over and holding my arm steady.

Ken, somehow reading my mind, examined me from across the long table. Me at one end in emotional shock and Ken at the other end displaying on his face the exact emotions I was feeling inside. "Because the alternative is horrifying to believe of our mother and father? Is that what you were going to say next, Kyra?" Ken barked.

"Exactly," I mustered in the heartbreaking thought.

"Dude..." Killian growled, the word clawing its way up from his gut, rough and leaden, like a warning dredged from a nightmare I couldn't unhear.

The quiet between us all was unsettling, as we each sat in our own dark thought for just one second.

"Perdita... it can't be," Aunt Dottie whispered, her voice aghast, as she regarded me with horror in her eyes.

"What is it, Aunt Dottie? What can't be?" Ken asked.

I was frozen, waiting for the next shocking words to expel from Aunt Dottie's mouth. She knew something. I could see it on her face. There was a child born from our mom and dad that we never knew about. I was afraid to discover something negative. Something that would tarnish their memory or reputation in the community. There was already mystery surrounding their death twenty years ago. With the invention of social media, I was petrified at the thought of another King family scandal reaching every home in Peaceful River Valley.

"They never told anyone, my dear," Aunt Dottie added softly with a tearful look in her eye, squeezing my hand. "Think of how terrified your mother must have been, so young and to be pregnant. Katherine grew up in the 1950's and 60's. There were strict rules and guidelines about the order of events. Having a child before marriage would have been pure embarrassment for her mother and father. They were very wealthy and very strict in their upbringing of Katherine. They were Catholic and Pittsburgh high society. Her being pregnant by a Palm Valley redneck that left to go fight in Vietnam would be a scandal of massive proportion. It would have rocked their small world. But she would receive the best care."

"What are you saying, Aunt Dottie?" Ken Jr. said confused.

I placed my hand on Aunt Dottie's forearm. "What kind of care?" I said with caution.

"Your mom was pregnant in the '60s, before they were married. The little girl only lived a few hours. She lost the child," Aunt Dottie said looking up at me, waiting for a response.

"Wait, what?" I shook my head as I said the words. "Mom really did have a baby before me, and the baby died?"

"The baby didn't really die?" Jess asked, sitting forward in her chair, staring at Aunt Dottie from across the table and waiting.

Killian, looked perplexed, "Mom named her first baby after the dog in *101 Dalmatians?*" His brows squeezed together as if he was intentionally trying to make them into a unibrow.

Ken sat back shaking his head. "The baby lived, and we found her fifty plus years later on a DNA website?"

"No way," Killian shook his head in disbelief.

Aunt Dottie gazed over at Killian shaking her head no, slowly, and then stared directly at Ken. "I think so... Katherine named the baby Perdita. Katherine spoke Latin. She loved Shakespeare." Aunt Dottie was waving her hand around her head as she had done a million times before when she was trying to recall a memory.

I chimed in "Yes... The Winter's Tale was her favorite and Perdita was the lost daughter of royalty." I gazed at Aunt Dottie and my eyes began to well with tears.

"Perdita means lost one," Aunt Dottie said with a cracking in her voice as she held back her own tears.

I put my elbows on the table and my head in my hands. *Mom, what happened?*

Chapter NINE

The next morning, I was late to meet Jess at the Peaceful River Valley Kayak Launch, where we set out to kayak the Intracoastal Waterway every Saturday at five in the morning. The guest room door, where Aunt Dottie was staying for the weekend, was still closed. I quietly made my way to the kitchen. I did not want to wake Kat before 5:00 am, since she probably didn't get to bed until midnight. I envied her youth and energy. I had 15 minutes to make a cup of coffee, hitch the kayak trailer to the truck, and drive to the Peaceful River Valley kayak launch. I started the coffee, then popped over to the mudroom at the side entrance of the kitchen to open the garage doors. Ken's truck was gone.

I pulled Dad's old Ford truck out of the garage and backed it up to the toy garage. After Mom and Dad died, I had a hard time getting rid of Dad's truck. I opted, instead, to invest in an upgrade by OTT Hot Rods. The transformation took a year, but it went from a rundown, beat up work truck to a sweet refurbished 1940s Ford pickup truck in my favorite Florida color... custom Bora Bora blue. I had air conditioning installed, of course, because Florida was not habitable without AC. I hopped out of the truck and threw the trailer onto the hitch of Dad's Ford. Once attached, I hopped back in the truck and pulled the trailer out of the garage.

I found water rolling to a boil as I re-entered the kitchen, perfect timing. I added the hot water to the French press to steep the coffee grounds. The only way to make coffee in Florida was with a French press. If you've ever experienced no power the morning after a hurricane, then you've been driving around in the receding floodwaters, taking your life into your own hands, desperately searching for an open coffee shop. The result being no coffee, a hangover from the hurricane party, and a vow to find a new way to brew coffee with no power. Hence, the French press coffee steeper... the only way to make coffee in Florida during a hurricane. While waiting for the water to steep the coffee grounds in the French press, I wrote Kat a note. I made myself a cup to go and left the remainder for Kat. I stuck the note to the French Press and left it on the island facing the hallway to her bedroom. Kat rarely got up before 8 am. I'd be home to drink it before she even got out of bed, but just in case, I left the note.

Went kayaking. Coffee is for you. Luvu, K

Peaceful River Valley was 14,000 acres of previous swamp land that was now dried out and developed into housing, parks, pools, roads, schools, library, retail, and commercial space. The 2,400 acres of glorious quiet preserve along the ICW in Peaceful River Valley stretched 3.5 miles. Jess and I kayaked 3 miles south and 3 miles back north each Saturday on the Tolomato River and the surrounding tributaries.

I pulled into the parking lot at the northern Kayak Launch Park and maneuvered the trailer to the water. Jess was standing knee deep in the ICW ready to release and hold the kayak next to her own as I parked the truck and trailer. I jogged over to Jess.

"Thanks, girl, I got it," I winked at Jess snagging the kayak as it bobbed toward me.

"Morning. Wild night last night, huh?" Jess winked back at me. "You King's really know how to throw an exciting party."

"Aren't you glad you had that front row, VIP, popcorn seat?" I snickered as I wiggled into my bright orange Hobie kayak.

"Yep, I must admit that was some twisted nest." We both pushed off and started south on the canal. We paddled quietly, passing the homes on the water with their long boardwalk docks jutting out from the marshy land to their small boats and yachts. Both sides of the canal went from docks to swampy marsh and pine trees in a quick second. We left civilization and floated down the ICW in the darkness, enjoying the calm and peace of the morning.

At 5am, in Ponte Vedra Florida, it was still dark and quiet. Gliding down the canal, the gentle rocking of the kayak and the quiet lapping of water against its hull lulled me into a tranquil peace and serenity. It was my priceless meditation moment. This early in the morning, we humans were the intruders to the natural environment. The canal and surrounding preserves were full of life, including frogs, birds, turtles, alligators, deer, fox, coyotes, and the occasional boar. The dark sky above us started to ombre to the east. First a dark blue melting into a slim light blue line followed softly by an ever-so-dull white shimmer just peaking over the pines and oaks that hugged the eastern shore.

We drifted toward the Peaceful River Valley South Launch Park, the faint sound of lapping waves guiding us to the small beach just ahead, barely visible in the distance. Southeast, the water stretched flat and glassy, a dim glow pulsing at the marsh's edge. I squinted as the light sharpened, splintering into dozens of flickering points—yellowish-orange, cold as embers in a dying fire. I blinked hard, willing my eyes to adjust, but when I looked again, the dots had multiplied, skittering across the surface like a swarm candle lights dancing on the water. I froze mid-paddle, my breath catching as I turned to Jess. "Jess," I whispered urgently, "do you see that glow on the water to our southeast?"

Jess halted, her paddle lifting silently as our kayaks drifted closer, hulls nearly kissing. We stared into the pre-dawn murk, the dark water now alive with a hundred pinpricks of orange light... unblinking, unnatural. The air thickened, pressing against my chest.

"I do. What is it?" Jess murmured, her words tight, swallowed by the silence.

"It's getting closer," I whispered and then held my breath as two of the orange lights were upon me. Only inches away from the front of my kayak. The stillness shattered... a soft bump jolted my hull, nudging me into Jess. My paddle trembled in my grip, still poised above the water. Then I saw it... not candles, not tricks of light, but eyes—slitted, predatory, glowing like lanterns. "Wow" I gasped in awe, at the baby alligator's glowing eyes as it traveled past me on the right. Then another on the left of Jess. Several passed in between us. Dozens of baby alligators traveling in a huge congregation. They floated by us with their orange eyes aglow in the dawn light. Several nudging into our kayaks as they swam on by.

Jess was stiff in her seat with her eyes wide, still holding her paddle out of the water. "That's never happened before. I'm afraid to put my paddle back in the water," she giggled nervously.

"That was the most remarkable thing I've ever seen on the Tolomato River. Dozens of baby alligators. Wow!" I said, a little bit louder now that the congregation passed me.

"Oh, I don't know," Jess countered with a brittle building laugh. "The bird snatching Captain's fish mid-reel might still take the crown."

"Oh yeah, Captain Brian was ready to declare war on that bird," I shot back, voice rising above a whisper as I dipped my paddle in, shaking off the chill still clinging to my spine.

We reached the south kayak launch and turned around to start back north. The sky to the east was bursting with light from the rising sun. The sky to the west was still dark blue. I glanced over and saw women poised on paddle boards like graceful flamingos. The sunrise yoga SUP crew met every Saturday at Peaceful River Valley South Launch Park. Yoga on paddle boards? Not my jam. I can barely salute the sun on solid ground without toppling like a drunk toddler. Yoga on water sounded like a one-way ticket to an unplanned swim lesson.

"Did you want to break for five?" I said to Jess while sipping my coffee.

Jess nodded and moved closer towards me. We hooked our paddles together. "How are you feeling today, girl?" Her voice filled with empathy and concern.

"Yes, I'm okay. I appreciate you asking. Every year is tough, but yesterday was... well... I don't have words yet for it," I said wearily.

"Two decades after they die, you find out you have an older sister... there are no words for that scenario. Do you really believe it?" Jess said sipping her water with a skeptical squint.

"As hard as it is to believe... I think yes... I do believe it. The site is reputable and apparently this is not the only time this has happened." The sunrise caught my attention, and I paused, taking in the first rays of the day. "She looks like Mom, doesn't she?"

Jess adjusted our paddles to shorten the distance between our kayaks. "Oh yea, identical to Momma Katherine."

"Since I started treating this anniversary as a celebration, it has turned my grieving to hope. I like reminiscing about who they were and our experiences together. I love sharing stories about them, even if I heard them a thousand times already." I closed my eyes, tilted my head back and felt the warmth, love, and security of a moment as a child when they both held my hand as we waited for a funnel cake at the town fair.

"The annual celebration is a wonderful way to honor them and retain your history," Jess interjected. "New history is a bit of a surprise."

I rejoined the moment and looked over at Jess. "Yesterday was an un-expected overload of emotion. Kat processed it at warp speed. One mo-ment we were at the kayak launch sharing our disbelief, then she picks up pizza and returns excited about a new older sister. She gave me emotional whiplash. I'm obviously still processing having a sister."

"Oh boy I've not seen her that giddy since you gave her that Emerald green 10-speed bike for her birthday when she was thirteen." Jess smiled and then stared into the east at the sun coming up behind the tall pines.

"Perdita looks like Katherine. Aunt Dottie confirmed she knew of a baby. It seems surreal, but also obviously true at the same time. Do you know what I mean?" The gentle sounds of lapping water accompanied my view of the yoga ladies gracefully posing on their paddle boards; all grace while my mind was doing cartwheels.

"Totally. It's like opening your family tree and realizing someone stapled an extra branch on when you weren't looking." Jess let out a laugh and pointed at the SUP Yoga group. "Splash, she's in the drink. I guess that happens when you try to balance on a board on water."

I looked over and watched the woman lift herself back on her board with ease and form the sun salutation pose without missing a beat.

Jess continued... "Ya know... it is blatantly obvious to look at Perdita and know she is a King. Do you think Aunt Dottie knows more?"

"She is a mirror image of Mom. I'm not sure yet about Aunt Dottie. You know how well she keeps a secret. Although... she went white as a ghost when she heard Perdita's name."

"Someone must know something." Jess secured her water bottle.

"It's a mystery that I feel compelled to solve for my mother's sake. Kat said she would help." I looked forward to spending time with Kat even if it was to research how we lost a sister 50+ years ago.

"Yea, I did notice she was excited about finding Perdita's photo online," Jess offered. "But what I really want to know is how Kat is adjusting to being a graduate from law school?"

"Oh, my word. In that department, Kat has not adjusted yet. I keep asking her if she is going to get a job with a law firm. But she avoids the conversation," I confessed to Jess.

"Well, it's only been a few weeks. Law school seems like an intense place. A few weeks to decompress is probably a good thing for her," Jess said, picking up her paddle.

"Agreed. Although..." I stopped and drank more coffee. I looked over to Jess with a side smirk and a raised eyebrow.

"Uh-oh. I know that look," Jess laughed at me while untangling her paddle and giving me a little slap on the bow.

"Yes, you do. Although, I want her to pay rent and start a budget. She needs to understand the real world. I may have sheltered her too much."

Jess laughed out loud. "Ya think? Between Kenny and you, Kat is a princess. You've both protected her and given her everything she wanted."

"Shhh... you're gonna wake the gators," I snickered, trying to pick up the pace to keep up with Jess.

"Seriously, Kyra. You did everything you could for Kat. No one could have done better. You were an amazing faux mom. You were busy working a full-time job, plus being a mom to Kat all resulted in you never meeting a man or becoming a mom yourself. I know you wanted children. It's time to twist the focus back to you. Kat is amazing. You did a great job raising her. She needs a beat to regain her focus and that's all. It's time to start focusing on you for a change."

"I guess you're right. It could have ended a lot worse for Kat," I shuttered as my mind went to scary thoughts.

"Like what... gang affiliation in Peaceful River Valley? Come on now," Jess snickered.

I glanced over at Jess and she knew my mind was dancing with the irrational, so she pushed it right there to the edge. Good best friends know how to slap the evil chaos monster out of your mind to snap you back into reality. I smirked back at her. "I was thinking... like a pink spiked hair punk rocker with a dog collar, but yes... yes, gang affiliation would have been worse."

"Ha... but no... don't do that to yourself, Kyra. Take a bow, won't you. She turned out amazing, and that was partially good genes. But mostly it had to do with you being there for her and providing her a rock-solid foundation," Jess said as she started paddling harder and faster.

"Thanks, Jess. It means a lot to me to hear that," I was proud of my little sister, Kat, who was not so little anymore. I struggled to keep paddling at Jess's Olympian pace.

"Now, it is time for you to do something with your life. Maybe follow one of those dream businesses you keep thinking up. A second income could help in retirement," Jess said.

"Huh? What does that mean?" I suddenly felt lost in the conversation as I started paddling and peddling with my kick-up fins at the same time to catch up with her.

"You know what it means, Kyra King. This is your time to shine, girl. Can't wait to see what you do next," Jess shouted back at me. She, clearly, was the stronger kayak peddler.

I paused peddling and paddling, admiring the sky as it glowed soft golden-orange along the east canal, yet the west sky clung to bluish-white with a low moon lingering. Sipping my coffee, I watched Jess's kayak skim across the water, a good two boat lengths ahead of me and getting further out in front of me. If I want to keep up with that woman... I need to drink more water and less coffee. Welp... that's a dumb idea. I tossed back one last motivating sip of java, secured my tumbler, and took to task as I tried to catch up to Jess.

Chapter TEN

After kayaking, I returned home to find everyone awake. I pulled the note away from the counter and tossed it in the garbage, as I heard slippers scooting across the floor. "Good morning, Aunt Dottie. Coffee is ready for you in the French press. I'll put water on to make more."

"Good morning, Kyra girl. Where's my favorite mug?" Aunt Dottie yawned on her way to the cabinets.

"Cabinet above the coffee. First shelf, right side," I guided her as Kat, energetic for before noon, be-bopped into the kitchen.

Aunt Dottie pulled a coffee mug out of the cabinet that said "I came, I saw, I forgot what I was doing... went back. Got distracted & have no idea what's going on. Is this my cup? I have to pee..." and giggled as if she had never seen it before.

"Kyra, I'm glad you are back. I want to talk to you," Kat said without even saying good morning.

"Good morning, Katherine-Anne. You're up early. Have some coffee and relax," I urged her.

"I think we should talk about Perdita and this situation," Kat added her coffee to a French press she pulled out of the pantry.

I sighed. "Yes, I agree," I pulled up a counter stool and sat at the island. "I gave it some thought while I was on the water this morning."

"What did you conclude?" Kat poured honey in her empty coffee mug, while she waited for the water to boil.

"I think we should call Perdita and ask her to meet us. I would like to confirm for myself that she is who she really says she is."

"You think she's an imposter? Kyra, I don't believe you." Kat snarled with a perturbed shock she reserved for only the worst of sins, like not allowing her to livestream me twenty-four hours a day.

"I agree with Kat. This woman looks like your mother. She has the name. The timeline matches up. Why are you so hesitant to believe?" Aunt Dottie asked while cleaning her eyeglasses.

"I'm skeptical by nature, of course. But...I do believe she is our sister after hearing your tale of Mom's lost child, Aunt Dottie." I sighed and got up to start making breakfast. "I understand the data. I just don't understand how Mom kept this to herself. Why didn't she tell me?"

"Katherine was in pain. She grieved. Maybe she couldn't share that with us. Maybe she thought you were better not knowing than feel her pain. Or maybe like all of us with pain in our heart... it was too painful to say mutter out loud." Aunt Dottie wisely confessed all the right options. All the right pain points.

"Later today I'm going up into the attic to pull down all their stored personal effects. Then on Monday, when the bank opens, I'm going to look in the bank security deposit box. Maybe Mom left a trace... of something that will help us understand what happened."

"What if you don't find what you are looking for, my dear? Will you accept and be content to not know?"

I stopped to consider the question. How would I feel not knowing? I don't like not knowing and it would make me feel wretched. "I guess I will have to be... ok with it... as you say. I'll have no choice. I want answers and will search for those answers, if I have to."

Aunt Dottie sighed loudly and put her coffee mug down. "Kyra, can't you just have faith that you were meant to have your older sister, revealed to you now, and that is the plan... so enjoy it? Must there be a quest for more information that may pick at old scabs and wounds?

"I see no harm in doing a little digging into Mom and Dad's life to find out how Perdi was lost. What are you afraid I will find? Because you are staring to sound like you don't want us to know any more about this situation, Aunt Dottie."

All three of us stopped and looked at one another. What was it about Aunt Dottie... what was she holding back? "Aunt Dottie, do you have anything else you want to share with us? Anything else you can remember about that time in the late 60's?" I raised an eyebrow as Kat glared at me and shifted her gaze to Aunt Dottie with a look of intense interest.

"Oh stop looking at me like that KitKat. I don't know anything more than I already told you. I'm just old enough to know... that some things are better left in the past... dead and buried." Aunt Dottie retrieved her ebook from the coffee table in the living room. I returned to shifting the food in the frying pan.

"Mom's understanding aside," Kat started to say as the kettle whistled. "It is serendipitous to find out this way... on a website... via technology," She turned off the gas and poured the water in the French press over the coffee granules. The velvety chocolate coffee scent wafted through the air. "I mean, just think about it. Can you imagine all the factors that had to align perfectly to result in this chance meeting? Kyra, you had to give me the *Ancestry.com* present. I had to take the DNA test. Mac had to sign up. He had to decide to provide his DNA test. This all happened on the same site. What if he decided to join *23 and Me*, instead? We would still be in the dark about our new sister," Kat said, bewildered at the string of incidents that had to come together to inspire this reunion.

"Praise God, yes. You are so right KitKat," Aunt Dottie bellowed from the living room. "The odds of all these events aligning to make this disco very... it's just a modern day miracle."

"Nothing happens by chance, Kat," I added, watching the bacon on the stove top carefully.

"What do you mean by that my skeptical, yet hopeful, sister?" Kat teased me, as she sat at the island with her coffee mug and her French press.

"She means it was God's plan all along, KitKat," Aunt Dottie piped up loudly and returned to the kitchen island where she provided Kat a reassuring gentle rub on the back.

"Well... that is an intricately weaved tapestry, right there, I tell ya," Kat said as she plunged down on the French press and poured her coffee. Her trademark grin and head bob made me smile every time.

"So, yes. God placed her in our path. Therefore, we must meet her. What time is a reasonable time to call a new sister on a Saturday morning?" I asked.

"We should probably wait until at least eight, right," Kat said as she checked her phone for the time.

"Aunt Dottie, are you going with us to meet Perdita?" Kat asked eyeballing her over the coffee mug.

"Oh... well... I don't want to intrude. Ya know, Connie and I have a boatload of activities today. Plus, it's Saturday night. I have a hot date."

"What?" I whipped my head around, singeing my hand on the griddle as the tongs clattered into the bacon grease with a sizzle.

"Nice. I hope he is rich with one foot in the grave and the other on a banana peel," Kat jested.

"Kat, that is not nice." I said biting back a snort and smearing butter on my fresh burn.

"Oh, you know he is, my dear," Aunt Dottie winked at Kat.

I cooked breakfast while Aunt Dottie and Kat were as thick as thieves over on the island. "Don't you think we should meet this male suitor before you go gallivantin' off?" I asked, eyebrow arched.

"Psh, I don't know if I like him enough to introduce him to kinfolk yet." Aunt Dottie shot back, her face scrunching into a sass-soaked grin. "Don't rush me."

"Well... due to your age, I say step on the gas... a little bit," Kat snickered, dodging my glare.

"Where is he taking you tonight?" I asked, trying to steer the conversation before it devolved into the gutter.

"Ruth's Chris Steak House for supper at four o'clock. I need to be back in time for Cappers and Crimes podcast tonight at eight. Although, the last time, I had nightmares listening to those scary stories. Woke myself up with my own screams in the middle of the night. Next morning, my next-door neighbor, Ethel, asked if I was sacrificing animals in the middle of the night when I was screaming like a banshee."

"Maybe they are scarier because you're only hearing them and not seeing it play out on a screen. So, your mind makes up the stories and your mind can produce some pretty terrifying horrors when left to its own devices," I said, flipping the eggs over easy.

"They just ain't like the ole Twilight Zones, ya know? Pure fright fuel," Aunt Dottie said, mimicking Kat's signature grin and head nod. Clearly, Aunt Dottie had been rehearsing Kat's signature move.

"Well, maybe we won't even meet her today," Kat said, scrolling on her phone.

"True, maybe she has plans already," I said, plating breakfast for each of us.

"I have plans. I need to go to the Publix at seven o'clock when no one is there yet. It's my quiet time to shop," Aunt Dottie said, crunching on a piece of bacon.

"Why do you need groceries if you are going to dinner tonight?" Kat asked.

"Well, you know, for provisions... like whipped cream and strawberries."

I interrupted Aunt Dottie right there "Okay, we get it. You might have dessert. We will go with you. I need a few things for meals this weekend. Do you want to drive the Moke to the Publix?"

"I get to drive the Moke? Hot diggity dog! Oh, I'm so excited. Where is the key? Should I pick you up out front? Oh, I finally get to drive the

Moke. This is so exciting," Aunt Dottie said, grabbing the keys from the mudroom key holder.

"No, no, Aunt Dottie, not in your pajamas. Go get dressed," I said with a smirk.

While Kat and Aunt Dottie were getting dressed, I pulled the Moke out of the garage and into the driveway. We all met on the front porch. An excited Aunt Dottie hopped in the Moke with the keys in her hand, and we were off. As Aunt Dottie pulled out of the driveway, with the emergency brake up, I released the brake from the passenger seat and gave Aunt Dottie the evil eye.

Aunt Dottie hooted, "Wahoo, hold onto your britches!" as she gunned the Moke toward the stop sign... then stomped the brakes like she was squashing a roach. We lurched forward, my nose nearly kissing the windshield, Kat's coffee sloshing, and Aunt Dottie cackling, "Oh these brakes are touchy."

I made the sign of the cross and held on.

Aunt Dottie was already waiting for us in the Moke. Kat and I exited the Publix with a couple of bags in each hand. I was laughing with Kat about getting smoked by Jess on the water this morning and the Yoga ladies who fell in the canal. Just as I was enjoying the day, Kat's face turned from enjoyment to fear as her mouth made the 'oh no' shape and I heard the blaring of a horn. I looked toward the Moke.

I halted immediately when I noticed the Moke was not in the golf cart parking spot from which we left it. To my surprise, the Moke was moving backwards. "Oh, no," Kat repeated. Aunt Dottie was reversing into a security truck that was picking up money at the Publix. "Oh, no. She hit him."

I'm not sure why Aunt Dottie ever got out of the cart without first pulling it back into the parking space. But she carefully exited the vehicle. The cart was wedged up under the fender of the armored car. The driver was looking at her with his mouth open in disbelief while throwing up his hands. His partner grabbed his moneybags and quickly tossed them back in the rear of the truck, locked the doors, and ran around the side with gun drawn. "Oh, no. Wait! No!" I yelled.

"Awesome! I've got to record this!" Kat said, dropping the bags and preparing her phone for video.

Those men were very jumpy given the calm, safe area that we lived in here at Peaceful River Valley Publix. A crowd was now forming. Aunt Dottie was out of the vehicle, looking at the damage. She decided to push the cart just a little in hopes of dislodging it from under the truck fender. It popped out easily and with a jolt of energy sprang forward. "Oh, no," I said as I started running with my bags flapping at my side.

Aunt Dottie bounced up and down like a little bunny, stretching out her right hand, pointing and screaming to onlookers, "Look out, look out now," as my Moke rolled into a sign. I heard her play by play as the Moke jumped a curb. "Oh no, look out!" The Moke then rammed a sign knocking it down. "Ohhhhhh!" The Moke crushed a bush... and stopped just before it plowed into the bike rack, making all the bystanders jump back and the pigeons flew away.

Aunt Dottie's last words were "Ah... crapola."

Chapter ELEVEN

Needless to say, I drove us home from the Publix, after the police and fire department released us. They quickly realized this was not an armored carjacking with a golf cart, as it was falsely reported on the 9-1-1 call and posted on the Ladies of Peaceful River Valley Facebook page. I don't even know how these rumors start around here... the imaginations run wild.

As we hit the tumbled bricks, from the first Palm Valley bridge, that lined the front entrance of The Ranch, I glanced over at Aunt Dottie who still had a puss on her face. "Aunt Dottie, now, you are not still upset with me because I wanted to drive us home now, are you?"

Still pursing her lips, she sadly replied, "No, I guess not. I probably deserved the keys being taken away from me for that one." She looked away towards Lucy, my neighbor and book club president, waving at us as she walked her golden retrievers. Aunt Dottie returned the wave with a smile.

"That looks like a good idea. Kat, do you want to go for a hike through the Peaceful River Valley Preserve at Davis Park?"

"I don't know. I prefer to bike that trail because of all the boar," she replied not lifting her nose from her phone. As I looked closely into the rear-view mirror, I could see her eyes squinting behind her sunglasses, as she attempted to read the phone. She raised her sunglasses up over her head and closely examined her phone.

I went around to the passenger side to assist Aunt Dottie out of the Moke. Kat was still sitting in the vehicle staring at her phone. "Well Kat, what's going on now, did we make the news?"

Kat stepped all over my rear seats, as she quickly hopped out of the Moke "It's a text from Mac. He would like to talk with us again, but this time with Perdita on the phone."

"Perfect! Now?" I asked.

"Yes, they want to talk now. I'm calling him back," Kat said as we all made our way into the house via the front door.

"Kat, I know you are very excited right now. But I urge you to tread lightly. This may not be easy for her. She may not have had a mother or a father. We know nothing about her. Let's take it slow," I urged. "We know nothing about how she was raised, Kat. I had the love of our parents for 26 years before you arrived, and they passed away. How did she grow up? And... she may not know Mom and Dad are gone. We don't know how she will react. It could be very upsetting for her."

"Slow, tread lightly, lots of unknown. I got it," Kat scooted past me and practically skipped through the foyer to the kitchen.

As we entered the house, the Ring doorbell camera alerted me to motion on my phone. "We want to keep our guard up and take this on with caution," I said to Aunt Dottie. "I said don't sound so eager and she skips to the kitchen, dialing the phone."

Kat's phone was on speaker and started ringing. Mac picked up immediately. "Hello, Katherine-Ann. How are you doing today?" Mac asked politely.

"Yes, we are all here and doing fine. I have you on speaker phone... it's me, my sister Kyra, and my Aunt Dottie."

"I'm on speaker phone, too. My mother is here today, visiting me on the farm. Say hello, Mom," Mac encouraged Perdita.

"Hi Perdita, I'm your Aunt Dottie," she shouted into the air, as if the speaker phone could not hear her.

A voice filled with the sound of pure enjoyment replied on the other end of the phone, "Hi Aunt Dottie. I'm Perdi... I guess your niece, right?" She paused and cleared her throat.

I jumped in with calm professionalism, as to not seem overly excited. "Hello Perdita. I'm Kyra King, your eldest sister." As I said the words, I realized I was no longer the eldest sibling. I was no longer the head of the family. I had a sister who was older than me and now the head sibling of the family, if she wanted to be part of our family.

"Hello, Katherine-Anne. Hello, Kyra. Everyone calls me Perdi."

"Oh, yea... everyone calls me Kat. Perdi, I saw your profile online, and it says you are an attorney, is that correct?"

"Yes, I've been an attorney for almost 30 years now. First in Pittsburgh where I mostly grew up. Then I met Mac's dad and moved here permanently to Jax Beach to be with him while stationed at the Navy Submarine base in Kings Bay, Georgia."

"Perdi, this is Kyra. Sounds like you said permanently. Did you live here in Florida for a time?" I asked as I put away items in the refrigerator.

"Oh, yes. Mom and dad's old mid-century beach house in Ponte Vedra Beach. We traveled here every winter during my youth. We stayed for months at a time. I'm living full time in the old beach house now," Perdi reminisced.

"Does Mac really own a farm or was that a euphemism?" I asked, partially in jest and partially curious—who owns a farm at his age?

"I'm visiting Mac on the farm this weekend. And yes, he does own a farm. He is really trained as a chef but loved my mom's farm in Pennsylvania and decided to find some land in rural Northwest Florida to raise cattle and grow organic and natural crops. That boomed into a supply business for farm to table foods for restaurants and chefs throughout Northeast Florida and Southeast Georgia," Perdi said with pride in her voice.

"How wonderful, Mac. I love to cook. We will need to cook Sunday Supper one night here at my house for the whole family," I said inviting complete strangers into my home to cook meals with me. How could I protect my family from fraudsters if I'm cooking with them? "Well... when we all feel more comfortable with one another, that is," I quickly added to eliminate my eagerness.

"I was so excited to hear you were in law. I just graduated from law school. What type of law do you practice?" Kat sat intently upright, waiting for Perdi's response.

"Yes, Perdi. Kat graduated law school and passed the bar last month... without studying for it. She's a genius, and I for one can't wait to see her get her first job so I can officially call her Kat King, Esquire."

"That is quite an accomplishment, Kat. I know people who studied for months only to fail it several times. You must have a wonderful ability to recall information. To answer your question, my firm handles contracts, estate planning, elder care, business accounts, and I mostly manage the firm now," Perdita said.

"Oh, that's interesting. Probably not a lot of courtroom drama in that career," Kat laughed as she said it.

"Correct. It's more about keeping others out of court." As Perdita's little laugh rang out, it took me back to my mom's laugh.

Aunt Dottie whispered in my ear. "Doesn't she sound like your mom?" Then she looked at me and began nodding in agreement with herself. Yes, she did sound like Mom, and it made it more difficult to be skeptical and cautious. She seemed friendly and kind.

"Ladies, it was lovely chatting with you all. I had Mac call you all today because I would love to get together to meet you," Perdi graciously said.

"We were wanting the same, Perdi. We are available on Monday morning for a breakfast before the workday," Kat took charge, and I loved to see her eager to lead and coordinate us all. It was a delightful break for me.

"Perfect, Monday works for us. We should meet centrally, how about Ponte Vedra Beach?" Perdita requested.

"Yes, let's meet at The Metro on A1A in Sawgrass. Do you know it," Kat asked?

"I do. We will meet you there. How is seven o'clock," Perdí said.

I looked around at Aunt Dottie and Kat. We were all nodding our heads in agreement. "Done, Perdi. We are all available and can't wait to meet you both. Monday, seven, at The Metro in Sawgrass."

Chapter TWELVE

I seemed to be tossing and turning, unable to sleep. I looked at my phone, it was 3:30 a.m. There was absolutely no sense in lying in bed when I could be out in the kitchen pacing with coffee in my hand. I needed to admit to myself that I was nervous to meet this new woman who'd entered our world. I wondered if she was the real daughter of Mr. and Mrs. Kenneth King. It felt so bizarre to think about our worlds crashing into one another.

I threw off the covers as Kat startled me by banging on my door. "Kyra, are you up? I can't sleep." There was a long pause. "I'm so excited and nervous all at the same time. Are you feeling the same?"

I sat on the edge of the bed and tried to tap into my physical and mental feelings. I was skeptical but recognized that technology had advanced and most likely connected Kat and Perdi because of a sincere DNA match. Poof... a sister. A sister that could have been here all along had she not been lost to us.

I was sad to no longer be the oldest, and having missed out on the experience of an older sister. She could have cared for me. She could have helped me care for the twins and Kat for the past 20 years. I sighed, I could have used the help. No, I was not feeling excited. I was feeling dreadful.

Dreading that Perdita would take away my family. She already had more in common with Kat than I did, and I'd only known her one day. *Irrational thoughts*, Kyra, I said to myself in a whisper.

"Kyra, what did you say? I can't hear you. Get up and come talk to me."

"I'll come out as soon as I get ready," I said as I headed to the bathroom to take a shower and process what felt like impending doom in the pit of my stomach. Clearly not the same feelings as Kat. Why was she so excited? Why was I so scared?

This was not a typical Monday morning. I needed to take a personal day. I emailed my boss, warning her of the time away from the office this today. I decided to leave out the full reason. Some emotional traumas are just too personal to expose to the boss. Kat, Aunt Dottie, and I would meet Perdita first. We agreed that if the meeting went well and we were satisfied that this woman was our sister, additional meetings would naturally happen.

Kat and Aunt Dottie were sitting in the kitchen with coffee. Kat jumped up to pour me a cup, eagerly explaining her every sleepless hour over night. I turned on the TV to Fox News. I sat down in my comfy chair, and to my surprise, Kat was handing me my coffee. Behind her was Aunt Dottie sitting down on the couch and opening her book to read. "Thank you so much Kat for making me coffee," I said.

"I've been up all-night Googling Perdi and Mac online. I added her as a friend, and she did respond. She looks very accomplished. Her LinkedIn profile says, "Attorney and Entrepreneur." She seems like a free and independent career woman, like me," Kat said while holding her phone to her chest and looking proudly up in the air, waiting for praise for being her own boss.

Since it was my job to keep her positive and boost her ego, I quickly told her, "Of course. That seems natural that the entrepreneur's spirit would flow through all of us. Dad was so independent and self-taught. He instilled that in us. But I wonder how she would have learned that trait. Maybe there is more to Nature versus Nurture than we know about," I sipped my coffee and wondered if I would also be running my own business if life had not thrown me into a caretaker role at a young age. My life could have looked very different.

I smiled at Kat, who seemed mesmerized by the news. "We should go over to The Metro early and grab a booth," I said as I waited for Kat to burst with the next topic or jump up, ready to go. But she was just fixated on the TV screen.

"Oh, no," Aunt Dottie exclaimed from the couch with the same fixation on the TV screen. Then I heard Brian Kilmeade's 6 a.m. welcome, "Hello Fox & Friends from The Metro Diner in Ponte Vedra Beach. I missed my flight to New York, but The Metro Diner was happy to host us for Breakfast with Friends on short notice."

"What did he say?" Aunt Dottie asked as she blinked several times in dismay.

"Can you believe this?" Kat said pointing at the TV.

"Well... golly... I sure don't," I sighed watching Brian Kilmeade make his way around our hometown diner packed with happy Peaceful River Valley early birds. The diner, where we were to meet Perdi in just about an hour.

"Seriously? Golly? Golly? For real KayKay... what's next... Jeepers?" Kat sniped.

Interrupting Kat's outburst, my phone started ringing in my lap, breaking all our gazes on the TV screen.

"Well, I guess this is what happens when you live in a town with a famous news anchor," Aunt Dottie commented as I hit the mute button on the TV and answered my phone.

"Goodness gracious... why do so many famous people have to live here!" Kat exclaimed irritably. She was so cute when she got annoyed.

"Good morning, Perdi," I said into the phone.

"Good morning. Our location was commandeered."

"Oh yeah, we are watching it right now, too. Kat could start an argument in an empty house, she's so irritated."

"What a coincidence," Perdi said.

"Right? But it's okay, we can meet down the road some at Beach Diner. Do you know it?"

"Yes, I was thinking the same thing. Meet you there shortly," Perdi said. Then I hung up the phone and returned to the news and my coffee.

"Drat, foiled by Brian Kilmeade. I didn't see that coming," I said to Kat as I gave a little laugh.

Kat was still pacing around the living room. "How can you be so calm, Kyra? Why is your body not vibrating with excitement at the thought of a sister and meeting her? She is your age. You are going to have so much in common and so much to talk about." Smiling and almost glowing, Kat could not contain herself.

"Kat, how many cups of coffee have you had this morning?" I asked.

She put up 4 fingers as she sat down on the couch.

"I am still cautious. I am looking forward to meeting her," I said while I sipped my coffee and watched my little sister examine my face and reactions as if she was trying to decrypt a code.

"Let's go. I think we should go now," Kat was up on her feet again and headed to the mudroom for shoes. I looked at my watch. It was too early.

"Well... you seem too excited to sit patiently, so I guess we can go now," I said, looking at my watch.

"C'mon, let's go," Kat shouted from the mudroom, holding the door open. She practically bounced out to the garage.

"Let's go Aunt Dottie." I poured my coffee into a to-go cup and slipped on my fancy sandals that coordinated with my sun dress. If any occasion deserved more than shorts and flip-flops, it was meeting our older sister for the first time.

Chapter THIRTEEN

We sat, anxiously, at the largest table The Beach Diner offered towards the back of the restaurant. We waited for the arrival of Perdita and her son, Mac. Of course, we had more coffee because if anything reduces anxiety, it is surely more coffee. I could not imagine how this happened, but here I was sitting and waiting to meet my older sister. I was warming up to the idea of having an older sister, but I was cautiously optimistic.

I was still in somewhat of a state of shock. How could I have a sister? An older sister that I never knew existed. How did this happen to Mom? Did Dad even know Mom was pregnant? Did they really think she died that day on her birthday? Or was that a story they told Aunt Dottie, and they really gave up the child for adoption? No, that didn't fit my view of Ken Sr and Katherine. They could never give up a child. Maybe there has been a mistake in all this electronic DNA exchange. Or maybe this is really what it seems, and we have a sister we never knew about. A sister lost to us. The mystery was how... how was she was lost to us?

Today, we would determine if Perdi and Mac were part of the King family. I was about to meet my older sister who could, perhaps, tell me what happened to her at birth and how she was lost from the King family tree.

Kat had her head in her phone. "You are not going to record this or mention this personal situation on your channel or podcast, right?" I asked in more of a telling tone.

Kat's eyes looked up at me first. Then she put the phone in her purse. "I will not tell anyone until you are ready. This is huge news. I can't wait to introduce Perdi to our small world of people. Are you going to tell anyone?" Kat asked.

"No, Kat. We need to keep this quiet for now. We don't know if this is real. We don't know the full story. It seems too soon to make claims or tell people. If we do, then we will have to answer questions. Questions that we don't have the answers to at this very moment."

"Unless Perdita has more information," Aunt Dottie added.

"True. She may have all the answers. But if she doesn't, I am afraid we may never know how or why this happened," I sipped my coffee and sighed as I looked over at Kat. "I know you're exhilarated by this news and new opportunity. But for me, I can't imagine how something like this happened to Mom and Dad. They loved children. Mom tried many times to have more children after the twins but without success. When you came along, so unexpectedly, they were overjoyed that they were able to conceive again and so late in life. Well, back in the '90s it seemed late in life. Now it seems like women are having babies into their 50s." I stopped abruptly and downed my eyes to the table. What did I just say? Was I stating a fact or inadvertently confessing a wish?

Noticing my moment of inward reflection, Aunt Dottie began to nod her head and added "This is a private matter."

"I understand how you feel, KayKay. You knew them longer than I did. I don't really remember them the way you do. I have shadows of memories." There was a long pause as Kat was emptying her soul in a way I'd never heard before. She sighed and looked down at her hands. I enveloped her hands with my hands without looking up at her and said a silent prayer that this meeting would go well for us all.

We sat silently enjoying the few seconds of tenderness. When we released our hand holding, Kat was as bright and chipper as ever and continued on. "I'm thrilled just to meet her. I'll keep the news to our intimate circle, Kyra," Kat confessed quietly as the bell rang on The Beach Diner door and there she was... Mom.

My mouth parted open. Kat saw my shock and surprise. She spun around and swiveled back to me all smiles. Kat stood up as Perdita and her son Mac, who was much taller, walked towards us. There was no doubt we were related. Perdita was dark skinned like me and dad. But her hair was fair like Mom's. It was blonde with strands of grey. She wore an age-appropriate bob with long strands in the front that were cut bluntly on an angle to the back. Her son, Mac, was tall and slender but clearly muscular. He wore denim jeans and cowboy boots. His baseball cap brim was rolled round and pulled low on his face so that you could hardly see his eyes. His complexion was tanned from the sun, and you knew by looking at him he worked outside. He looked as if he smelled like fresh cut grass on a summer day. At first glance, I would have called him a Jacksonville cowboy. Kat squealed with a hello and a wave for them to come over to our table, as others stopped eating and looked over towards our table.

I had to smile at her sheer enjoyment of the situation. Her reaction was playful, sweet, and certainly differentiated from my calm and understated reaction. I found myself getting up and out of the chair. Before I knew it, I was throwing my arms around this complete stranger who was more my sister in appearance than the woman I raised, standing next to me.

We hugged and that hug lingered for many long moments. I felt Perdita's body ever so slightly breathing up and down into a slight sob. I knew this woman was my long-lost sister. I felt it in her hug. I separated myself from her and we connected our gaze to find we were both, indeed, crying.

We both launched into happy laughter tears when we both said in unison the same exact phrase. "Hello. I'm sorry."

Mac was right there with tissues. He pulled out more for me after he handed the first fist full of tissues to his mom. As I said thank you, I grabbed him towards me and hugged him too. He hugged me back like a man who graciously accepted affection and knew he was loved. He tilted his head towards mine as a small child or puppy would do when accepting affection from a loved one.

Giving them both a little more personal space, I stepped back and watched Aunt Dottie dive in for hugs. "This is Aunt Dottie hugging on you. I'm Kyra, and this is your little sister, Katherine Anne or Kat for short," I said locking eyes on Perdita. Mac and Perdita sat across from us.

"Kat, I love that nickname," Mac said. "We are happy you agreed to meet with us. We had no idea how this would go. But y'all seem real nice and kind. Thank you for that." Mac pointed at me and then to Perdi and continued "You both really look like one another." We all waited quietly for the coffee to be poured by the waitress. I watched Perdita next to me arrange her silverware and coffee cup exactly at the same time. Across from her was Kat, who was arranging her silverware and coffee cup in a mirror image. Their motions were nearly identical. They each moved the coffee cup to the center of their space. Next, they removed the silverware from the napkin. Each folded the napkin on a diagonal and placed the silverware on top of it, only then taking the spoon and placing it in the coffee cup. The waitress stopped by with more glasses of water.

"Do you need anything else for the moment?" she asked.

"Honey, please." Simultaneously both Perdita and Kat asked for honey for their coffee.

"Fascinating," I whispered with my eyes wide open. "You both take honey in your coffee."

"Wow. That's wild. No one I know except Mom drinks coffee with honey," Mac added with a smile that showcased his dimple in his left cheek.

"Our mom also drank honey in her coffee," I said, pulling photos out of my purse. I placed three piles of photos of the family on the table. Perdita and Mac looked at them all as we explained who, where, and when they all were taken.

After every photo was discussed, we sat quietly for a moment. Mac broke the silence and said what we were all thinking. "Do you know how this happened?"

Kat and I both let out a sigh and shook our heads no. "No. We are very confused by the entire situation," I said in a soft voice with remorse still lingering in the air. "I assume if you are asking us, then you have no clue as to how we were separated either?"

Both shook their heads.

As I looked from Mac to Perdi, there was a glimpse of something in Perdi's mannerism that made me think she knew more than she was offering. Was I reading into it? I didn't want to push on the first meeting. As curious as I was and as bad as I wanted information, I knew the time had to be right for Perdi to expose what she knew.

"Well, I hope you don't find this too forward, but we have dinner every Sunday night together. Can you join us for Sunday Supper at 3:00 at our home next week?" Kat blurted out to my surprise.

"Yes, you must come to family dinner on Sunday and meet Ken and Killian. Your twin brothers are working today," I smiled, and hoped the surprise did not show on my face. "Every day actually. They took over our Dad's construction business and built it up into a local construction company. Mostly focused on residential housing now. They run the business together and couldn't get away on such short notice. They can't wait to meet you both."

"Wait... not King Construction?" Perdita asked with interest.

"Yes, actually. You have heard of them," Kat asked?

"Fascinating. We have heard of them. There is a subdivision near our my home that has a King Homes sign out in front of it," Perdita said. "I drive by it every day."

"That's them," Aunt Dottie added. "My brother, your dad, would be so proud of how far they have taken the company since he passed. They started with individual lots all over town, building single family homes and selling them. Their latest project is in Peaceful River Valley, where we live. They recently got lots in West End, as a preferred builder."

"That is just wonderful. I would love to come to dinner and meet them. Mac, are you free Sunday?" Perdi shifted in her seat.

"Well, I'll need to check with the cattle, but yes, I'm available."

Aunt Dottie belly laughed. "A little farmer humor," she boasted.

Mac smiled, and asked, "What can I bring to my first King family Sunday Supper?"

And just like that, we were a family planning Sunday Supper together. I felt relieved and connected enough to wade into deeper waters. "Perdi, is there anything you can tell us about your birth date, adoption, or adopted parents? Maybe first we should tell you what we know from Aunt Dottie."

"Oh Aunt Dottie... do you have some information to share that may be helpful?" Perdi asked gently.

All eyes were on Aunt Dottie as she recounted the story of Ken Jr going off to Vietnam in the Army. Katherine lived in Ponte Vedra Beach at The Inn and Club of Ponte Vedra Beach. She was pregnant and barely showing when she visited Aunt Dottie in Palm Valley at the King plantation. The King plantation had been standing for almost 100 years. The drive was a long dirt road off Palm Valley Road. The drive ended at the A-frame house made of logs on top of cinder blocks. The year was 1967 and she knocked on the old creaking screen front door. When Aunt Dottie opened the door, Katherine looked frightened. Her mother found out she was pregnant and was going to send Katherine away to a nurse to care for her during the pregnancy. When Katherine returned six months later, she was a different girl. Katherine was melancholy until Ken proposed. Then they worked hard and lived in a little apartment near the beach until they could afford to buy some land here in Palm Valley and start a family.

Aunt Dottie finished the story with "You see dear... Katherine told me you had only lived a few hours and died. I don't think she ever knew you existed, or she would have found you."

Mac handed Perdi more tissues. Perdi stood up, rubbing her nose in the fist full of tissues and quietly headed towards the ladies room. "Should I follow her and go talk to her?" I asked Mac as I kept my eyes on Perdi. A woman at the table near the hallway to the ladies room watched Perdi go by, then stood up, and headed down the hall.

"No, I think she will be ok. If I know her, she just needs a minute to process the new information. We discussed this being one of the possible scenarios."

When Mac stopped talking, I focused on his face and focused on his slight dimple in his left cheek. "We do want to hear all about you, Mac. I hope you will share all the stories of your childhood and how you came to own a farm and love to cook. Maybe at our Sunday Supper."

"I look forward to Sunday Supper. I have not done one in a long while. Mom has been too busy with work and now she is thinking of selling that old beach house and it needs repairs. Her focus is not on a relaxing family event." Mac pulled out his phone and flipped through a series of photos including some cows, chickens, horses, and a little ranch home built nestled within a series of large old oak trees. It reminded me of the Palm Valley house where I grew up. His ranch was clearly built in the mid-century with clear signature architectural details like the celestial windows.

Perdi returned to the table, "Apologies everyone. Aunt Dottie, thank you for sharing that story of Katherine. I had, for a long time, thought I was not wanted. But clearly that was not the case. I imagined all the probabilities, and this was one that seemed plausible – that Katherine did not know I was still alive."

"This information, of course, sets off a series of questions to be answered about what happened in the room when Mom gave birth?" I said, flashing through all the events that could have happened.

Kat cleared her throat and asked, "But how do we find out for certain what happened? Perdi, do you know how your parents ended up adopting you? Is there a story there?

"No, I never asked. I didn't know until I was nine, that I was adopted. By then, my mom was already gone and dad was so melancholy. When he wasn't sad, he was angry. We never shared family history. I seemed to cease to exist to him after mom was..." Perdi trailed off and blew her nose.

"Someone must know something. Relatives?" Kat insisted.

Aunt Dottie was motioning to the waitress for more coffee and when she arrived, we all stopped talking. No one at the table was willing to divulge our secrets. The waitress poured more coffee into all the empty mugs while tidying up a few dirty items and exiting without saying a word. Aunt Dottie leaned into the table and whispered, "Kat, I'm not sure we will ever know what happened that day."

"Mom was adopted by loving people at birth." Perdi placed her hand on Mac's hand and I could tell she was on the verge of tears.

"You were adopted on your birthday? Then your parents must have some information about the birth, right?" I said almost excited to hear this could be a lead.

Perdi sipped her coffee and placed a napkin to her lips. "Sadly, no. Mom and Dad both have passed on now."

"That's what I was afraid of... we can't get info out of the dead." Aunt Dottie shifted in her chair.

"We never really talked about the adoption process either. I was raised by two people who loved me and that was enough for me. I wish I had asked more questions after mom died. It was tragic and unexpected. My dad became unreachable, emotionally. I went to work... burying myself in the history of law and the law itself to gain a relationship with him.... To try to reach him." Reaching for photos in her purse, Perdi shared a small collection of family photos, most taken when she was young at the Ponte Vedra Beach house. She pulled out several photos of Mac as a baby and at graduation and the day he got the keys to the farm.

Kat shared more photos of Mom and Dad. We all noted Perdi's resemblance to Mom and Dad. Perdi had visited or lived in this area her entire life, but we never once met. We marveled at several near misses and at a chance meeting with various events and locations going back to the '70s. Mac and Kat barely got to say a word while Perdi and I dominated the conversation exchanging tales from our histories. We talked for hours about our lives, our connections, and how technology pulled us into one another's universes.

Chapter FOURTEEN

We said our goodbyes in The Beach Diner parking lot. We exchanged information. We made plans. This was what normal people did when they met a sibling for the first time at the age of 50-something. This was totally normal.

I was deep in my thoughts as we drove home. Kat was catching up on all the buzz online as I drove us back over the bridge. I thought it was a quiet ride home given our interactions. When she looked up from her phone, I said "Well, was that meeting exactly what you had in your mind?"

"No, actually. I thought it would be more... me and her talking. I was so high-key about meeting her. But, maybe I built it up in my mind too much. Or maybe she was not what I was expecting."

"What were you expecting, Kat?" I asked gently. There was a long quiet pause. She was thinking, perhaps, or trying to choose her words carefully? I jumped in and said "I do feel like I bonded instantly, but perhaps it was our age. Or perhaps it was how closely she resembled Mom... except for her skin tone. I wasn't really expecting that."

"Didn't I show you her photo online? She looked so much like Mom... from one of the photos I have of Mom before I was born," Kat's enthusiasm diminished, replaced by a snarky tongue only reserved for me.

Yep, this was something that would need to unfold slowly. This was sensitive, and we had different ideas in our heads of how it should go. I should extend an olive branch before she shuts down, I thought. "Kat, it was such a good idea to ask them to Sunday Supper. I think the twins will enjoy meeting her. What do you think?"

"Sure, that sounds good. Maybe Ken and Killian can blubber all over Perdi, too so I have no opportunity to talk to her," Kat's wicked words stabbed me a little. Was I being overly sensitive? Was Kat jealous of my instant connection to Perdi? Would I get a straight answer out of her if I asked?

"Mind your tone with your sister. Respect, always," Aunt Dottie commanded and put a hand on Kat's shoulder from the back seat.

"Kat, Perdi was separated from Mom at birth for all we know, and she never knew Mom's touch or love. She never knew Daddy. I feel an immense amount of compassion towards her," I stated the obvious and prepared for a missile to be launched back at me. But she went quiet.

"You're right. I'm sorry I snapped at you." Kat looked over at me with puppy dog eyes. She was instantly forgiven. "I guess I was just surprised at how quickly you two connected. I could see there was a bond, instantly, between you both. I thought... I would be the one to bond with her, given you didn't seem to show much excitement about the situation."

Kat was right about the exchange. I had no expectations and almost dreaded the encounter while she was bubbling with excitement. This seemed more our personalities than anything to do with Perdi. I always walked cautiously into any situation and Kat blasts on any scene full of excitement and wonder. Changing the subject, I went back to her favorite topic. "What are you working on this week for content? Are you still doing your podcasts?"

"I'd like to see more alligator content. That Florida Guy stuff is funny," Aunt Dottie interjected from the back seat, drinking her Beach Diner coffee from a Styrofoam cup.

Kat, completely ignoring Aunt Dottie's suggestion, pulled her nose out of the phone and said "I don't know. I was going to do our Perdi finding. You told me to keep it on the down low, so I am exploring backup topics. Are you going to work today when we get home?"

"I'll check in, yes, after lunch. Today, I'll get the remaining boxes down from the attic and search them for an inkling of our mystery sister." I turned into The Ranch and as the tires hit the brick path in the entrance, I thought to myself... please let me find something that will help solve the mystery.

Chapter FIFTEEN

Once we arrived home, Kat went directly to her room. With a sigh, I made my way to the garage and pulled down the attic stairs. It was time to find all the boxes in the attic with Mom and Dad's personal effects. They were all in cardboard file boxes labeled by decade.

I was looking for photos, letters, cards, journals, diaries, or anything that might provide me with an inkling of information about what happened in the months leading up to the birth of Perdi in 1967. I sat back on a sturdy box in the attic. Pushing boxes out of the way as I eliminated them as possible suspects.

I pushed the marked boxes towards the hole in the floor. How would I get these down from the attic? Why are attics always up these dangerous stairs? Why can't there be normal comfortable stairs to an upper level with a normal door as an entrance to the flippin' attic? Huh... that's a good idea. I'll need to remember to give that design tip to the twins.

I loaded up my office with stacks of file boxes from the attic. Some were dated, most were not and just listed the decade on them. I picked the first one and dug into the box, ready to explore the history of the Kings. For the most part, I enjoyed seeing mementos and personal items including photos. I found photos of Dad when he was younger. A black and white photo of him in uniform in front of what I imagined was the Palm Valley house on Roscoe Road before it was demolished and sold for land in the late '60s. I found photos of Mom and her life up north. Her family must have been very wealthy. She and her brothers and sisters wore pretty clothes and shoes. There was a long-curved stairway in a foyer with a chandelier that looked extravagant. I could see Mom in the middle of her siblings. She was noticeable by her smile and the ribbon in her hair. I'd seen that ribbon. It was on her head in a photo that was in the den of the old Palm Valley home where Mom & Dad shared their entire lives.

In one of the last boxes I opened, I found my parents' marriage license, original birth certificates, and copies of each of the kids' birth certificates. Included were locks of our hair in envelopes marked with our names. I found a treasure box full of letters. Some were on military stationery. There were almost a hundred stacked in several piles and tied together with string. I organized them by post mark dates, for those that had them. I read each and every one in chronological order. The letters were of course full of love and romance. They reminded me of the faith my parents walked every day. They were tender towards one another. The letters were full of hope, loyalty, tears, and the imagination of a future life together. Exactly the letters one would expect to read between young lovers. It was like reading a story where you knew the characters at old age, but through reading the letters, you envisioned them younger and could journey with them through their youth. I could see them living their lives again through reading the letters.

One final item in the bottom of the letter box. A 10 x 13 envelope with the letterhead of Ponte Vedra Inn and Club. It was their old logo, but I recognized it. It was sealed with glue. It was the only thing in the box that was sealed. All other envelopes were open with a letter opener or torn open. A few had no envelope. But this one was sealed. I could only imagine why.

I got up off the floor and stretched my legs. I walked to the kitchen and laid the envelope on the island while I poured myself a glass of homemade sun tea. I knew whatever was in that envelope needed to be shared with the family. Maybe they should be there with me when I open it. Maybe I should just open it with Perdi. Maybe I should not open it at all. Why would there be one sealed envelope? What was mother concealing?

Boop-Boop. The Ring alerted me to the front door opening. Ken yelled out, "Sis, you home?"

"I'm in the kitchen," I said loudly into the air. "What are you two doing here this afternoon?" I glanced at the clock on the microwave and realized I spent the entire afternoon and into the early evening looking in boxes.

"We wanted to hear how the meet went this morning with Perdita. How was it?" Ken asked.

"Yea... what is she like, dude? Give us the four-one-one." Killian said as he plunged his hand into the nuts on the counter, capturing a fist full. Killian referred to everyone as 'Dude'. I could only surmise that this was behavior left over from me allowing him to watch *Fast Times at Ridgemont High* too many times when I babysat them as children His favorite character was Jeff Spicoli. Killian emulated him as a young boy, took up surfing, and became a Palm Valley version of Spicoli. Spicoli's influence would manifest part in very funny ways, within Killian. I imaged Killian in his board shorts, chest and arms tattooed, with zinc oxide on his nose wrangling an alligator quoting the famous Spicoli line *"If you're here and I'm here... isn't it our time?"*

Kat found her way into the kitchen as Ken was pouring sun tea drinks for everyone and adding sugar to his own. We piled into the living room, making ourselves comfortable in the chairs overlooking the lanai and pool. It was a lovely evening for the sliding glass doors to be open. The sky was darkening, the jasmine was blooming in the courtyard, and the breeze pushed the palms softly around as if they were dancing. It was a perfect May night.

"Well... I was skeptical at first," I said, "but as soon as I saw her in person, I dropped my guard. She looks exactly like Mom except for her skin tone. To be more accurate, she looks like an older version of Mom. She's charming and sweet. She's absolutely lovely. She grew up in Pittsburgh and wintered here in Ponte Vedra Beach."

"Oh... really? The Beach Club?" Killian asked.

I nodded my head yes as we all knew only well-off people vacationed to Ponte Vedra Beach in the winter at the Ponte Vedra Inn and Club. "The interesting tidbit of information she did tell us was that she had no idea she was adopted until much later in life."

"Her parents didn't tell her she was adopted? She never thought to ask why she didn't look like her parents?" Ken asked, sipping his sweet tea.

"When she was nine she found out and while she didn't go into detail, I sensed it was a difficult time or subject. Apparently her dad didn't take the death of her mother very well." I was hesitant to say more as I wasn't certain why Perdi hesitated this morning. I could only assume it was either too painful or she didn't want to share too much in front of her son Mac.

"We didn't touch upon some of the more sensitive areas of all our lives. We still have no idea what happened to her as a baby. She doesn't seem to know. She has no family left; they have all passed away. We didn't tell her how Mom and Dad died. Only that they had passed away." Kat looked over at me and seemed almost sad that we didn't mention the accident.

"Well, in all fairness, we don't know what happened to Mom and Dad that day. No one does," Killian added.

"Then there is her son, Mac. He's a real sweetheart. He is, maybe, a little younger than you guys. She must have had him young. Perdi said she was shocked when Mac told her that he found relatives through a DNA match. She was eager to know us, given she thought her family was all gone. She submitted her DNA and found the 50% match to Kat."

"Wow, that is crazy," Ken said while Killian shook his head in disbelief. "I still can't believe that we have a sister we never knew about. It is even more shocking that y'all met her and she looks like Mom. Unbelievable. I can't wait to meet her."

"Yeah, what's the plan. When do we get to meet them?" Killian asked eagerly.

"Kat invited them to Sunday Supper," I said smiling at Kat.

"Yep, they were thrilled. Y'all will meet them Sunday. Oh… and they knew your construction company," Kat said proudly.

"It's the logo. Everyone loves the crown," Ken said boosting a smile.

"I still think the best logo was the one where we spelled construction with a K," Killian said straight-faced, prompting us all to laugh.

Ken just shook his head and mouthed '*No*'.

We sat quietly for a moment, and I realized we had not laughed since we found out we had a sister. It felt good to share this moment with all the original sibs.

"So, we have no new information. And she has no idea what happened when she was born? Her family had no idea who the birth parents were when they adopted her?" Killian asked.

"No, she has no idea. Her family was not forthcoming with information about the adoption. She did look through all the photos and papers that were left after her parents died. She found some paperwork, and at the time, was too involved with her grief to read it or look through it. She is going to go through it now. I've promised the same. That's the project in my office… all those boxes were in the attic. I'm going through all the cards, paperwork, birth certificates, and letters that I can find. Hoping to find something that will help us understand what happened."

"Did you want me to help you?" Kat asked.

"That would be great. I still have several boxes to go through," I said looking over at Kat. "I found all the letters Mom and Dad wrote to one another while he was in Vietnam. You can read them for a journey into their young love and lives together."

We all went quiet as the night was winding down. The breeze into the house was cooler. It was an emotional day, but I suddenly felt very relaxed surrounded by my family.

"Well, now you will find out how it feels to have someone older bossing you around all the time," Ken laughed. "Let's get going, Killian."

"Oh yeah... you're not the boss of us anymore... you're not the oldest," Killian sang out.

"Not sure how I feel about that just yet," I said playfully but truthfully.

I watched them back out of the driveway and pulled my sweater tighter around my neck. The pavers beneath my bare feet were cool, sending a slight chill up my body. A man was standing on the opposite corner from the house smoking a cigarette. I stepped down the front stairs and watched his expelled smoke waft up to the street sign that read Littlewood Rd and Cross Branch Dr. I winced as he put out his cigarette in his hand under the streetlight. He walked across the cul-de-sac and disappeared into the darkness of the Peaceful River Valley preserve. I went back into the house and locked the front door as I looked out the four lite glass door. Kat surprised me in the gallery as I left the foyer.

"Did you see that guy put a cig out on the palm of his hand? Who was that, KayKay?"

"Oh, you startled me. I thought you went to bed, Kat."

"No, I was closing down the electronics in the podcast room and saw the glimmer of something across the street. I mean... who smokes cigarettes anymore? Yuck!"

I laughed as I recalled a time when I smoked cigarettes before Kat was born. I would sit at the bar with my colleagues and open my brown faux crocodile cigarette case that was adorned with gorgeous brass around the perimeter. It was a magnet for young men to come over and talk with me after they lit my cigarette. Oh... those were the days. When men and women talked to one another at a bar instead of burying their nose in a phone. "I love that you have commandeered my guest suite and call it your podcast room."

I heard my phone ringing. I searched for it in my purse on the kitchen island. "Ken, did you see that guy on the corner."

"You know I did, that is why I called you. Lock the doors."

"Yes, I did." I smiled at the thought of Ken still protecting me and Kat. "He put his cigarette out in the palm of his hand. Kat was more freaked out that he was a smoker than where he put out his cigi-butt."

Ken laughed on the other end of the phone. "Did you want me to come back to the house?" I watched Kat return to the kitchen and look at the sealed envelope on the island.

"No. No, we are safe. I locked the door. This is Peaceful River Valley after all. Nothing wicked ever happens here."

"It would make me feel better if you would load your gun and keep it in the bedroom with you tonight."

That was a good idea, I thought to myself. "Yes, I will. Thank you, Ken."

"For what KayKay?"

"For always watching out for us," I gushed.

"Of course. You're my family. Call me if there is any trouble."

"Goodnight, Ken."

"Goodnight, Sis."

I hung up the phone. I quickly called Perdi. As it rang, I wondered if she would be excited to hear from me. "Perdi, this is Kyra."

"Hey there, Sis," Perdi replied, like we knew each other for a lifetime. I smiled. I was not certain if it was the tone of her voice or what she said but it warmed me like hot cocoa with marshmallows on Christmas Eve. I'm someone's little sister now and it felt natural to talk to Perdi. Hopefully, she felt the same.

"Perdi... do you feel comfortable showing me your birth certificate?"

Chapter SIXTEEN

K at was pouring more sun tea into her glass as I walked into the kitchen. I tapped my fingers on the envelope on the kitchen island after I hung up with Perdi. I touched my finger to the embossed logo in the corner. I turned the envelope over. I ran my fingers over the top flap and felt the glued edge disintegrating with age. It was not open but it was starting to come unglued. I wondered how long it had been sealed. I opened the island drawer and reached for the letter opener. With the top sliced open, I felt inside and removed the contents. One slender white envelope, one white stuffed envelope, and a third envelope, in mom's signature peach color for her writing paper. But it didn't seem to have anything in it... until I looked more closely.

Inside the peach envelope, that was not sealed, was a perfectly snipped tiny ribbon around blonde strands of hair. The hair was short and baby soft. The inside of the envelope flap had the words *'Perdita 1967'* written in pencil.

"Wow... do you think that is Perdita's hair from the day she was born?" Kat asked as she looked on with me.

"I think so. I found envelopes like this with all our hair tied in this same little ribbon. Look... it says Perdita, 1967." I handed Kat the envelope to examine the contents.

"Whoa... that's amazing that we never found this before... don't you think?" Kat was astonished, but I wasn't. I knew why we didn't find this before now.

"Well... after mom and dad passed, we packed up a lot of their belongings and we sold so many things. We are actually lucky this is here with us and wasn't sold with a jewelry box or in a shoe box or something." Knowing that I prolonged the clean out of my parent's house until the very last moment. I packed these boxes over 10 years ago and never went through them. I just knew they had records and important items in them... that I would someday go through... when I was ready.

The next envelope contained only a small piece of paper. Much smaller than the actual envelope itself. On the first paper was Perdita's birth certificate. The second paper was Perdita's death certificate.

"Look... birth and death certificates for Perdi." I handed the contents of the envelope to Kat and picked up the last envelope. The smaller envelope felt thick in my hand. Like it was stuffed with wads of paper.

"What's that?" Kat asked as she gulped down her sun tea.

"I'm not sure yet," I said as I carefully pulled out pieces of paper from the envelope. Kat moved beside me to see for herself.

I unfolded the pieces of paper, carefully. It seemed like quality writing paper, and it was peach in color. I'd seen this paper before. Mom had a box of peach writing paper when I was a little girl. She let me write letters to our grandparents on that same paper. I smoothed the paper out. Eagerly, I read the top page. The page included a name, date, and the name of a man and a woman under it. Then below was the name of a city in New York. The next page included a different name, date, and names of a man and woman with a city in Pennsylvania. I counted seven pages in total all with the same format but different names and places. The last page, that seventh page, included the name Perdita King, Perdi's birth date, and the name of her adoptive parents Susie and David Boyle. Under the parent's name was the word Pittsburgh.

I pushed the pages towards Kat. She looked at each one. She came to the last page, finished reading it, and looked up at me. "What do these all mean? Are these other children who were adopted?"

"I don't know. I'll need to research them all. But if this pattern is birth name, adoptive parents, and city in which they lived, then mom knew that Perdi was alive and taken from her.

"Whoa... that's unbelievable. We need to call Perdi," Kat said in disbelief.

"I called her earlier. We are having lunch with her tomorrow," I said examining the fronts and backs of each piece of paper. "I asked if she would bring her birth certificate so we could examine it."

A close up of a stamp

Description auto-matically generated

Perdi met Kat and I for lunch the next day. I called out from work, again, taking another day off to dive deeper into the mystery of the lost sister. We met at South Kitchen on the patio and ordered salads. When Perdi arrived, she presented me with her birth certificate. I was eager to check the authenticity.

I was disappointed to see it was perfectly normal. I put on my reading glasses and noted the hospital. She was born in Jacksonville at Riverside hospital. The certificate was worn but looked legitimate. Born in 1967 at Riverside. "Riverside Hospital was where I was born and so were the twins." I smiled at Perdi. "Thank you for showing me your birth certificate. I thought maybe there was a mistake about the year or authenticity."

"Authenticity? Why did you think it was going to be a fake?" Perdi asked as her face went from a smile at the thought of absurdity to a genuine look of concern.

"Perdi, there is no easy way to say this," I began.

"We found your birth certificate last night in Mom's belongings," Kat said softly and then added "along with your death certificate."

"Your birth certificate is identical to the one we found at home, except the last name of course," I pushed the certificate back across the table to Perdi. "There is something else," I whispered, as I pulled the piece of paper out of the envelope. "We found the name of your adoptive parents on a piece of Mom's stationary... written in her own hand writing."

"Wait, what!" Perdi put her hands on the table and sat up right. We clearly caught her attention.

"I know. It's startling information. It was in a box with all the copies of the kid's birth certificates," I handed Perdi the manilla folder with the certificates fastened to the inside.

She took the envelope from me without breaking her gaze. Searching my face for any movement that would convince her this information was not true. Perdi opened the envelope and examined the contents.

"She knew I survived and was adopted? But Aunt Dottie told us that Mom told her I only lived for a few hours and then died." Perdi's mouth was open and her gaze from me to Kat and back to me made my heart hurt.

"Mom's family was well off for the time," I said. "They were from the North. She had family in Pennsylvania and New Jersey. We never met Mom's family. She once told me that she came here to Florida with her mother to look for a winter home in Ponte Vedra Beach, fell in love with our dad and never looked back. Her family did not approve of dad. They basically disowned mom and never talked to her again."

"Dad was from Palm Valley, and they were blue collar, and his family lived off the land. Our family came here from Ireland. The King family goes way back. We owned a lot of land for like hundreds of years," Kat added.

"We don't have much information to go on here. We don't know when she wrote this note. There are no dates on any of the pages that indicate if she wrote this the day you were born or years later," I said knowing this was not helpful information.

"So, Aunt Dottie was told that I died on the day of my birth. You found both the birth and the death certificate. But now we have this piece of paper with my parents and Pittsburgh PA, which is where I grew up, mostly," Perdi repeated it. It sounded worse out loud than it did in my head.

"Mom and Dad didn't talk about their courtship or their lives before we kids were born. We have asked Aunt Dottie, as our only living relative, on my dad's side. She doesn't remember much because she was married at the time and traveled a lot between Palm Valley and her home with her husband. She knows that her brother was very much in love with our mom."

Perdi looked down at her salad being delivered. After listening to my short little love story, her shoulders slumped the smallest amount and her head drooped. I could not see her face. Her short blonde hair was softly swept back behind her ear just enough that I could not read her eyes. She seemed somber or in deep thought. I continued, "We were all born at Riverside, except for Kat. Riverside is gone, obviously."

"It's a Publix now," Kat chimed in.

"We have an appointment this afternoon with the state records manager for Duval County. I want to meet with them and see if there was any more they could tell us about the birth or this birth certificate," I pointed down at the envelope on the table containing Perdi's birth certificate. "They may have records. When I called yesterday, they said most were still in folders and boxes. Only a small portion are digital records. I think it's worth investigating, Perdi. Will you go with us this afternoon?"

Perdi shifted in her seat. She was looking at my hand on the envelope. Her hair was slightly covering her eyebrows and eyes. I could not get a read on her emotions, but I assumed she was upset. She looked up at me with watery eyes. "I would like to know what happened back then. But this is all so shocking to hear I have siblings. I always knew it was a possibility when I was told I was adopted." She paused, locking her gaze on me and softly placing her hand on mine on top of the envelope. My heart seemed to stop, and I held my breath as I impatiently waited for her next words. What was she about to divulge?

She said softly and slowly, "Your words really impacted me when you said Mom and Dad loved babies and children and you knew in your heart that there was something not right about this entire situation. Knowing Ken and Katherine the way you did... one of us will be shattered here when we find the truth. Your image of who they were might shatter you. Or... I may learn something that will shatter me to pieces."

I grabbed her hand hard. "No, Perdi. You were not given up for adoption. Don't even give that thought any energy. I believe we are both feeling the same way, Perdi. I'm nervous and eager to find answers... to resolve this mystery. But, at the same time, I think that the people who raised me and who I thought I knew better than myself... well... they may not be at all who I thought they were. What we may learn... the idea of it scares me," I paused.

I swallowed hard because I was about to be vulnerable to a stranger I barely knew. Ultimately, with every fiber of my being, I felt an instinctive connection towards Perdi. "I trust my family. I only met you, but I trust you. Please know, whatever the answer is here to our mutual question, we will find it together. We will deal with it together. Let's never let one another go. I need your support, personally," I saw the tears run down Perdi's face and she gripped Kat's hand as Kat reached out.

"Agreed. I need your support as well. I don't feel as though I can do this alone. It is painful how scary it is to not know the truth but to seek it, despite the fear," Perdi confessed.

We smiled at one another with tears in our eyes. The waitress came up to the table, took one look at us and said, "Oh no, I hope it wasn't the salad?" We all burst out in a sigh of relief and little laughs. I wiped away my tears with my napkin from my lap. I could not contain myself and started giggling like a child. To my surprise, Perdi almost mimicked me perfectly. There was no doubt we were sisters. Only sisters could find such joy and laughter in the sorrow and pain of life.

Chapter
SEVENTEEN

Perdi, Kat, and I jumped in Perdi's car after lunch. We were off to find the Duval County records at St. Vincent Hospital. Riverside hospital, where we were all born, closed in 2001. It was purchased by St. Vincent. The records woman I spoke with sounded very confident that all records were provided when Riverside combined with St. Vincent. She couldn't promise anything, but she was going to research all birth and death certificates for the King family, and Perdita's adoptive family name of Boyle.

Armed with our driver's licenses and our newly uncovered records, we took the elevator to the basement where only the morgue and records room were located. The cement blocks were painted in a high gloss light blue color. The floor was checked in royal blue and white instead of black and white. It seemed calming and vibrant all at the same time. We entered the records room and were instantly greeted by Doris Adams, the record room keeper. I'd spoken with Doris on the phone yesterday. I was curious if she would remember me. She was well beyond retirement age, short and a little round with curly short hair. Her glasses were on top of her head. As I glanced down at her face, I noticed an additional pair of glasses hanging low on her nose, as she read a document held in her hands. Oddly, there was yet a third pair of glasses hanging from a chain around her neck. Doris was turning out to be a fascinating woman. Her movement was slow as she looked up and greeted us.

"Hello ladies, how can I help ya today?" Doris asked in a deep South accent, most familiar in the more rural areas west of Jacksonville. I was about to answer when a jolt of movement caught my eye—an orange tabby cat, a blur of fur and muscle, had somehow appeared on the counter. It then gracefully strolled toward Doris, rubbing its head affectionately against her shoulder and chin, a low purr rumbling in its chest.

"Ahh... a furry co-worker that knows no personal space boundaries," I said with laughter. "Hello Doris, I'm..."

"Yes, yes, Kyra King. I recognize your voice. Plus I don't get many visitors around here." She, in fact, remembered me. I was touched and impressed. To my surprise, she turned back around and headed slowly, almost shuffling, over to a large file box on the rear counter. Doris picked up the box with no issue and hoisted it up on the lower counter where there was no Plexi glass.

While leaning on the top of the box, Doris took off the glasses that rested on her nose, closed the arms, and began tapping them on the top of the file box. "Dears, I did look up your records for birth and death within Riverside. I need to check your driver's licenses to make certain you are able to receive this information."

Perdi, Kat, and I produced our Florida driver's licenses. Doris took them and hardly looked at them, pushing all three back across the counter. "Now... I did find something peculiar in the paperwork that we should talk about before I hand off these copies. Give me a moment, I'll come around. Sit at that table right there and let's chat a moment." Doris pointed her folded glasses towards a small round table in the corner of the room opposite the door.

I glanced over at Perdi and shrugged as we shared a look of uncertainty. We sat down at the table as instructed and waited for Doris. The cat watched us from the counter, licking a paw. Doris disappeared behind a wall and re-appeared through a doorway to the records room. She sat down across from us at the table placing a manila folder in between both of us. "Now, dear, you say your name is Perdita Ryan, born May 28, 1967 in Riverside Hospital? Is that correct?"

Perdita was wide-eyed and hanging on every word Doris said. "Yes, ma'am, that is correct. I'm Perdita," I took Perdita's birth certificate out of the envelope and handed it to Doris to confirm the authenticity of the document.

While still holding a pair of glasses, Doris reached up on top of her head and put her head glasses on her nose and examined the document. "Well dear, I suspect that this is not going to be easy to hear. I don't want to jump to any conclusions. I will just tell you what I found." Opening the manila folder, Doris began, "I found a birth certificate for one Perdita King. I found one death certificate for an infant named Perdita King. Born to one Katherine Edwards, prematurely by approximately 1 month. The father on the birth certificate is Kenneth King. The baby lived 6 hours."

"Oh my gosh, it is true." Kat gasped.

"Yes, we found evidence suggesting as much in Katherine's belongings," Perdita said as she inspected the information in front of her. "But then how do I have this birth certificate? It even looks exactly like this other birth certificate. The signatures are the same. The dates are the same. The only thing different is the parents. I was born to David and Susie Boyle. My mother, Susie Boyle, while dying in a hospital, told me that it was all a lie. I was not born to them... to David and Susie that is, Ma'am. I was adopted by them with no paperwork."

Kat burst out in shock "What? I'm shook."

My mouth was gaping open, and my eyes were wide as saucers. I could not believe what I was hearing. No one wants to hear these things. Especially not on someone's deathbed. I threw my arm around Perdi and comforted her. I told myself to remain calm, but it was not working. "Doris, is there anything else in those files that indicates what transpired on that day in

May 1967? Does it say if both Katherine and Kenneth were present? Does it mention the Boyles at all?"

"No, dears. This is the most interesting thing I've come across in 50+ years at this institution. Well, I was with Riverside for a long time. Heck, I started at Riverside in the '60s. I can tell you one thing and one thing only. There was a nurse at Riverside. She was a middle-aged witch. No one liked her. She had a reputation for being sly."

"Sly?" Kat said, interrupting Doris.

"That's right, sly. Ya know, shifty. Tricky. She was a nasty woman," Doris said with emphasis on nasty, using her hand with her folded up glasses to bang on the table. She was your nurse during the delivery. Her name is on your file. Agnes Flannery, but people here called her Aggie." Doris went on to deliver more absurd news.

"But... that is not the crazy part," Doris relayed as Perdi and I looked at each other almost in horror. Could we take any more?

"Okay, Doris. Lay it on us. Because this story can't possibly get any wilder," Perdi said with a stone-cold face.

"It can and it will. You had no doctor present during your birth. I have no record of a doctor being on duty that night to deliver a child. I have no doctor in the records that admits to being your doctor of birth or death. The nurse is the only name that appears on any of your paperwork."

My mind was racing with questions. No doctor? Who was this nurse? How did a baby get born with only a nurse present. Did a priest provide the last rites for the baby? Mom being Catholic, she would have insisted. I fiddled and tapped each one of my fingertips with my thumbs on both hands from pinky to forefinger while repeating to myself to stay calm. It wasn't working. I was jumping out of my skin. What happened to my mom that day?

"Doris, is this nurse, by any chance at all, still alive?" I said almost pleading for a positive answer.

"If she died, I don't have record of it here. She may still be alive, but it would make her older than me and I'm as old as God's dirt," Doris said.

She slowly stood up as if it took all her might. She shuffled towards the box on the counter. "Here are all your copies. I don't know what your story is, dear Perdita, but it sure started out with a scandal."

"Truer words have never been spoken, Doris. Thank you for your help," I said, getting up and picking up the box and handing it off to Kat. Perdi sat still for a moment, looked up at me with puppy dog eyes. Pleading to make it stop? Pleading to find an answer? "Let's go, Perdi. We have more pieces of the puzzle to fit together."

"Family secrets are best left as secrets... and that's the truth," Kat sad quietly while consoling Perdi gently. Kat placed her hand on Perdi's back, soothing her slowly.

"Bye-bye now, dears. Oh, wait... Perdi? Perdita, do you know your name means 'lost' in Latin? Do you think your mother, perhaps your real mother, Ms. Katherine King named you Perdita because she lost you?" Doris said with such genuine inquiry.

With a long pause, I watched the energy drain from Perdi's body as if it was physically holding her up and now released... her body had no will to stand on its own. Her head went down and when her chin reached her chest, it stopped. Kat wrapped her arm around Perdi's back as if to hold her up right.

"Did Mom know Latin?" Kat looked at me quizzically. "Perdi was the momma dog in the children's book 101 Dalmatians. Mom read it to me all the time when I was a little girl," Kat said in a low, uncertain voice.

"No Kat... Mom was very well educated. She attended some fancy private school in Pennsylvania. She loved Shakespeare. Perdita was the daughter of a King in the Winter's Tale," I said looking up at Kat.

"I believe your mom believed you did die shortly after you were born. Child, you were loved by your mother, and she desperately lost you on that day with a name like Perdita," Doris lovingly hypothesized.

"Hmmm... yes, Doris, you might be right," Perdi sniffled and put her head up high while she stood up. "The name does tell it all now that you put it together for me that way, Ms. Doris. Thank you." Perdi smiled. It was like watching Mom smile 20 years ago.

Chapter EIGHTEEN

I t was a very quiet ride home. Perdi was concentrating on the road. I
was looking through the box of records. There were actually a ton of
records in this box. Apparently, we were all born at Riverside and some
of our family died there. Neither of us had any more family. They were
all dead. We were all we had left. Our small little family plus Aunt Dottie.
"Why is this box so big and heavy? And how in the world did Ms. Doris
manage to lift it like it was full of cotton balls. Ms. Doris must do Burn
Bootcamps to keep herself so fit and able to lift such heavy stuff at her age,"
I said with a snort of laughter to ease the drive home. Looking over at Perdi,
I could tell there was a faint smile on her peanut face.

"Why did she have so many sets of glasses?" Kat asked.

"Right? Do you think the cat lives there, or does she bring him to work
with her every day? She sounds like she is from Palatka, but she knows
Latin. Doris is an enigma," I said, still going through the top folders of the
very large pile.

"How about we go to your place. We can spread out the files and do
some research," Perdi said, ready to get down to work.

"Love that idea. Back to The Ranch," I said as I continued thumbing at
the folders.

"What about the Moke? We left it at South Kitchen," Perdi said.

"Oh I'll have Ken and Killian get it and drive it back home," I put down the box to message the twins.

"Let's stop for provisions first. Go to the Beach Publix. We need ice cream," Kat said, no doubt thinking of bonding sister time over a dessert.

"I could use some Mint Chocolate Chip," Perdi said as if she was in love and longing for a sugar fix.

"Perfect," I said as I texted the twins to get the Moke. By the time I was done with that conversation, we were at the Publix buying ice cream.

At home, I dropped the box in the dining room. I started heating leftover homemade chicken soup for our dinner. I opened the box and sorted the folders into three piles. "Are you hungry, Perdi? I just put soup on the stove to reheat."

"Soup sounds great. Thanks," Perdi said politely. "I can't wait to review some of these files. I'm not confident we will find anything else. But just talking through this with you... well... it might help me process, sis." Perdi grinned and her mood seemed a little lighter. "This house is fantastic; do you mind if I look around?"

"Sure! Don't miss the courtyard," I said as Kat came into the dining room and sat down at the table.

"How could I miss the courtyard? There is a gorgeous pool in it surrounded by lush tropical foliage. It's fabulous. My beach house is a courtyard style home." Perdi peered through the sliding glass doors that stretched 16 feet wide and 10 ft high.

"Oh really? Was it built at the mid-century?" Fascinated by courtyard homes—the architectural design concept of bringing the outdoors in—I was truly intrigued by the possibility of finding this concept alive on a beach, with the sounds of the waves and the smell of salt in the air.

"Yes, my parents built it in the 50's in Ponte Vedra Beach. The homes surrounding my home are all enormous mansions now. No one appreciates the quaintness of the homes built originally. But clearly, this is a new build and maybe there is at least one modern day architect giving a nod to Frank

Lloyd Wright." Perdi smiled at me and then ducked into the master wing of the home.

Boop Boop. The Ring alerted me to the garage door opening. Aunt Dottie appeared in the doorway of the kitchen. "Moke is returned to the garage."

"Hi there. You are just in time for some soup," I said pointing at her with my ladle.

When Perdi returned from her tour, she said hello to Aunt Dottie with a hug and they both sat down. "I love this house. But it's really a lot of space. Is it just you and Kat now?"

"It is just the two of us. Aunt Dottie stays with us most weekends. I'm waiting for the day Kat wants to move out." I winked at Kat as she looked up at me.

"Kat, you took the bar but don't want to go into law?" Perdi asked.

"Oh no, I do. I'm just taking some time to apply. While I'm waiting, I have a podcast and a channel I'm growing."

"Interesting. You know, I own my own law firm. We currently have open positions, if you would be interested. If not, tell me where you are looking, I have a well-established network and can put in recommendations for you," Perdi mentioned. She was going to help Kat. This was the best news. Perhaps Perdi could be a mentor for Kat.

"Really? That would be terrific. I'd love to hear about what you have available and how I can apply my talents," Kat said while she closed a folder and put it in a pile at the end of the table.

The aroma of simmering soup filled the air as I watched them, their intense conversation about law punctuated by the gentle clinking of china. I collected napkins as I thought to myself, I've been trying to get Kat to take a law career seriously for weeks. Five minutes with Perdita and Kat is converted and ready to work in the field. My ego was bruised. I was clearly just replaced. Or maybe I'd been irrelevant for some time, and I was just now finding out about it. Having a new sister was lovely but I'm not sure I'm ready to be replaced as the sole caretaker and boss lady to my little sister, who I raised since she was five. There was a break in the conversation.

"Perdi. Tell me how you chose a career in law," I said.

"Actually, my dad was an attorney and practiced law. I think I chose it because it was familiar. I also saw that it provided a nice living for him and mom. I lived here at the beach house after college for the entire summer before law school. That was the year I met my husband, Mike. He was stationed here in Jacksonville while in the Navy."

"Oh, what happened to Mike, where is he now," Aunt Dottie asked curiously.

Immediately we heard displeasure from Kat. " He died a long time ago," Kat said to me with her perturbed face.

"Oh, Perdi, I'm so sorry for your loss." I looked over at Kat and asked, "How did you know that?"

"Oh, that's tragic, Perdi. When did that happen?" Aunt Dottie asked.

"I talked to Mac about it," Kat said as if they had become as thick as thieves.

"It happened almost twenty years ago." Turning to Kat, Perdi asked, "Mac talked to you about his dad?"

"Yes, why?" Kat looked concerned, as if she said something wrong.

"He doesn't talk about his dad. I'm relieved he conversed with you about Mike," Perdi looked up at me obviously hurt or shocked. I knew how she felt. "He died in a Naval accident. Then I went back to Pittsburgh to practice contract law with my father for a year, but I was miserable. We came down here that next winter and I didn't want to leave. I raised Mac in the Ponte Vedra Beach house and worked. I started the Ponte Vedra Beach office of the law firm and ran it for my dad until he retired. Now that he is gone, I run both offices. I'm thinking more about retirement now. I wanted to give Mac the business. But he has no interest in it. He just loves to farm and create recipes and cook.

"I understand his passion. I, too, have a love for tending to my garden and cooking all my own creative recipes," I said.

"Peaceful River Valley has a community farm. You purchase a plot and you can grow whatever you want on it. Kyra grows a lot of our food," Kat said.

"Do I detect a hint of pride, Kat?" I asked.

"Well... yeah, you are a superb cook and you seem to really enjoy it."

"Yes, I do love it," I said as I sipped the last of my chicken soup.

After supper, Kat cleared the dishes and loaded the dishwasher while Perdi and I reviewed folders and papers from Riverside Hospital. Perdi took the Boyle family. I took the King family stack. We continued getting to know one another as we looked through folder after folder.

"Hold the phone," I said looking at the King files. "What is this?"

I announced, "Dad had a twin brother. We have an uncle we never knew about. He was Dad's twin brother, named Conor, who, apparently, died in Vietnam in 1967."

"What? Dad had a brother?" Kat asked as she was digging into the Hagen Das.

"Aunt Dottie, you had another brother? Why didn't you ever tell us about him or say anything?" I was flabbergasted and my voice elevated.

Aunt Dottie looked shocked and sat upright in her chair. "Well... I... it was a long time ago. Your dad didn't like to talk about it."

"There is not a single photo that I've ever seen with the two of them. Why the secrets?" I expressed while holding the birth certificate in one hand and the death certificate in another hand.

"We just didn't have cameras back then. People had to be rich to have their picture taken and we never had that occasion. Ken and Conor were twins and close. They did so much together. When Conor came home and said he joined the Army, Ken felt he had no choice but to join right beside him. Then they were shipped off to Vietnam together."

"Uncle Conor never came back?" Kat asked as the room went quiet.

"Neither did your dad... not really," Aunt Dottie said. "He physically was here, but he never got over what happened over there... of which he would never talk about. And I don't know about... before you go asking me," Aunt Dottie added gruffly.

"I can't stand all these secrets and lies," I said dramatically, tossing the papers on the dining room table.

"Dad never mentioned him, at all. How horrible for dad that he spent his life separated from his twin and unable to talk about him, even to his own family," Kat said as she passed me the Hagan Dass

"This does explain the twins in the family. It doesn't help with the Perdita mystery. It does confirm this family is chock-full-of-secrets," I said as I shoved a spoon full of Hagen Das in my mouth.

Chapter NINETEEN

After Kat retreated to her suite and Aunt Dottie to the guest room, Perdi and I were left alone to have an intimate conversation about the findings of the day. It was remarkable how easily we could talk with one another, as if we had known one another our entire lives. I lit a candle on the outdoor table. We sat in the swivel chairs on the lanai, enjoying the salty air, and sipping our green tea. We quietly watched the night fall upon us with a strong refreshing breeze blowing the heavy wind chime to play a deep melody. The palms were swaying in the strong tropical wind. The flame of the candle flickered with each breeze and gave off a coconut aroma. The air was getting cooler.

Both of us enjoyed the comfort of silence with a loved one in the room, that cozy feeling you get when you are with someone you love, but no one is talking... like being alone but better because you are together. I didn't want this night to end without a resolution to the Perdi mystery. Instead, I found more mystery relatives. When would this trend stop? Once is a freak accident, but twice is, in the data world, a trend. My mind began to race again in the direction of dad. I knew he was in the service in the '60s, but I didn't know he had a brother. A twin brother, Conor King, who was killed in Vietnam. Dad must have been devastated. Is that why Dad never talked about him?

Then there was the Perdi saga. Although our new lovely friend, Ms. Doris, was able to supply us with evidence that Perdita was officially born and died the same day, we still had no answers to what really happened. "There was no doctor present at the birth... only a nurse. Nurse Aggie Flannery. I think Aggie Flannery is a lead," I said to Perdi as I sipped my tea.

"Yes, but she is deceased. I don't think we can question her," Perdi said with a straight face.

"Luckily, we may not have to." I picked up my tablet and began a Google search. "Thankfully her name is not prevalent. Aha... I found a Jacksonville Beach woman with the same name and similar age. She looks to have had one child. Oh.. but he is incarcerated. Blast it... she's deceased, some years ago. Interesting... twenty years ago."

Yawning, Perdi said, "So, how do you get information from the dead?"

"Indeed. She's probably the key to all we want to know, but dead and buried," I said, clicking on her birth and death dates on the public records website. "That's strange."

"What's strange," Perdi questioned as she sat up intrigued.

"This can't be possible." I looked up at Perdi. "This woman died on the same day as my parents ... er... our parents."

"No, that is too coincidental," Perdi stated logically.

"Well... butter my butt and call me a biscuit!" I exclaimed. "She did die on the same day as our parents, but one town away at her home in Jax Beach." I jumped up.

"Okay, no need to get excited. Keep calm," Perdi said, grabbing for the tablet.

"I don't believe this. Do you?"

"It's shocking to hear, yes, but we don't know what it means. It is just a date. A date in time," Perdi said looking at the records.

"A date in time, in which three people died that were possibly linked," I said, jumping to conclusions.

"Kyra, her son is still alive. Why don't we go visit him in jail and ask questions," Perdi asked. "I don't think it is smart to make assumptions nor jump to conclusions."

Shocked, I caught a glimpse of something in the palm trees at the edge of the courtyard near the corner of the house and did a double take. I looked hard into the darkness, squinting. Great, now I'm seeing things. I turned back to Perdi and sat down. "That is a good idea, yes. I wonder why he's in jail. I hope he's not dangerous." I cringed a little and pulled my hoodie together at the neck and crossed my arms to my chest.

"Leave me with his name and I'll look him up. I'm a lawyer. I can access any information we need," Perdi winked at me and put her tea down, collecting her things. "I've got to go to bed. Too much emotion today. My brain needs a reset."

"Would you like to stay here tonight? I think Aunt Dottie is staying the night. I can make up the sectional. I'd love for you to stay, and I know it's been an exhausting day," I offered.

"Oh, it would be nice not to drive home right now. Yes, if it won't put you out," Perdi said sweetly.

"Please... we're family now. It's expected that you crash on my sofa. I'll get you some sheets, blankets... and pajamas," I smiled.

We entered the house, and as I closed the glass sliding doors, I looked back out to the palm trees at the end of the courtyard. There was nothing there. Their long bushy palms just swayed in the tropical breeze. Then the sound of breaking pine straw snapped loudly through the courtyard, and I slammed the doors shut as the neighbor's dog started going wild, barking from within the fenced yard next door. I locked the door. The hair stood on the back of my neck and tingled down my arms as my body quivered with a scare I'd not felt before. Not since living in Peaceful River Valley.

Chapter TWENTY

When I woke the next morning, I tipped-toed past the rear den with the sectional and my sleeping older sister. I smiled once I entered the living room, knowing my older sister was sleeping under my roof. I sat down at my work computer in the dark of the office in the front room. The laptop light lit the small area. I typed my boss to let her know I was out again today on family emergency. I updated my out-of-office reply and quickly scanned my inbox for anything urgent. I was feeling a bit anxious, having not been at work all week. At the same time, I felt compelled to continue my quest for how Perdi was lost to us. I could not ignore that my personal world had been turned upside down... in the most delightful way with the discovery of a big sister.

With another vacation day in front of me, I knew exactly how I wanted to spend it. I grabbed my tablet to do more research on Aggie Flannery. I returned to the lanai, where I looked out into the courtyard in the morning dusk. Nothing there. Probably was nothing last night too.

I opened my tablet and started to research our mystery nurse Aggie Flannery again. With a rare name like Aggie, I could easily find her in old public records and any news articles at the online Ponte Vedra Beach library. I started with Duval County real estate purchases. A hit immediately for

Agnes Flannery purchasing a home in 1940. An article of her and the Davis family at their Dee-Dot Ranch. Then, she died, and her home was left to her eldest son, Robert Flannery. A news article reported Robert Flannery as the murderer of his mother, Agnes Flannery. I guess that is why he is in jail.

I needed Kat to do this research. She was much better at it than me. I would leave the legal items to Perdi, and Kat could research and investigate until we unraveled this mystery. We had a nurse, Aggie Flannery and her address. We had a convicted felon, Robert Flannery. I was suddenly confident we could find out how Perdi was lost to us. I was confident we would find Mr. Robert Flannery.

Perdi appeared in the doorway of the lanai. "Are we the only ones up so far?"

"Yes, Kat will not be up for hours. Her lights were on last night when we went to bed," I said, smiling at Perdi in my pajamas with her tousled hair, looking so comfortable already in my home.

"Are you up for a walk or a run," Perdi asked as she walked around the lanai, stretching her arms out and yawning?

"Yes, great idea. I'd love to get some exercise before everyone gets up. I'd like to bring Kat into the research mix today. Perhaps she can help you with the legal research of our Mr. Robert Flannery.

"What about Aunt Dottie? She can help too, right?" Perdi inquired.

"Hmmm... I'm still a little perturbed with Aunt Dottie at the moment. She has always been secretive, but I feel her omission of our Uncle Conor King is a blatant betrayal."

"Oh, I don't know, Kyra. I think you're treating this too harshly. You don't know why she kept this information from you. Maybe it was to protect you," Perdi said wisely. It was true that Aunt Dottie was always withholding information to keep the family mentally and emotionally healthy. I suddenly imaged each individual in the family inside their own giant bubble Zorb ball for protection against the world. I snort laughed.

"What was that?" Perdi inquired.

"Haa... nothing... my imagination. Perdi, you might be right about Aunt Dottie wanting to protect us. At the same time, I've known this woman a long time. She is keeping something more from us."

"Let's go for a walk, and everything will look better, after exercise." Perdi said, "Do you have some leggings and a t-shirt for me? I have gym sneakers in the trunk of my car."

"Absolutely." I said as we went into my room and pulled out all the workout clothes from my drawers.

Halfway through our walk, I realized that Perdi was in much better shape than me. When was the last time I went for a speed walk or a run? I was huffing and puffing just to keep up. "So, you are a power walker, eh?"

"Yes, why? Am I walking to fast for you, KayKay?"

Aww... she used my nickname. A nickname that only my family used. I felt all warm and tingly... or was I having a heart attack? "Um... yes, a little. The most cardio I get is standing around the stove stirring things... or running to the sink to put myself out if I'm on fire."

Perdi belly laughed hard like Aunt Dottie does, and they both had the same laugh for sure. It made me smile to see family resemblances in her. Thankfully, she also slowed down a little. I just need to make her laugh more and I'll be able to keep up with her.

It was still dark, but the sky to the east ignited a slim array of purple, pink, and orange as the sunrise peeped over the trees. I heard something over my shoulder to the west and jerked my head quickly as alligators were prevalent around the retention ponds. I could see some movement next to us in the brush. We both slowed as the rustling became louder.

"You ever see any bear or dangerous animals on these trails," Perdi asked quietly.

"Shhh... what is that?" I peered into the darkness at something large with a bunch of little somethings. "Boar!! Run!" I screamed as a large mama boar charged at us full steam.

I physically jumped up in the air and backwards at the same time, knocking poor Perdi down to the ground. I tripped over her and found us a tangled mess of limbs rolling on the sidewalk desperately trying to lift our old bones onto all fours in order to spring to our feet. I was the first up and pulled Perdi up by the arm pit, throwing her into the air, with some freakishly strong Momma strength. Thankfully, she landed on her feet. She stepped backwards elbowing me in the ribs causing me to double over. She, then stepped on my foot, sending me straight back up again. I caught sight of the boar steps away while we both shuffled wildly into one another, trying to get our bearings. Before I knew it, we were in a full dang gum sprint down 20 Mile Road with a boar nipping at our butts while her little baby boars chased after their mama.

"Okay... okay... we can stop running," I said gasping for air as we reached the entrance to The Ranch. "It's gone. It went back into the woods."

Perdi bent over and put her hands on her knees. "Gosh, darn it. That scared me. I almost wet my pants."

"Those are my pants," I laughed. "Yea... that was a ruckus if I ever saw one." I laughed louder.

"You can run really fast when you want to," Perdi laughed, putting her hand on my back.

"Faster than a scaled haint," I laughed harder.

"What is a scaled haint? Is that a southern term?" Perdi was still looking behind her on the path, checking for boar, with her head on a swivel.

I straightened up quickly when I heard the police car nearing The Ranch, screeching past us. "Wonder what that's all about?" Another police car came down the road with lights on and no sirens. As we neared Littlewood Road, I could see the police cars all surrounding an ambulance in front of my house. My smile and laughter turned to sheer panic as I grabbed Perdi's arm and stopped in my tracks. "What... oh my God. What's happening?"

I sprinted down the street and hopped between the police cars as I reached a covered body on a stretcher at the base of my driveway. "What is going on? I'm Kyra King. I live here," I pleaded with the police officer holding me back from reaching the body.

"You live here," said the Sheriff's deputy, taking off his hat and holding it to his heart.

I watched as he put his hat to his heart in slow motion, and I could hear my heart beating in my chest. I could feel the gun belt of the officer holding me pushing into my ribs right where Perdi elbowed me. Every sense I had was on high alert. I saw the officer's lips moving. What was he saying? "What?"

"Ma'am, I said you live here," pointing at my house.

"Yes, sir. My sister, Kat. Where is she?"

"Ma'am. Ma'am, I'm sorry to tell you this, but a body has been discovered on the premises."

Chapter
TWENTYONE

"Oh my God, no," I blurted out. I felt Perdi behind me with her hand on my back comforting me.

"What is going on, sir? I'm Perdita Ryan, attorney," Perdi said so calmly.

"Yes ma'am. I need you to identify the body, if you can. There was no identification on the body when found."

Stop calling my loved one *The Body*, I thought angerly. At that very moment, Kat came running out of the front door and down the driveway in her pajamas. I struggled to get past the officers. "Kat! Kat! Let me go, please. That's my sister." Kat reached me before the muscular officer would let me go. She ran into my arms hard and took my breath away. "Oh my gosh. You have no idea how scared I was that something happened to you."

"No, I'm fine. I found the body," Kat said stepping away from my embrace and hugging Perdita.

"Oh no, that could only mean..." as I looked at the officer and turned to the dead body under the sheet. He pulled back the sheet.

"Who's that?" I asked in unison with Aunt Dottie who was suddenly standing next to me with a cup of coffee in her hand.

"Oh my goodness, Aunt Dottie. You gave me a scare." I hugged her.

"Why, dear? Oh... you thought that was me under there?" Aunt Dottie said with small chuckle. "No, no. we found him. We found a dead body... in your garage. In the driver's seat of your Moke."

I hugged her hard. I was so relieved to see her alive and kicking. "What?" I asked, very confused. "I don't understand. How did this person, who we don't even know, get into my garage?"

"Oh, well, that is the mystery of the day, isn't it? We are having quite an intriguing week," Aunt Dottie said loudly over the noise of the stretcher buckling up under itself as a stranger's body was enclosed in the back of the ambulance.

The officer was trying to pull me over to the side of the road as the ambulance left with no lights. A crowd of neighbors, in pajamas, formed around the house. I watched an officer tape off my garage with yellow caution tape. There were men working in my garage looking in my Moke. Possibly looking for prints or any other evidence that would help them determine how a dead body ended up in my garage in the wee hours of the morning.

"Ma'am, are you okay?" the Sheriff's deputy asked.

"I'm having quite a day sir, I am not okay. I'm frazzled," I said.

Perdi reached for my arm. "She is fine. We were just chased by a boar down the road while out for a morning walk. It was quite alarming. She is fine." Perdi was standing beside me with her arm around my waist and holding my arm tight. I looked at her, and her eyes looked stone cold.

"Ma'am. Do you know the man that died in your garage," the officer said as I refocused on him.

"I'm certain I do not know him. I did not recognize him at all."

"Do you know how he got into your garage, ma'am?"

"No, sir," I kept my answers short. I suspected Perdi wanted me to keep calm and my mouth shut, although I could not imagine why. I didn't have anything to do with this man's death, and she certainly knew that fact.

"I see you have a Ring doorbell and cameras. Would you offer up the content for your address to help solve this crime?" Oh my gosh, did he say crime? Oh, no... I was getting a hot flash. This deputy is going to think I'm lying as soon as he sees the first drop of sweat hit my brow. I started to wipe my forehead with my arm sleeve.

"Crime? You can't possibly think that this was a crime. What evidence do you have?" Perdi used a lawyerly tone that suddenly made me afraid of ever facing her in court.

"No, none, ma'am. You are right. Right now, it is only a mystery. I'm sure dead guys walk into people's garages all the time. Where are you from, ma'am?"

"Oh, excuse me, officer. Sometimes I can't switch off the lawyer in me. Certainly, I'm Perdita Ryan and I'm from Ponte Vedra Beach."

"Is that your car in the driveway, Mrs. Ryan?"

"Well... yes it is," Perdi replied.

"When did you leave the premises this morning, ladies?"

"About an hour ago." I looked at my watch. It was only eight in the morning, and there was already another mystery to solve. I used the collar on my tee-shirt to wipe the sweat from my upper lip and chin. Oh God, please just let me pass out right here.

"Well... the coroner will give us approximate time of death, and then I will have some more questions for you ladies. Don't leave the county."

"Yes, of course," I offered.

"Here is my card. I'll send you a request for your Ring account information shortly." I took it and used it to wipe the back of my neck.

"Um... okay," I replied as Perdi ushered me away from the police officer.

"Why are you hoovering over me like a hawk?" I asked.

"Why are you sweating like you were caught in a monsoon?" Perdi asked.

"Holy hot flashes, Batman. Get me to the AC, stat," I said. I was rapidly cooling down as I said the word *AC*.

"Kyra, I'm sorry to be guard dogging you. I just didn't want you to say anything that would land you in custody," Perdita said, still stone cold.

"Wait... why would I be in custody?" I asked as all the detectives working the case stopped what they were doing and watched us walk up the stairs to the porch. Why were they staring at us?

"Were you telling the truth? You don't know the man who was removed from your garage?" Perdi questioned me.

I suddenly became terrified of what Perdi was accusing me of. What did she mean? What was she saying? Did she think I had something to do with that man's death? I searched her face for answers as she walked me through the front door. "No, Perdi. I don't know him."

Once inside the house, Aunt Dottie asked, "Are you okay, my dear girl? You looked in a state of shock when I saw you arrive home to see all the police cars."

"Yea, I looked shocked because I was shocked. I was horrified that something terrible happened to one of you. My heart was in my throat. What happened, Aunt Dottie?"

"Well, I went out to the garage because I left my purse in the Moke last night when I drove it over here for you. I just wanted my ebook and reading glasses."

"Yep... then I heard her scream. I knocked over my coffee on the kitchen island and I ran out to the garage. I thought it was a snake or a spider or something." Kat interjected.

"Nope, it was a dead body. I tapped him a little to see if he would move... but he didn't budge." Aunt Dottie said as she reenacted the tapping on my shoulder.

"You mean to tell me he was sitting up-right in the driver side of the Moke, dead?" I inquired.

"Exactly," Aunt Dottie said, nodding her head up and down.

"You touched the body?" Perdi asked in that lawyer tone again.

Aunt Dottie was nodding yes. "Tapped him and then screamed."

Kat eagerly interjected, "Then I came out. I screamed when I saw the body. But then I ran back in to get my phone and started filming it all."

"What? Kat... you did not?" I said shocked.

"No, I didn't but I wanted to. No, I called the police and they sent an ambulance even though I told them he looked dead. And squad cars... a lot of squad cars."

"Well, let's go look at the Ring cameras and see what we see," I said as we all moved from the foyer to the kitchen.

I put on the kettle for hot water, and we all gathered around my tablet to watch the various angles around the doorbell and the house.

Chapter TWENTY TWO

P erdita was on her phone while I was setting my tablet up so we could all watch the videos on my Ring account. When she was done, she hung up the phone and turned around to us and said "Okay, I got one of my assistants running point on research to find out more on Aggie Flannery and Robert Flannery. We will have something soon," Perdi sounded very professional.

"While you've been leading that front, I've been looking for my password for my Ring account," I sounded much less together than my rockstar sister. I was flipping through my secret notebook with *Passwords* in big bold letters on the front of it.

"Oh my goodness... how are you in technology," Kat said grabbing my tablet and pulling up the login. She stroked a few keys and we were in. Kat hit the History tab.

We watched video after video only to see the flag waving in the wind, a kid on a skateboard, and a random cat with a lizard in its mouth, until we saw doorbell video footage at five p.m. yesterday afternoon.

We watched Aunt Dottie speed up the driveway in the Moke, hitting the bumper of Perdi's Mercedes Benz. "Hey! You hit my car." Perdi cried.

"It just jumped out at me," Aunt Dottie claimed shyly, her eyes wide with her lips grinning into a one-sided smile.

We watched as Aunt Dottie backed up, pulled forward again and makes the hard left into the side entry garage bay nearest to the house door. Then, next video, was of Aunt Dottie looking at Perdi's car. She had a hoodie in her hand and began to clean the spot on the bumper where she just hit Perdi's car. We all turn to her and waited for an explanation, as she sucked in her cheeks and puckered her lips around a hard butterscotch candy. She looked up at the ceiling, trying to whistle unsuccessfully.

"I'm gonna keep an eye on you from now on," Perdi laughed, as she pulled Aunt Dottie into a snuggle hug.

Kat hit play on the next video. This video showed Aunt Dottie entering back through the garage bay with her hoodie. The garage bay door began to close. As the garage door starts to go down, a man resembling the dead guy exits a car. The car pulls away.

"An Uber maybe." I said pointing at the car driving away.

The man begins walking up the driveway. He was wearing what appeared to be a suit and jacket with a white or light-colored button-down shirt. Coming from the direction of the cul-de-sac, another unidentified man, in a dark hoodie, was following behind him about 30 feet back.

"Where did that second guy come from?" Perdi asked, pointing to the screen where Mr. HoodieMan was walking.

"I don't know. I didn't see him get out of a car," Kat answered. "But... KayKay... is that they guy who snuffed his ciggy in the palm of his hand the other night? He is wearing the same hoodie, I think."

The next video showed the man in the suit walk into the view of the Ring doorbell. I recognized him immediately as the dead body on the stretcher. He was looking down at a thick piece of paper, maybe an envelope. He folds the envelope and places it in his jacket pocket. He looked directly up and into the camera at the front door. He placed his foot on the first step and then was startled by the motion behind him.

The man in the dark blue hoodie charged up the driveway full speed and puts his foot under the garage door catching the sensor. The garage door stopped and began to roll back up while Mr. HoodieMan darted towards the front porch. The dead guy then rushed towards the door with a surprised expression on his face.

We couldn't see what happened next because Mr. HoodieMan jumped on the guy in the suit and pushed him into the doorbell camera. The only thing we could see was a hand, then a partial face, mostly chin, and then all dark clothes.

"Did we just witness a murder?" Kat asked as we all stood motionless with our eyes on the screen and our mouths hanging open. Aunt Dottie lost her butterscotch candy.

"I don't think so. It just looked like one guy jumping another guy." I said, trying to convince Kat of her lying eyes.

The video came back in focus. The man with the hoodie had his back to the camera and was picking up the man in the suit. He was apparently strong, because he used a fireman-carry to transport the dead guy to the garage. We could see him drop him in the Moke front seat and then the camera cut off, probably due to inactivity in the immediate zone on the camera.

"Wow. That was crazy. Who are these guys?" Perdi said as she backed away to answer her phone. "Okay, send it through. Thanks. That is what I wanted." There was a long pause, and we all looked over at her. "What do you mean, he was released yesterday? Are you kidding?" Perdi hung up her phone and checked her text. "Oh, no."

"What's going on, Perdi?" I asked as I paused the video.

"Robert Flannery was in jail for killing his mother twenty years ago. He was released, just yesterday from jail." Perdi clicked on a photo and made it bigger, holding the phone up to my face, so I could see it. "I just got the photo for Robert Flannery."

"Oh, no." I said, surprised to see the dead guy's photo in my face. "Are you kidding me? The dead guy? The dead guy is Flannery?" I looked up at Perdi. "Perdi, why would a killer be coming here to my house?"

At that moment, an email notification popped up on my screen from the Sheriff's Deputy asking for access to my Ring videos.

Chapter
TWENTYTHREE

I sent the Ring video information to the St Johns County Sheriff. I swallowed hard as I hit send. I'm not sure what was happening on my front porch last night but it didn't look good. Perdi was reviewing the materials sent by her research assistant.

Boop. Boop. "KayKay, Kat? Why is this door unlocked?" Ken shouted from the foyer.

"We're in here." I hollered back, thinking I probably need to lock my doors more often.

"Kyra, I need you to lock your doors all the time. There was a murder here last night, and you were apparently not even aware of it. That psycho could have walked right into this house." Ken was heated and rightly so. He was serious about keeping us safe.

"I know, Ken. You're right. I'll lock it from now on. Did you want to take a breather and meet your sister?" I asked as I did my best Vanna White impression towards Perdi.

"Oh snap!" Killian walked in behind Ken and started walking towards Perdi hand extended to politely shake it.

"Hi Ken! Hi Killian! So nice to meet you both. Call me Perdi." Perdi ignored Killian's hand and dove in for a hug as Ken approached them and waited patiently. Killian stepped back and Ken hugged Perdi hard and choked up, covering it as a laugh he stepped back.

"Oh... wow... Perdita. I... um... I'm Ken the older, my protective, twin. Wow... you look just like mom."

"Yep, she sure does." Killian fascinated by her resemblance to mom, put his hands in his pockets and assumed the 'awe shucks' position of his childhood years.

"We were not expecting you here. I came over as soon as the news spread that a dead body was found at my sister's house." Ken turned his head towards me with outstretched arms. "What gives?"

"I found him." Aunt Dottie interrupted.

"I was there too!" Kat chimed in.

"Now that y'all are here... we found out some things. I think we should tell you," I said as we all gathered around the dinning room table. "Here it is in a nutshell. Perdita has a birth certificate and a death certificate, under the name Perdita King. She also has a birth certificate under the name Perdita Boyle."

"We know all this... get to the new information, like who is the dead guy?" asked Kat.

"I'm getting there. No doctor was present at her birth, only a nurse. The nurse's name was Aggie Flannery. Ironically, she died on the same day as Mom and Dad twenty years ago."

Perdi interjected, "I learned from my team this morning that her son, Aggie's son, was convicted of murdering her twenty years ago. Apparently, he was released, yesterday, from jail."

I felt like I was in the Twilight Zone. "This story doesn't make any sense Perdi. As his first act of freedom, Robert Flannery shows up here, at my home. Why?" I asked.

"Well we don't know why. I stick to facts not assumptions." Perdi used that lawyer tone again.

It was quite fascinating that Perdi was so calm while I was jumping out of my skin. "Right, facts. We do know he was knocked out or possibly killed right here outside my home by a man in the dark hoodie. Then he was aggressively stuffed into the driver seat of my Moke. Which I will now need to thoroughly detail to get the dead guy ick out."

"Wait, what do you mean killed right here?" Ken questioned.

"We have the videos... wait till you see these!" Kat exclaimed and hit play on the tablet in front of Ken and Killian.

"Is anyone at all concerned that we slept the entire night in the house with a dead guy in our garage?" Kat blurted out.

"Last night while we were out on the lanai, I got the sense there was someone moving around on the side of the house, watching us. The neighbor's dog was going wild. I think someone was out there," I said, giving myself goose bumps again.

"Who was the guy with the hoodie and where did he come from?" Perdi asked as she pointed to other videos.

"In this video, when Mr. HoodieMan leaves the garage bay, he heads towards the front of the house in the opposite direction of the camera. He never looks directly into the camera except that shot during the scuffle on the porch. We get a great shot of his chin," I joked, flipping my hand up at the video playing in loop.

"Well... maybe let the police investigate it. They will figure it out," Aunt Dottie said as she slid from the counter stool and walked towards the guest bedroom.

"Where are you going, Aunt Dottie? There are still more videos to go through," Kat said, watching her walk through the living room.

"I'm going back to the old Starling. Who is going to take me?" she shouted, disappearing into the back hall.

"I think she knows something, and she is not saying," I whispered to Perdi and Kat.

"What do you think she knows, KayKay?" Kat whispered.

"All I know is that we are sitting here looking at film, and then she takes off as soon as I start asking questions about the guy in the hoodie. We look closer and she leaves the room." I stated the facts.

"You think she knows him?" Perdi asked as she hit pause on the video at the full frontal of the chin.

"I don't have a clue. I just sense her evasion. Look at us... we are all hanging on every video and morsel of information, trying to figure out what is going on in the King universe. Aunt Dottie... she just walks out of the room, saying let the police handle it," I whispered. "I'm not buying it."

"She is being more secretive than usual. Plus, she is usually more interested in solving mysteries and crimes. She loves *Murder She Wrote* and *Quincy*. Watches all the reruns," Kat added, and Perdi laughed out loud.

"No, she does. She is always up for a good sleuth show." I emphasized sleuth for effect.

"I'll take her home. I'll see if I can pump some information out of her on the way to The Starling," Perdi said as she collected her things and knocked on Aunt Dottie's door. "Ready when you are, Aunt Dottie?"

I picked up my phone and called my auto detailer and explained I needed to schedule an emergency visit to the clean the Moke... as soon as the police were done with it.

Chapter
TWENTYFOUR

It was four hours since the discovery of the dead body in the garage. The crowd in front of the house dissipated. The investigators were all gone. The sheriff's deputy had all the video from the Ring. I had a visit from Mr. and Mrs. Packer, who were very concerned. They told the police the time of the dog barking wildly last night but that they did not see anything. They also returned my lasagna pan, so I could make another dish for them. Reggie, my auto detailer, was finishing up a full cleaning of the Moke. I agreed to take Kat in the Moke for photos for her content, while I was off work for the day. It would be a relaxing deviation from the dark mysteries usurping my existence.

The Moke looked shiny and new. One would never know there was recently a dead body sitting in it. We made a left out of The Ranch and headed towards the back entrance towards Crosswater Parkway. "Hard to believe I was running for my life as a boar and it's offspring chased us just a few short hours ago, right over there," I said, pointing to the spot. Kat laughed at me.

"I would have loved to get that on video. That would have been pure Florida gold," she giggled.

"What are you taking photos of today, Kit Kat?"

"I want to go visit Ken and Killian while they are building houses in Town Center," Kat said while adjusting her camera lens.

"Oh, that sounds like a fun visit," I said, wondering if she was doing a podcast on their company.

As we got closer to Town Center, gun shots rang out to our left. Kat stopped what she was doing and looked up. "Sounds like folks are at the gun range on Moonshine," I said to Kat and kept going.

"There is a gun range on Moonshine? How can they allow a gun range in a major subdivision like Peaceful River Valley?"

"You live a sheltered life here in Peaceful River Valley, sis. There are actually two gun ranges in Peaceful River Valley. I think there used to be three." I was thinking back to the one that closed near the business park we were about to pass on Crosswater Pkwy. "The other one is a private range. It is south of Town Center. We should go. You should know how to handle a weapon and become certified to carry. I could teach you," I said as I flashed back to a shadow in the courtyard last night. Was there someone there watching us or was I seeing things?

"I don't think so. I like shooting photos, that's it," Kat laughed.

"Aha... I see what you did there. Clever girl." I smiled at Kat and accelerated down Crosswater Parkway.

The light near Village Drive turned green, and we hurried across the street, the sound of traffic fading as we entered the Publix shopping center. Kat wanted to take photos of the Town Center with good sunlight. We stopped at several places for her to record video, snap photos, and create some content. I drove her while she took video from the passenger seat in the Moke. She had a lot of selfies in the content, and I wondered how she would pull all this together. Perhaps I should take more of an interest in her work, I thought. As we turned towards Town Center, I smelled a fire. It was not cool enough in May to have a fireplace burning. I was wondering if it was an illegal burn when I heard the firetrucks and first responders in the distance.

Turning west on Village Drive, we could see flames several blocks in front of us on the right. At the stop sign, I decided to get off the road and head onto the golf cart path. I did not want to be in the path of a firetruck trying to get to a fire. We sat idle on the corner waiting for the firetrucks to roar by. They were now turning down Village Drive. To my surprise, I spotted Aunt Dottie on her golf cart, sitting on the path across the street from us. She began to wave when she saw us. Then she floored it across the road in the path of the fire truck, waving to us and saying hello even as she slammed on the brakes only feet from us. The firetruck immediately passed us by within seconds of Aunt Dottie landing on the golf cart path beside us.

"Aunt Dottie, you are a maniac on that thing. Did you see or hear the big firetruck barreling down on you?" I stood mesmerized by her lack of awareness.

"I saw y'all and got excited. I wasn't paying attention to traffic," Aunt Dottie said loudly above the sirens.

"Looks like another house fire in Town Center," Aunt Dottie said, pointing at the smoke a few streets away.

"Why do houses in Town Center seem to spontaneously combust?" Kat motioned towards the empty plot of land across the street from us where a family's house burned down last year. It was still a pile of dirt and no house had been rebuilt.

"I do not know, Kat. It's another mystery," I said.

Aunt Dottie was inching forward on the golf cart path. "Probably all those electric cars people own nowadays. This wasn't an issue years ago when we all had gas powered vehicles. Maybe your brothers will build better houses in West End and then people's homes will not burn down."

"What are you doing over here, Aunt Dottie." Kat asked.

"I'm heading to Publix for some groceries for tonight's crafts. It's hard to eat while crocheting. We typically eat first and then once we are full, we get down to the craft business."

"Did you have a nice ride home with Perdi today?" I asked.

"Oh yes, she is a lovely woman. And so accomplished. Just like you, KayKay. Kat, you would be lucky to go work for her. She has her own firm and hundreds of people working for her," Aunt Dottie bragged.

"I didn't know her firm was that big," Kat admitted.

"Several offices and they do a variety of legal work for corporations in addition to that estate law stuff," Aunt Dottie continued.

A police car flew by us down Village Drive into Town Center. "Well, it sure is a busy day for the St. Johns County Sheriff's office," I said as we watched another police car whiz by us. "Want to go see what the excitement is about?"

"Yep, let's go." Kat said, taking the lens cover off her camera.

"Bye, Aunt Dottie. Love you," I said as I mashed down on the accelerator. We headed west past the street with the fire. It looked like the police activity was in West End where all the new construction was going on.

"Look, the police cars are all in front of the model homes there... by Killian's truck," Kat said as she pointed towards the mayhem of people.

"What is going on, here?" I asked as I parked the Moke in the middle of the street. "Stay here. Do not leave this vehicle," I commanded Kat. I hopped out and ran over to Killian's truck. He wasn't in it.

I shouted "Ken! What's going on?" as I watched as the police lead Killian, handcuffed, towards a squad car. "Ken, what happened?"

"I don't know. They were looking for Killian. They cuffed him when he couldn't provide an alibi for last night.

"Last night? What happened last night? Were you with him?" I asked.

"No, I wasn't with him or I would be his alibi. They think he killed the guy at your house." Ken looked at me confused.

"Oh no. Why would they think Killian killed Flannery?"

"They said, they have a video of him attacking a guy on your porch."

"No, that wasn't Killian."

"We know that... but why do they think that?" Killian pointed to the St Johns County Sheriff was watching us as his deputies put Killian in the back of the car.

Chapter
TWENTYFIVE

I t was Thursday morning. I had not slept a wink since Killian, the younger twin, was arrested for the murder of Robert Flannery at my home. I had not worked in three days, and I dreaded contacting them and telling them I needed more time off. At the same time, the work was piling up into a mountain of tasks waiting for me. I had to call out again. I would need to tell them something. I have a new sister I never knew about. A stranger was murdered at my home and left in my garage. My brother was arrested for the murder of a murderer. These all seemed like flimsy, the-dog-ate-my-homework type of excuses to call out of work. I decided to say I needed a mental health week, which was true. My mental health was on the brink of collapse.

The house was quiet. When I walked out to the living room, I noticed the courtyard was full of fog. It was eerie. Fog rolled into low-lying areas and covered the ground some mornings. Peaceful River Valley was actually a bog or a swamp or a palm thatch, at one time. I was used to lots of things, like thousands of frogs in the spring keeping me up at night, and lizards, gators, boar, wild fox, and coyote roaming the community with us. Quiet and fog were an eerie mix.

My phone rang, startling me to a little jump. Where did I leave my phone, and why was it ringing at this early hour? It was before 6 a.m. I hit the answer button and then speaker as I moved around the kitchen from the island to the stove, preparing the morning coffee. "Ken, it is very early, my brother."

"Kyra, have you seen the Facebook page for *The Parrot* yet this morning?"

"No, I have not. Why? Did Mr. Johnson's dogs poop on Dr. Merritt's lawn again?" I laughed at the most common content in *The Parrot*, our local weekly fluff paper. Every week there was an article about dog poop. Who knew it was so popular a topic? Maybe Peaceful River Valley was just too small a place to garner actual news. The paper and online readership was small and all local to our community.

"We are all over the front page," Ken said. "I'm looking at it now. They have Perdita's photo. It looks like one of her online profile pictures."

My eyes blinked hard. My throat strained to swallow. "What do you mean, Ken?"

"Exactly what I said. Perdita's story is out. They are dragging our name through the mud. They know all about it and published it."

"I'll call you back," I said as I hung up the phone and opened my tablet. Quickly finding the link to the Ponte Vedra Parrot online. I clicked the search button and started typing P E R D I , when my eyes lowered to the center of the page below the search to see a photo of Perdita from her Linkedin profile smack in the middle of the front page with the headline *Local Family Secrets*.

I read the article as quickly as I could. It did not seem to cite a source. I had no idea how the paper came across this information. The article was vague. It did not divulge much information, but they had Perdi's name and our name. The author speculated that Perdi was given up for adoption at a young age by my mother, who was named as the birth mother, and the Boyle's were named as the adoptive parents. Whatever information the writer had was a guess, I supposed. There was no adoption record, so I hoped that Perdi could sue her for slander and demand a retraction. This journalist had no information about the birth and death certificates. She did not mention the Ponte Vedra Inn and Club. She did not mention any of the people noted on the pieces of stationery that Katherine King left for me in the box of mementos we perused.

The article was written by an author named Krystal Kelly. Her photo was in the upper right corner of the story. She looked familiar. I knew I'd seen her before but could not place where I saw her. I noted the author's name and flicked her photo with my middle finger. Oh that was juvenile, Kyra, I said to myself. I felt the anger raging inside me. I was angry. I didn't want my family accused of things that were not true, even if they were dead. The King name had a long and illustrious history in Palm Valley. This story was not supposed to get out. My poor mother's reputation will be tarnished without merit. I wanted to strangle that writer. Or at the very least send her a very nasty letter.

I tried to tell myself to calm down. I had a few deep breathing exercises between sips of coffee. This resulted in a vicious cycle of revved up anxiety throttled by inner soothing, followed by another sip of coffee which ignited my anxiety again. I sighed. This was not relaxing. Maybe Perdi was right, and I should switch to tea. I needed to postpone my inner spiritual journey of peace and tranquility. I decided there was nothing I could do about it at that moment. I took my coffee to the living room and sat down with my tablet.

Please forgive me for my anger, Lord. Please don't ever let me meet this woman. I felt better giving my anger up to the Lord. However, the article left me feeling exposed. Perdita's face and name were exposed. She was a successful lawyer in Ponte Vedra Beach. I could only hope the Ponte Vedra Parrot had a very small following.

We'd agreed to keep this quiet and just between us. I didn't say anything. I knew it was unlikely that the twins said anything. It could have been Aunt Dottie or Kat. Both were the most likely source of the leak.

Kat was not up yet. I went to her Insta page and looked for any posts about our family. Nothing. I called Aunt Dottie. It was early, but she had probably been up for hours. No answer. I breathed out heavily, trying to explain in my own head how to tell this to Perdi. It was 6 a.m. I didn't think I should call her. She might have been up, but I didn't want to take the chance. I decided to call her around 8 a.m. She is probably up and at work by 8am.

For the next two hours, I looked at the clock between sips of coffee. It was taking forever to reach 8 a.m. I occupied my time researching the names on the peach paper. My assumption was they were also victims of the ugly Aggie Flannery. Kat walked in the kitchen, and I looked over to her from the living room and said, "Good morning, Kat. Glad you are up. I want to talk to you about who you may have told about Perdi and Mac," I said as I was getting up and in route to the kitchen to replenish my cup of coffee.

"I have not told anyone about Perdi. I'm waiting for you to give the go-ahead before I tell anyone." Kat said as she squeezed honey into a mug.

"*Ponte Vedra Parrot* has the story. They released it last night online and in the print version this morning. Ken saw it on his way out of the house," I said opening my tablet to the site with Perdi's photo and pushing it in front of Kat's mug.

With a sleepy but shocked look on her face, Kat pulled the tablet near and scrolled as she read quickly. I had no idea Kat could read so fast. She was like a speed reader. She repeated *"Oh, no"* several times until the end. "That is not too bad. At least she doesn't know anything real. She only has part of the story," Kat said.

"It's unfortunate, Kat. I have no idea where she got this information, and I'm not sure why they didn't contact us to get our comment. Don't journalists do that anymore? They have a story, then contact the people in the story to get comments?" I was rambling.

"I don't know why you are upset about it. It is hardly the full story," Kat said without connecting the dots.

"First, it is not the truth. Or not the complete full story, anyway. Second, this is our family's name. She slanders Mom and Dad's reputation by suggesting that Mom put Perdi up for adoption. That is simply not true. Lastly, Perdi is an attorney here and has clients and well-known connections. I've not talked with Perdi yet, but I think we can sue for slander," As I said the words out loud, Kat laughed and looked over at me as if I was joking.

"What... you are serious? Who are you going to sue? The *Ponte Vedra Parrot* is not even big enough to sue. You can probably write a retort and have more of an affect. They are small, and no one reads it anyway. The most play it gets is the salacious stories that float around Facebook groups which then become fodder for the barflies in Peaceful River Valley. It won't go anywhere."

Kat was calming me down. She made some good points. "I hope you're right, lil' sis. I would hate for a more regional or national news outlet to pick this up and run with it. It could ruin Perdi's business, your business, and stain our family's name and reputation. This is far more difficult because we don't know what happened. It's far more intriguing because of the stationery with the names. We don't know the connection to Ponte Vedra Inn and Club. We need to keep those items to ourselves and not divulge any of that information until we know more," I said apprehensively.

Kat poured her coffee into a mug and stopped to look me in the eyes as she said, "I'm starting to think Aunt Dottie has a valid point here about you letting go of this investigation and letting the police handle it. It's making you crazy."

"I'm not crazy, Kat. Why don't you want to know what happened to our family and possibly these other families?" I held up the peach papers with the names written on them that Mom left in the sealed envelope marked with the logo of the Ponte Vedra Inn and Club. "I believe there was a crime committed with multiple victims."

"We don't know that. You're jumping to conclusions, which is why you should hire a private investigator or hand it over to the police."

"Hand it over to someone else? Is someone else going to be personally invested in finding out what happened to mom in 1967? Or what's behind the weird coincidence that she died on the same day with this nurse Aggie Flannery, the woman named on Perdi's birth certificate?" I said in an animated tone that indicated I needed to calm myself down.

"This is what I'm talking about, KayKay... you are scaring me." Kat paused and stepped back as she circled her arms around me and hugged me hard. "You haven't worked in days. You are up early researching people online."

"I just need to find out what happened, Kat. Did you research any of the families on the peach paper that Mom left?" I said, trying to convince Kat to stick with me. "This feels personal to me, Kat. Mom suffered a loss, and she knew something about it and left us a clue." I separated from her embrace. "I can't just ignore that, especially not now after Aggie Flannery's son died on our porch."

"I know. It's crazy to think about, but I just think we are in over our heads here and need help."

"Then you believe this all fits together somehow?" I said, a little bit more excited. "Perdi wants to find the truth, too. I need to call her."

"Are you certain we don't want to hire a private investigator?" Kat suggested.

"I think we can investigate it ourselves. I found a lot of information about four of the names we found. I think we can get public records for each with little issue. Why are you not taking this seriously, Kat?"

"I didn't find anything on my names. Although, I wasn't looking hard." Kat was sipping her coffee and yawning. "These are all old people, and these old people don't have social media," Kat complained. "I think we need better sources, like what a private investigator would use."

"Okay, I'll take them back from you. I found all these people on social media," I said, wanting to keep moving forward with my investigation on my own.

"How do you know they were the exact people you were looking for? I typed in John Andersen and got over 100 results on Facebook. I can't sift through all those results to determine which one is the John Andersen that I am looking for from this piece of peach paper." Kat said with clarity. I instantly realized maybe the people I researched were not the same four people that I needed. I sighed and poured another cup of coffee. I'll give up coffee next week.

Kat went back to her room and returned with the stationery. She left the peach pieces of paper on the island, with a new page. It said *P.I. for Perdi. Sam with a 904 phone number under it.*

"You talked to Perdi about hiring a private investigator?" I asked, a little shocked that Kat and Perdi were colluding.

"Yes, she thought it was a good idea to bring in someone who could help us with real tools like databases and access to records."

"Really?" Kat had several good points. I had no idea if any of these people I researched that morning were the actual people that Mom had named on the sheet. I somehow had to get access to a database with names and birth dates. Kat and Perdi both agreed bringing in a third party would increase our chances of finding these potential victims. If those dates on the stationery were actually birth dates in the same format as Perdi's page, the research would be a lot faster and potentially more accurate. Ugh, it was after 8 a.m. I grabbed the phone and pushed call on Perdi's name. I took a big sip of coffee.

Perdi was very quiet on the phone when I sent her the link to the article via text. I'm sure she was reading. I knew I needed to find out how this woman Krystal Kelly got our information. This situation was only known by the family. I trusted us all not to say anything. Aunt Dottie was a question mark. She understood the sensitivity of the situation for sure.

But she could talk to anyone and everyone and did. She loved to share and overshare.

"Perdi? What is going through your mind? How will this affect your career and business?" I asked softly.

"This is unfortunate. I don't think it will impact my business. It would be fantastic to make this go away, but I doubt it will," she whispered.

"You don't sound upset at all, Perdi. I'm flippin' mad about this, and it is not even my photo on the front cover. It is not accurate information. I want to sue this paper and this so-called journalist. Do we have a case?" I was fired up.

"I need to think about it and consult with counsel. I doubt we will want to sue. Litigation is not a pleasant option, but maybe we can have an attorney send a letter requesting a retraction. But that does not help us in the situation. The word is out. Containment is now what we need to do. We need to control the message."

"You sound very calm. I'm normally the calm one. Are you not upset that the author of this article printed that our mother gave you up for adoption?" I asked, wondering what was happening to me.

"I don't know what happened the day of my birth. We don't know for certain that mom thought I was dead or that mom gave me up for adoption. We may never know and it is very upsetting. But, in my heart, I believe that she thought I died. That is the only thing that explains the other names on the peach paper."

We were both silent for a moment. We both believed that mom thought Perdi was lost to her. But we had no proof or way of knowing for sure. I needed to find out more about the lives of these people on the peach pieces of paper and immediately.

Perdi broke the silence and asked "Can you meet for lunch today. I'll come to you. Meet you at Treylor Park at 11 a.m. Maybe Kat can join us. Let's think through this and determine how to best handle it. In the meantime, I'll contact a friend who knows best how to deal with the press."

"Yes, I can meet you for lunch today. I'll ask Kat to join us."

"Ok, I'll see you at 11."

"Perdi, one more thing... did your attorney friend go see Killian last night?" I asked.

"Yes, he advised him not to say anything. Kyra, Killian could not identify Flannery in a photo. It was all a surprise to him that he was being accused of murder. He didn't do it."

"Thank you, Perdi. I know that, but it is good to hear you say. What are the next steps to get him out?" I asked.

"They have not charged him yet. Apparently, this was just a discussion."

"Why would they handcuff him if they were not arresting him?" I asked honestly.

"I don't know. The attorney thinks this is all a big mistake. They may be waiting for the coroner's report to come back with the time of death and cause. There is nothing we can do there until they charge him or his holding time is up."

"Alright. I need to go check my blood pressure. Kat and I will meet you at 11 at Treylor Park."

Chapter
TWENTYSIX

K at and I took the Moke to Treylor Park, and found plenty of golf cart parking spots. We parked in front of the neon Cocktails and Dreams sign and I wondered if Kat even knew the reference. Perdi, dressed in a very nice grey suit, was already standing outside the front door with the phone up to her ear. She wore a pencil skirt that landed just below her knees, coordinated with black kitten heels in patent leather. They had a sophisticated little black and red bow across the top. She looked very sharp and professional. She carried a huge red leather hobo bag that matched her red beads around her neck. The bag was two times the size of a normal bag, but it looked amazing with the dark suit. Very classy look. I suddenly felt underdressed in my typical Florida uniform of jean shorts, t-shirt, and flip-flops.

She waved at us as we pulled into our spot. I waved back.

Kat waved and said "Hi Perdi!" As Perdi turned to face Kat she raised up an index finger and mouthed "One sec." Knowing this was the universal symbol for *I'm on the phone*, we guided Perdi to a table as she chatted on her call. We chose a patio table overlooking the vibrant green space, enjoying the warm sun and gentle breeze on that glorious May day. While she was mostly listening, we did hear her say several provocative *I understand* phrases to clue us in that she was still on the phone.

Finally, Perdi hung up. "Hi, sis," I said. "So, how does your attorney friend suggest we put the genie back in a bottle?"

Smiling at us like it was just another day, she said "Hi, ladies. So happy to see you, no matter the circumstances. But, sadly, no... that genie can't be stuffed back in the bottle. My defamation and internet attorney, Marty, was able to provide some guidance. He will send a letter to the Ponte Vedra Parrot asking them to issue a retraction and apologize to your family and me. He doesn't believe the Ponte Vedra Parrot is big enough or has enough reach to sue. With a small push, Marty is certain they will acquiesce. Good news, right?"

I blinked and grimaced at how little that helped. "That only solves one item. Now, do we have any idea what our message is to people about this mess? I've been avoiding calls all day. Plus, I need to prep Aunt Dottie with what to say before someone approaches her about it."

"We are family. I don't think we need a message about it," Kat said without looking up from the menu. She took a drink of her water.

"I agree, Kat. We are family, and I am not going to deny our relationship. But I don't know what to say about how we became a family, just recently. I would like to say, we are looking into it, but right now we have no answers about how this happened," I said, confident that I loved my new sister and that I would claim her. I just don't want to answer any further questions... just now.

Perdita chimed in with the best idea. "I think we tell everyone we are family, we connected via *ancestry.com* and we are looking into what happened. We don't go into detail. Keep responses at a high level. We admit we don't know the exact truth."

We all agreed and nodded. I was relieved we were not lying. I didn't want to lie about Perdita being family. I loved her already.

"Perdi, we can't thank you enough for sending over the attorney to see Killian yesterday evening, on such short notice," I said.

"Yea, that was really nice of him to drop everything and go talk with Killian," Kat added.

"Well, I did send an attorney, but I met him there and we both sat down with Killian," Perdi confessed.

"You saw Killian? In a jail cell?" I gulped and imagined that was an uncomfortable meeting.

"Yes, he was very gracious and sweet. He has no idea why they are questioning him," Perdi stated as she put down the menu and took a sip of water from the glass that was perspiring.

"That's our sweet Killian. Is he in with other inmates? Is he safe where he is being kept?" I asked, concerned about his physical safety.

"Yes, they have him in a solitary room in a holding area. He is perfectly fine. He has not been arrested, this is just a lengthy discussion so far. Although, he does not have an alibi for the night of the murder," Perdi dropped on us.

"Why would he need an alibi. He didn't do anything?" I said naively.

"They have not charged him yet, correct?" Kat jumped into the conversation, and I felt helpless as they continued to talk about timing, medical examiner reports, and fancy attorney words that went over my head.

"Can we see him? When do we get him out?" I asked.

"We need to get the medical examiner's report back with the cause of death. If it was murder, they will likely charge him. If it is vague, they will run out of time to hold him without charges and let him go," Perdi said, pushing her sunglasses to the top of head like a headband.

"Okay, so how long before we get the medical examiner's findings?" I asked.

"Could be today or tomorrow," Perdi replied.

"Why did they take him into custody in the first place? They don't really believe that was Killian on the video, do they?" I asked, waving down a waitress. We all ordered fish tacos and sat quietly while we waited to be alone again.

The waitress walked away and Perdi started answering questions based on what she learned at the police station. "They do believe the person on the video was a King. Face recognition software comparisons threw a high likelihood match. But I'm not sure about this technology they are using for recognition. My office technology staff will research it. We will need to combat it, if it comes to that." Perdi sighed and shrugged her right shoulder. "I just don't think it will though. When my attorney spoke to the police, they were told this was just a friendly conversation and that Killian agreed to go to the station with them."

Wow, Perdi was impressive. She thought of everything. Even the private investigator. I suddenly felt small in her presence. I wondered if Kat felt that way over the years with me. Do older sisters seem bigger than life to little sisters?

Kat jumped in with very good questions, "Why did they cuff him if this was a friendly conversation? Why hold him?"

"He apparently got in a dispute with one of the officers, who he has a past history with and that officer cuffed him. He did the right thing at that point and did exactly as he was told and went with them willingly."

We finished lunch, and we all walked out of the restaurant towards the Moke. We were saying our goodbyes when Kat hit my elbow with the back of her hand.

"What, Kat?" I said, looking over towards the Treylor Park door. Standing in the exact same spot Perdita stood one hour ago was the woman who kicked off our day with her wild Ponte Vedra Parrot news article. Krystal Kelly in the flesh.

Kat whispered, "That's her. That's the woman who wrote the article. I don't believe it."

We all stared for a few seconds while we watched her on her phone. Before I knew what I was doing my anger got the best of me like a momma bear. I walked over to Krystal Kelly shouting "Hey, you... Krystal Kelly."

"Oh no, Kyra. Don't," Kat said following me.

Perdi asked "What are you doing?" as she tried to catch up to me.

Ms. Kelly looked my way and separated the phone from her head a little. She started to back up as I decreased the ground between us. "You irresponsible hack. You wrote about my family!" I pounded my fist on my chest as I confronted her seething with anger. "You'll burn in the back forty of Hades for your slanderous trash. You... you... mudslinger." That was the best a Christian girl could come up with in my fury.

"Yea... you tell her KayKay." Kat cheered me on.

I was waiting for her to retort, when all of the sudden, Perdita, in her pretty professional suit, was in between us. "Kyra, take a beat." But that huge purse on Perdi's shoulder bumped into Krystal Kelly and took her out. Krystal teetered backwards into the daily specials sign by the front door.

As if in slow motion, I watched the look of surprise turn to shock on Krystal Kelly's face as she tumbled back over the sign, flailing her arms around in mini circles trying to keep herself from crashing backwards. Realizing she was about to fall, I grabbed for her to steady her, but collided with her flailing hand, accidentally sending her phone skyrocketing into the air.

"Oh, no," I said as I tried to pull her long gangly arms towards me, preventing her from falling back. I heard a crack and both Krystal and I shot each other a shocked look. Krystal's stiletto heel wedged into the diamond shaped gap in the concrete and cracked in half, sending her collapsing down... pulling me down with her as I didn't quite let go of her arms. My face and shoulder hit the glass door, breaking my fall.

"Oh, there she goes," I heard Perdi say as her purse swung around and pummeled me in the face on my way down causing me to finally let go of Krystal Kelly. I felt Perdi's arms encircle my waist and yank me back. My flip flops went flying off my feet from the abrupt pull. The hostess inside was shaking her head and rolling her eyes as she witnessed the ordeal.

Poor Krystal Kelly teetered up against the daily specials chalkboard sign and fell over it, keister first. Her boney behind on the ground, head up against the glass door and feet flailing around in the air on top of the, now collapsed, sign with one broken heel kicking furiously, as she tried to get up.

My face instantly flushed red. "Oh... oh...oh, no... oh, my gosh." I bent over to help her up. Perdi on one side, me on the other, offering our outstretched arms to the poor girl on the ground. "I went too far. That was too far. Goodness... gracious. Let us help you up."

"Are you hurt?" Perdi asked, trying to move the sign out from under her knees when all of the sudden Krystal's head was smashed against the same glass door by that uber-large red hobo bag as it came flying off Perdi's shoulder. "Oh my gosh. This bag is too big," Perdi exclaimed as she pulled the bag off Ms. Kelly and set it down on the ground beside her.

"Those things should really be illegal." I said as I picked up my flip flop and stumbled back a few feet, backing into Kat. When I turned around, Kat said, "Smile."

"What? Oh Kat. You are not filming this are you? You would be," I said snidely as I turned around with my flip flop in my hand and realized Perdi needed help picking Ms. Kelly up off the ground.

"Seriously, girl. Are you okay? My bad," I rubbed my head which was forming a lump. I saw her phone on the ground and picked it up, rubbing the dirt off on my denim shorts. "Did you break anything?" I handed it to her once she was on her feet.

"You... how dare you attack me?" the journalist said with a pursed lip, waiting for a reply.

"Oh yeah, that's an exaggeration... much like your article. I didn't attack you. It was a huge purse that took you out. Then that daily special sign was an accomplice." I paused and tried to smile, letting her know I was not a threat. "Gravity... it was all gravity... really," I said trying to lighten the mood. "Here... here is your phone, hon."

Krystal snatched her phone assertively while giving me the stink-eye. I picked up her sunglasses and handed them to her. She flipped her sunglasses up on her head and took a good look at the phone. "It's not broken or else I'd call the cops."

"I wouldn't blame you at all... let's call them," I said trying to do my best to bring the tension down. Suddenly, I was very aware of Kat's phone in all our faces. "Kat, please. Don't make the situation worse," as I pushed down on Kat's arm and shook my head no.

"Let's all just take it down a notch, shall we?" Perdi said, getting in between us again to pick up that huge purse.

"That thing is not even a purse, it's more like a carry on. You could really hurt someone with that thing, Perdi." I whispered to Perdi, as Krystal was wiping off her behind and pant legs. She stopped and looked up intently at Perdi.

"Krystal, do you recognize me? Do you know who I am?" Perdi said, taking off her sun glasses and flipping her hair back. Krystal stepped back and leaned up against the glass when she recognized Perdi. "You had my photo on the front of *Ponte Vedra Parrot* today with your article. You told some lies about me and my family. I just got off the phone with my attorney and he is calling your boss right now. You didn't identify yourself as a journalist when you asked me if I was alright in the Beach Diner ladies room."

"I do know you. Attorney, widow, not raised here, but one heck of an interesting origin story," Krystal spouted out.

"That gives you no right to write about me or my family. Where did you get your information from anyway? Why would you run an article smearing my name and my family?" Perdi continued.

"You should be thanking me. Do you know how many comments we got on your story? Everyone wants to hear more about you," Krystal said, motioning with her hands to her chest as if she were to be thanked from the bottom of our hearts for putting us on the *Ponte Vedra Parrot* map.

"No one is going to thank you. I've called my attorney. He is contacting your editor now for a retraction," Perdi snapped back, using the sidewalk as her courtroom.

"More like lies you told," Kat jumped in, still filming. I just threw my arms in the air and hoped this would not end up as evidence for harassment.

Krystal's face changed from defensive to pure excitement as she said, "You don't understand. We had real readership engagement with your story. Everyone wants to know more about how you could be the lost child of famous Palm Valley folk." Krystal used air quotes with the word folk. Folk was an unnatural word for her to use given that Northern accent.

"What? What famous people?" Kat said as she dropped her phone down to her side then quickly raised it again, not wanting to miss the action. Kat was now interested in the topic. It included famous people.

"Yep, we would like to know what you are talking about. So far, you have not made one lick of sense." I said as Kat stood back behind me with that stupid camera over my shoulder filming every action and reaction of Ms. Kelly.

Krystal smoothed out her suit jacket, then pulled her hair behind her head and let it all go, tucking the strays behind her ears one side at a time. She was looking up at the sky as if searching for words. Then she finally clapped her hands together, cleaning them off. "Look. If you people don't want your interesting secrets exposed, you should not talk so loud in a diner. I was one booth over, next to you all and heard it all. I saw the entire exchange. Your name is really unique. Not a lot of Perdita Ryans in this area. You have no one to blame but yourselves. I was just lucky enough to be the person at the next table," she said as she shook her phone at us.

I was rolling my eyes and smacking my forehead with the palm of my hand. I walked a little circle and realized I was still barefoot.

"You made some assumptions. Those assumptions are slander. You should have contacted us before going to print. It would have been the magnanimous thing to do in your profession," Perdi said and then began walking away.

"Exactly." I shook a flip flop at Ms. Kelly, as I backed up my big sister.

"I did call you. Several times. Your phone number kept going to voice-mail. I'm not obligated to get your statement, but I did try," she said with what seemed to be genuine honesty.

Ahh... this was all happening at the same time I was out of the office and my work phone was in my office drawer. That did make sense. I put my flip-flops back on my feet.

"I believe you. Still, not a nice thing to do to people, Ms. Kelly." I grabbed Kat's arm and said "Let's go," I watched Perdi drive away without saying goodbye to us. She seemed emotional. Maybe she was mad she talked to Krystal Kelly in the bathroom. I hit the horn impatiently as I waited for Kat to get in the Moke. I sensed the heat rising in the pit of my stomach. This was not Perdi's fault, and I hoped that Perdi was not mad at herself.

I watched Kat have an exchange with Krystal. They were of a similar age. Maybe they even knew one another. I snapped my seatbelt, turned the key, released the parking brake, and shoved the shifter into reverse. I started to back up. Kat ran to catch up and jumped in the Moke as I was pulling away. "What was that about? Do you know her?"

"Yes, college. We had an English class together. I didn't know she was writing for *The Parrot*. I never saw her at the diner. Or I didn't recognize her. I was too distracted," Kat said, looking down at her phone to check her video content. I turned the corner to the left towards the traffic light. A police siren blared, and we both were startled by the sound of the siren. "Heavens to Murgatroyd, that startled me." I was being pulled over.

"Fan-freaking-tastic," I said out loud while Kat smiled and laughed at me.

With my head back and eyes closed, I tried desperately to re-center my positive energy by whispering, *This is not happening to me, not now, please Lord, bless me with your strength,* until the officer arrived beside me. I smiled, opened my eyes and turned to my left to be face to face with a belt buckle. Wow, he was tall.

"Hello Officer. Are you having a good day so far?" I said, looking up out of the golf cart.

"Out of the vehicle, please, ma'am," a very handsome officer with his cap pulled down over his eyes said with an absolute straight face.

Oh, brother. Aunt Dottie drives a golf cart like an Indy car racer hopped up on Red Bull and rum... she never gets pulled over. I make one turn without a directional and I'm goin' to the pokey.

Kat watched from the passenger seat while the officer asked me to step out of the vehicle. He asked me to place my hands on the hood of his cruiser. Oh my. Thank goodness I'm not carrying concealed today. He frisked me up and down while keeping his body tight to mine but not touching. He smelled delightfully yummy. Like suntan lotion and espresso beans.

"Didn't this vehicle recently have a dead guy in it?" he asked sarcastically. "It should be in evidence."

"Is that what this is about? The dead guy?" I asked trying to peek over my left shoulder.

He put his hand on my lower back and stepped away from me when he was done frisking me. "Turn around," he said.

"Thank you." I turned around and gazed into his eyes. Oh my stars, he was really handsome. His eyes were rich caramel mixed with dark chocolate and staring directly at me. They stood out on his tan skin. He smiled at me. Oh wow... dimples. I bit my lip as I admired him. Then... I felt it... the heat in the core of my body raged like a fire. My face suddenly turned heated. "Oh, no. Not now." Was I about to have another hot flash?

"Not now what, Ms. King?" He continued to grin at me. "Did you just thank me for frisking you?" He asked quizzically.

My lips quivered as a silly grin unconsciously appeared on my face without my dang permission. Was I smiling at him? I cocked my head to one side and giggled. What was happening to me? This was very disconcerting.

"I'm so sorry, officer. Was I speeding?" My eyelashes fluttered as I invaded his personal space and unconsciously reached for his arm with my left hand.

"I saw the whole thing. You knocked over a woman and then fled in a golf cart," he said, looking down at my hand on his arm, removing it with his opposite hand.

"It won't happen again, officer. Uh, I mean, Officer Menendez," I said as I quickly read the prominently displayed name plate on his well-formed chest.

"Pete," He smiled and looked down at my hand and touched my ring finger. "You're starting to perspire... am I making you nervous?"

"Ha... no... I'm just hot. And now it comes in flashes, at my age." I shut my eyes hard. Why did I just tell him that. When I opened my eyes, he was smiling at me.

"Get back in your vehicle Ms. King. Drive safely."

Huh? He knew my name.

"Kyra. Call me Kyra. Or KayKay. Thank you, Pete. Have a good day," I nodded. I slowly walked away with a new swing to my hips that I never noticed before. I hopped in the Moke. Kat was filming, again. "Gosh darn it, Kat" Must she capture every moment on film. I was embarrassed. Why did I thank him? For frisking me? Well... for that, he deserved thanks.

"Well, that was fun. I've never been frisked before." Smiling, I pulled onto the road with Kat laughing at me.

"Kyra, I've never in all my life seen you so red as you are right now," Kat said, snapping a photo of me smiling.

"Oh, zip it. You don't know me. You've been at college a long time, little sis." I said, trying to defend myself and sound more grand than I really ever was or will be.

"Oh, yeah? Are you trying to tell me you weren't in bed by 9 every night while I was away?

"I have a life, Kat." That was an outright lie.

"Okay," Kat said, still smirking.

"What were you talking to Krystal about? What did you say to her?"

"I asked her what she meant about us being a famous family," Kat pulled her sunglasses down off her head to her eyes. She tossed her phone in her purse as I drove onto the golf cart path from the light at Village Drive. "She said she knew how Aunt Dottie made her money."

"Aunt Dottie doesn't have a penny to her name," I said in a huff.

"That is what I told her. She looked surprised and said you really don't know about her fortune?"

I slammed on the brakes in front of one of the seven Peaceful River Valley Banks. I was in utter shock. I looked over at Kat without saying a word.

Kat continued, "That is what she said. Krystal said it was easy enough to look up how she made her money at the state registrar's office," Kat tossed up her hands. "Who knew?"

"Well, I would like to have known. The entire reason I sold Mom and Dad's estate in Palm Valley was to take that money and pay for Aunt Dottie's independent care facility and a bit of your undergrad degree. That property was in our family a long time and I would have rather kept it. It was sold to dad by the Landrums. Dad loved that property. But I had no choice. I needed money after Aunt Dottie had her first heart attack and needed to be in a better care facility."

"The Landrums, like the middle school," Kat said quizzically.

"Yes, Alice Landrum, the first post mistress in Mineral City in the '30s," I said proudly.

"Mineral City?" Kat looked forward.

"You need a history class if you don't know Ponte Vedra Beach was once called Mineral City before it became Ponte Vedra Beach. Ms. Alice was the first postmaster of Ponte Vedra Beach. Heck, you went to the Landrum school. How don't you know the history of your own school?" I was overwhelmed but that was no reason to belittle my little sister.

"Oh," Kat said quietly.

"I'm sorry, Kat. It's been quite a... week." I turned the golf cart around and pointed it in the direction of Aunt Dottie's abode at Starling. I was going to talk to that woman and get the truth out of her. How could she be wealthy? That just didn't add up at all. "We are going to see Aunt Dottie and talk to her about this right now."

"Why don't I just look it up online?" Kat pulled her phone back out and started searching the will and probate office web site. "Or we could call Perdi. She has so many resources. Are you going to hire that P.I.?"

"Don't call her. Give her some space. She was irritated when she left, I think. We don't have to take every piece of advice from Perdi. Just because she is older and has resources, we should listen to everything she says now?" I said, angry at Kat for fawning all over Perdi like she had all the answers. Oh what is happening to me... I'm coming unglued.

"I just think if she recommended a P.I. to track down all those names of people who may have been victims, just like her, then... well... we should follow her lead, that's all. "

"I know... you're right. I'm a hot mess," as I sped down the golf cart path towards the Starling Independent Living facility on the circle.

Chapter
TWENTYSEVEN

I called Aunt Dottie, and she surprisingly picked up. I tried to remain calm about being in the dark. "Aunt Dottie, what are you up to this afternoon?"

"Well, Connie is here at my condo, and we're waiting for Ethel to bring her homemade cookies so we can play some Yahtzee before dinner."

"That sounds fun. Great. Kat wants to talk to you, hold on." I handed Kat the phone. I stopped the Moke near the intersection of the circle. I decided to go back home. I needed to confront Aunt Dottie, but now was not the time to do it while I was a hot mess and she was, apparently, entertaining guests.

"Hi, Aunt Dottie. We just wanted to tell you we spoke to a woman today that said you were rich and inherited a bunch of money. We didn't know about it. How 'bout that rumor mill in Peaceful River Valley, huh?" Kat said nonchalantly.

I was shocked Kat just came out with it as easy as drinking sweet tea on a hot summer day. I couldn't hear what Aunt Dottie was saying. "Put her on speaker phone."

Kat extended the phone out between us and pressed speaker. "Y'all found out, huh? I was wondering when you all would put it together." Aunt Dottie sighed. "Look, I didn't tell you because it was not something I ever wanted to be known. I didn't want it to change how people treated me or us. It's really not a big thing. Hardly no one knows."

"Uh huh... not a big thing, Aunt Dottie?" I said about to become unglued.

"Look, can we talk about this later. Ethel just showed up with the cookies. I have entertaining to do."

"Aunt Dottie, please don't do that. Don't hang up on us and make us go read about this in the county records." I said as the golf carts piled up behind us honking their horns. I pulled off into the grass as folks went whizzing by, no doubt picking up kids from school.

"Girls. It's simple and now that y'all have birth certificates, you know. Your daddy and I were from the same mother but not the same daddy. My father left me land when he died in the '80s and I found out who he really was. Ya know... back then there was no internet to tell you your DNA story. I had to find out via the lawyers."

"What?" I mouthed to Kat who was shaking her head.

"That swamp land was in my name, but had a clause. I couldn't sell it to no one but the Ark group. It was tagged for sale to the Ark group in phases for development..."

"Of Peaceful River Valley." I finished the sentence.

"When did your parcel of land sell, Aunt Dottie?" I said, almost feeling my blood boil just thinking about being forced to sell the King family property in Palm Valley.

"Well... that's the funny thing about it. That land has been sitting there in my name, growing in value each year for decades. Then COVID hit us and there was a slowdown... before the miraculous boom. So those poor suckers had to pay me almost quadruple what the land was worth just a few short years ago." I could hear her laughing and her friends joining in. I swear I heard a man say *cha-ching*.

"Aunt Dottie... Aunt Dottie... do you mean to tell me the land just sold recently?"

"Yes, dear. For the next phase being developed in Peace River Valley called Sea by The Brook Village. They purchased almost all of it. I still own a small patch of a few hundred acres between the Guana preserve and Palencia with a cabin on it. Some of it is tagged Commercial and ready for sale if they ever want the rest of it.

"What?" I was floored. This just happened. This woman can keep a secret. I'm not sure we would have ever known this information if not for Krystal Kelly, a complete stranger. "Absolutely and completely accidental that we found this information out today."

"Now you heard it all... can I go play Yahtzee now, dears?" Aunt Dottie complained.

"Yes, ma'am," Kat said respectfully.

"Bye, Aunt Dottie. Love you." I said as I heard her hang up while blowing us kisses into the phone. "Do you even believe the week we are having?" I asked Kat with my mouth still open. Aunt Dottie had kept this secret from us all... a very long time. The woman should be in the CIA— she is so secretive and evasive. The wind, completely taken out of my sails, made me feel like I couldn't be certain of anything anymore.

Chapter
TWENTYEIGHT

K at and I arrived home to find Perdi pulling into the driveway. I pulled the Moke past her and into the garage bay. "Hey, there! What brings you back over? I thought you were going back to work."

"Yes, I did... I went to get the medical examiner report for Flannery. Unfortunately, no luck. They are not done yet and tests are pending."

"Well, that is really nice of you. Thank you, Perdi. I know you can probably send one of your assistants to do that." I appreciated her referring an attorney to us for Killian. "Do you want to come inside and sit down?"

Perdi nodded and followed behind me. "My assistants stopped to see him again today. They said he seems to be in good spirits, given the circumstances."

"Oh, I know Killian keeps to good spirits in any circumstance because he doesn't know the weight of a feather. He is the least serious person I know. He doesn't know what can happen to him." Kat seemed alarmed, as if now we were both coming unhinged.

"They will let him go soon, right? I mean he didn't do it, and they will need to charge him with something to hold him much longer," Kat said so confidently.

"He's been there 24 hours. They can continue to hold him another day without charging him."

"They are waiting on the coroner's report to show cause of death so they can charge him with murder," Kat said.

"Yep, they found his fingerprints on the Moke. And he has no alibi, which is a problem." Perdi said pulling out a day timer from her huge purse. "The most concerning thing, to me, is that the facial recognition software has such a powerful match to Killian."

I interrupted, "Ahh... but, he has been all over this house and the Moke. His prints will, of course, be found throughout."

I stopped abruptly as I considered what Perdi just said. "Wait... the video from the doorbell... where you can only see the guy's chin?" I questioned smugly. I suddenly was pumped with excitement about my ability to contribute. Perdi tilted her head to one side and squinted at me. I put a glass of sun tea in front of Perdi and shared "It is absolutely not Killian in the video. Killian has a scar. On his chin."

"The scar... yes." Perdi kept her eyes on me as I sat at the dining room table. "I noticed his scar when I talked to him at the jail."

"The scar on his chin. The man in the video doesn't have a scar on his chin. It can't be Killian in the video... there is no scar," I said as I went to the living room bookcase and grabbed my favorite photo of Ken and Killian when they were six years old.

The two boys were in overalls with no shirts and holding fishing poles about to get into a canoe at the end of Canal Boulevard, where the water crested into the road at high tide. It was now Mickler's Wharf but back when this photo was taken... Palm Valley was still the swamps where country kin divided up the land and lived off the land all year long. I was instantly transported back to the day I gave Killian that scar.

I was an immature young lady with tomboy tendencies. I fished in the river, trapped alligators in the swamps, kayaked in the ICW, built cabinets with my dad, and fought with my little twin brothers. One afternoon, Killian, the youngest twin, and I were pushing each other while jumping on his bed. He said something mean to me and hopped up onto the headboard and sat down. To this day, I don't recall what it was he even said. But I grimaced at him, tightened my ponytail, and charged for his feet, which were dangling from the top of the headboard where he sat. I pulled up his feet to the sky, and his butt slipped off the headboard into the crevice between the wall and the headboard. He folded like a taco shell behind the headboard, his legs and feet flailing in the air.

I, of course, instantly started laughing hysterically while also trying to help him out by pulling on the collar of his shirt. He was stuck in that crevice so tightly, I ripped his collar clear off the t-shirt and he fell back laughing even harder as he looked up at me, saying "KayKay, I'm gonna get you... as soon as you get me outta here."

I tried, again, to rescue my little brother while also trying not to pee my pants from laughing so hard. It was no use. I was not strong enough to pull him out. In the meantime, Ken, the older twin brother walked into the room. Seeing his brother's feet up in the air and the screams coming from behind the headboard, he too, bust out laughing. We all have such a warped sense of humor. With Ken's help, we pulled both socks off Killian, trying to budge him loose.

I sat on the floor next to the bed. Being a caring older sister, I placed a pillow behind his head. "Be quiet while I think. There's got to be a way to get you out without running to Mom and Dad." I said to him. Mom and Dad would surely punish me. Then I had an idea.

"Ken, come here and help me push this bed," I said as he joined me on the floor. "Push," I said, straining. The bed frame started to screech across the floorboards, and the crevice widened. I heard a thud followed by a yelp and ran over to the pile of arms and legs crumbled on the floor.

Killian's head popped up "Heavens to Murgatroyd, Killian! Why are you bleeding?"

"I'm bleeding?" Killian said as he searched the spot on his face under his lip. Ken took one look at the blood and started to cry. Killian was squeezing his hand hard against his chin and the blood was trickling over his fingers. He started to mumble, "I felt a sharp pain when my head hit the post."

I held Ken Jr. close to me to comfort him. "Don't cry, little man. You are not hurt, right?" My word, babysitting is hard, I thought. One is crying and one is bleeding... Dad is gonna break the wooden spoon on my butt.

"Come on, Killian. We need to stop the bleeding. Bathroom, now." I pointed across the hall at the bathroom as I picked up Ken Jr. and placed him on the bed. I pulled out a lollipop and tore the wrapper off. Handing it to him he looked at it wide eyed and said, "I won't tell Mom and Dad you tried to kill Killian."

"Great." I tousled his hair. "Now that is not exactly what happened, Kenny." I tilted my head and looked at the smirk on his face while his free hand waved for more lollipops. This was a shakedown, by a six-year-old, who didn't actually see anything.

I gave him another lollipop and headed across the hall into the bathroom. Killian was standing up on the step stool, looking in the mirror. Drops of blood peppered the avocado green sink basin. I grabbed a bright yellow washcloth and dabbed gently.

It was a large gash across his chin where his dimple started and his lip ended. Mom and Dad were going to punish me for certain. I would never have phone privileges again. I could say goodbye to that push button phone in my room for Christmas, too.

"Hold this against your chin," I said as I pressed the washcloth hard against Killian's wound until he took over. I grabbed another washcloth and took it into the kitchen. I opened the freezer and cracked three ice cubes out of the ice cube tray. I placed them in the washcloth and headed back to the bathroom.

The bleeding was slowing. I exchanged out the bloody washcloth for the homemade ice-filled sunshine yellow cloth pack. I held it to his face as I held the back of his head. He shook off my motherly attempts and held the ice pack on his own with both hands cupped over the ice. "You still gonna get me?"

"No, but you're gonna owe me," Killian said. "Big time," he added as he removed the ice pack and looked in the mirror. "Cool."

"What's cool, the ice?" I asked, quizzically looking at Killian admiring himself in the mirror.

"No. Cool that I'll have a scar. Like Daddy," he said proudly and smiled.

Perdi was saying my name. "Kyra. Kyra?" Perdi handed me the photo back and said "I didn't link the scar to the video. I'll tell his attorney. That may be enough to get him released."

"I don't understand why the police didn't make this connection?" I questioned.

"I think they are relying on technology, which is showing a high correlation match to Killian and Ken. Because Ken had a strong alibi, they assumed it was Killian." Perdi filled us in on the specifics as she dialed Killian's attorney. Once he picked up the phone Perdi paced the living room floor in front of the sliding glass doors to the courtyard.

Kat was sitting at the kitchen island facing the dining table when I got up to add ice to my sun tea. "But, also... what could possibly be Killian's motive? It's not like he knows a convicted felon."

Kat sounded so smart. I beamed with pride and stood a little taller and started to smile at Kat. She was so good at this lawyer thing. She just needed the right mentor. Perdi might be that good mentor for her to sharpen her innate skills as an attorney and grow in her career.

"We need to go to the police station and get Killian. He shouldn't be questioned so long when he clearly was not the person in the video," Kat continued, defending her brother.

Perdi hung up the phone and joined us at the kitchen island. "Motive, right. No motive for Killian to kill a murderer that was just released. This leads me to the next topic. I wanted to talk to you both about the birth and death certificate we got from Doris." Perdi said, opening up.

Perdi sat at the kitchen island. She looked like she had a sour taste in her mouth. Her eyes squinted and her mouth frowned down on both sides. "I have given it a lot of thought... about what may have happened the day of my birth. The odds of uncovering the truth are slim to none, with everyone else in the room now deceased except me."

"Perdi, what are trying to say?" I asked.

"I think we are investigating the wrong mystery here. We have focused on what happened to me on the day of my birth, when we should really be investigating the life of Aggie Flannery."

"Aggie Flannery? Really?" Kat said, putting her arm around Perdi to console her as her eyes filled with tears. "Why?"

"I need to face that mom gave me up?" Perdi said with a crackling to her voice. "She left nothing here to indicate why. I just need to accept it."

Perdi pulled tissues out of that huge purse. I got her some water while Kat hugged her.

"No... no... we don't know that," Kat said, trying to console her.

I put the water glass down next to her, and when Kat backed away a little, I moved in to hug Perdi. "No, no, Perdi. I don't believe Mom gave you up for one moment. It is the least likely scenario," I said.

"What do mean? Are you talking about the death certificate?" Perdi asked as we separated, and she continued to tap her eyes gently with tissues.

"Yes, that is exactly right. The only reason for a birth certificate, a death certificate, and an alternate birth certificate issued the same day is theft or fraud," I said.

"Fraud?" Perdi said, standing before me swallowing her full glass of water.

"Yes, that is what I think. I think Aggie Flannery was deceiving young women and stealing their babies."

"That is a really a stretch, Kyra," Kat said, knowing I had no further proof.

"Does anyone else have a better deduction after seeing the names on the stationery inside the Ponte Vedra Inn and Club envelope?" I said quickly as I was suddenly pumped with passion for this topic. Kat and Perdi just looked at one another, shaking their heads.

"I believe, at my core, that you were born to Mom and Dad. We know Dad was not here in Palm Valley that year because of his letters to Mom from Vietnam. We also now know that around the same time, Conor was killed in Vietnam," I went on as I paced back and forth next to the dining room table.

"Mom gives birth to you. The only one present was the nurse. Aggie Flannery. The nurse takes you away. She tells Mom you died and presents her with the death certificate. Then the nurse, and I do mean Aggie Flannery here, takes you and gives you to an illegitimate adoption agency. You are adopted by your parents with a false birth certificate in their name to prove that the baby is their baby." This makes perfect sense, from the trail of the paperwork, thanks to Ms. Doris.

"Oh, I don't know, Kyra. That sounds like my adoptive parents were in on the fraud. They just would not have done that. They would never take a baby away from its mother. You didn't know them. They were good Godly people. Family was everything to them," Perdi elevated her voice as she defended her adoptive parents.

"Perdi, I know it is hard for you to believe because you did not know our mom and dad," I said, as I moved my hand back and forth between me and Kat. "But I did. These are two people who believed in family first. Mom loved babies and children."

"So, what are you saying? That my mother and father knowingly paid for me?" Perdi said abruptly.

"No, I am not saying that. It may be that your mom and dad never even knew the circumstances. If Aggie Flannery was willing to falsify records for you and maybe others, then she would lie to your parents." I said quietly, trying to ameliorate the situation.

"I do not want to believe that the people who raised me paid for me in some illegal scheme to defraud the real parents!" Perdi raised her voice, as if she was getting out some real anger.

"I understand that completely, Perdi," I said reaching out for her hand. "I do not want to believe that my mother and father abandoned a child. Not even if they were un-married at the time. Not even if they were poor and had limited or no means. Not even if they were paid to." My breath drew inward and my heart jumped out of my chest. What did I just say? It came out of my mouth without even thinking it. I had never thought it before. How did it tumble out of my mouth as if I had no filter or control of my thoughts? The look on Perdi's face was pure anguish.

"That's it, isn't it?" Perdi said. "I was bought and sold. I was a transaction. There was money exchanged somewhere? By people in our lives who put us here and raised us up in the church, who changed our diapers, who fought for us through various schooling, teenage years, financial hardship, and apparently even war. You are telling me that one of these people or even more than one of them exchanged me for money?" Perdi shouted. She was physically shaking as I watched her come unglued for the first time since we met her. She was visibly angry.

Kat gasped and reached for Perdi's hand. "Oh, my gosh. That is a terrible thing to say, Perdita. It can't possibly be true," Kat said naively.

Perdita and I were locked on one another. Did I say something I needed to apologize for or was this a real question we should be pursuing? My shoulders slumped and my arms went out towards Perdi who stepped back slightly.

I recoiled and my hands began to fidget in front of me as I looked down at them. When I looked up at Perdi, I could see she was waiting for me to say something. "Perdi, we are only hypothesizing here. There is no way for us to know the exchange. We have no evidence. No proof. We both know that we were both raised by loving parents. We don't know what happened that day. We don't know the reasons. We just need to keep looking and exploring possibilities," I said.

Kat let go of Perdi's hand and as Perdi pulled away and collected her things. "I agree with both of you. KayKay is right, we are just hypothesizing. But Perdi, you are also correct. We need to continue investigating Aggie Flannery. If you have a false birth certificate and others do too... well we need to find them. Someone must know something about Aggie Flannery."

There was a long pause as Perdita finished gathering her items and walked to the front door. She put on her pretty kitten heels and stood back up. She let out a huge sigh and looked stressed.

"Maybe," Perdita said, sounding tired. "I think I need some time to be alone. I need to go back home to talk to some people who knew my mom and dad in Pittsburgh. I'll also search the boxes from the beach house for clues into their past." Perdi pulled her sunglasses down off her head to cover her tear-filled eyes.

"Perdi, don't go. Please stay," Kat said with such sweet compassion. "I think we are better able to find the truth if we are all together and sharing information."

"Yes, please stay, Perdi. This is painful for all of us. We understand it better than anyone. We don't want to do this without you," I said, hoping that she would reconsider a trip to Pennsylvania.

"Y'all are so sweet," Perdi said softening some but not fully. "I know there are people in my neighborhood that I can talk to because they lived there all their lives with my parents. I need to talk to them before any of them die and the secret is buried forever. I think it is a good idea for you to continue looking through your parents' effects. But please don't go trying to find Aggie Flannery without me." Perdi partially smiled as best she could. "I don't want you researching that part without me."

"But you won't go to Pennsylvania, right? You will just contact them via email or phone?" I asked as I thought to myself that I really needed some alone time. I still have a few boxes to go through, too. Mom and Dad lived their entire adult lives together. If we were going to find something that could give us a clue, it would be in one of those boxes, and I was not done yet with them.

"No, no. I'll contact them from here and if they have something I need to see, then I will make a trip up north," Perdi clarified.

"But will we still see you and Mac on Sunday for dinner? Please say yes," Kat said, walking over to Perdi and throwing her arms around her waist while putting her head against Perdi's chest.

"I don't know. I feel like I need some time apart. This is all too much." Perdi walked out the door with no plan to ever see us again... or so it felt.

Kat and I watched Perdi pull out of the driveway, sad to see her go after such an emotional conversation. I desperately needed some alone time with my thoughts.

"I can't believe you, Kyra." Kat shouted at me. "We don't know what happened that day and all your thoughts were speculation. You clearly upset Perdi and you practically chased her out of the house with your insistence that Mom and Dad would never..." Kat dramatically clutched her heart and pretended she was shocked. I guess that was her way of imitating me. I didn't like it. "Why didn't you try to make her stay? UGH, you make me so angry sometimes."

"What?" I paused for a moment and then realized emotions were high and I should walk away. "Let's both calm down, Kat."

Kat threw her hands on her hips. "KayKay... has that ever in the history of our conversations worked? Do we ever calm down because you say it? No. You do this all the time. I'm so tired of it."

"What?" I was so confused. What conversation were we actually having right now? "Kat, I understand you are mad. I know I didn't handle this conversation with Perdi very well... but..."

Kat interrupted me. "Kyra, you do this all the time. You get into people's business, you start taking care of them, and then when a serious event happens you withdraw and tell everyone to go calm down. Did it ever occur to you that I want to talk to you about this right now. I don't want to calm down. I have something to say to you."

"Ok... Kat... say it. What is it?" I said snidely.

Kat took her hands off her hips and pushed her beautiful long strawberry blonde hair off her face. She took a deep breath. Then laid it on me right there in the foyer. "I'm moving out."

Kat walked down the foyer, down the gallery, and into her room. Stunned, I stood in the foyer, my face frozen in shock, a whirlwind of emotions battling within. I didn't want her to move out this way. I don't want her to be mad at me. I want to be sisters. Here I am standing alone in the foyer with both sisters having just walked away from me. Was it me? What did I do wrong? Sigh... *This could not be more perfect a time for a relaxing glass of wine.*

I went back into the kitchen and chose a pinot noir from the wine fridge and uncorked it. I poured a small sample into the glass and thought it needed a few minutes to breathe. I opened the glass doors to the lanai and put the outdoor fan on. I lit a few candles and turned on some lounge music. The sky was turning dark, and the light was on in the pool already. I turned on landscape lights in the courtyard. I sprayed a few of the air plants and watered the bamboo palm on the lanai. It looked like the perfect setting for a glass of wine and some deep relaxation.

I turned around, walked through the lanai doors, and was startled to see Aunt Dottie sitting in the living room chair looking at me. "Aunt Dottie, you scared me. How long have you been here?" At that moment, I realized we were not alone. There was a grey-haired man sitting on my sofa. He stood up, turned around, and stared towards me. My eyes focused and blinked and refocused on the man walking towards me. "What is this?"

I suddenly felt light-headed. My knees started to buckle, and it was hard to keep myself upright. I tried to grab the chair in front of me. Sweat started to bead on the back of my neck at my hairline. He was walking towards me. My vision went hazy... as my body crumpled beneath me... "Daddy?"

Chapter
TWENTYNINE

I woke on my couch with a cold compress on my forehead and someone holding my hand. I tugged off the compress with my free hand and tried to sit up a little on the pillow. My vision was hazy, and when it cleared, the man holding my hand was my father. "Dad... am I dead, too?"

"Kyra, how ya feelin', love?" He smiled at me and patted my head with the compress as he removed it from my forehead. "I'm not your Dad. I'm Connie, er... um... Conor. Your Dad's twin brother," he said as he rubbed my hand gently.

"Who died in Vietnam, then?"

"Conor died in Vietnam. Or at least that's what he told everyone," Aunt Dottie chimed in from the chair besides me. "You're not dead, KayKay. Although you almost smacked your head on that fireplace mantle, and that sure would've killed ya."

"Aunt Dottie... what happened? I'm so confused." I said, sitting up on one elbow.

"I know you are. It's confusing. But we thought it was time to tell you because you caught me on the doorbell camera. We figured it was only a matter of time before you pieced it all together," Conor said with a smile and gentle voice, like Dad's voice.

"Or you would've jumped to the wrong conclusions and thought that he was your dad and if you had gone and told the police that it was your dad on the doorbell camera, they would've likely put you in a padded cell," Aunt Dottie said, joking.

"Jokes, Aunt Dottie? Right now while I'm dazed and confused, you're riffing your next standup routine?" I whispered as I sat all the way up. Conor was handing me a glass of water. I was thirsty. I stopped as I put the glass to my lips and pulled it away. "This isn't poisoned, is it?"

"I thought you said she was smart," Conor asked Aunt Dottie but kept his gaze on me.

"Dang girl, maybe you did hit your thick skull. Why would we go and poison you after we tell you the family secrets?" Aunt Dottie asked as she handed Conor a glass of wine. "Here, give her this, Connie."

"Connie? You're Connie, Aunt Dottie's best friend of 60 years?" I asked.

He smiled with a crooked little grin like he was a little boy keeping a secret. "Yep. Aunt Dottie can keep a secret."

"For sure," I said, sipping my wine. "Kat was home. Does she know you are here? Has she seen you?"

"No. I'd like to keep it that way," Connie said as he sat on my reclaimed wood coffee table. He was in very good shape for a dead man. He was slender but muscular like he never hit the gym and only did body weight conditioning.

"Well... I don't have secrets from my sister. So, that, is not going to be possible," I quipped. "Plus, the minute she finds out about you, she'll want to put you on her podcast." I sat fully up on the couch and put my feet on the floor.

"Well... that would be entertaining, but I got some people looking for me, so no," Connie said with confidence.

"Who's looking for you, Connie?" I asked with a stone-cold face.

Connie moved up the couch closer to me as I clutched the pillow where my wine glass was perched. "That is not what I came here to talk about tonight. It was just time to meet. Dottie and I agreed that we would bring you into this because you need to know."

"What do I need to know?" I whispered.

"There are some things you need to know about the day your parents had their accident. It will clear some things up for you and your sisters," Connie leaned in closer to me, looking directly in my eyes.

I was enthralled with him. My uncle Conor, who I had never met and who supposedly died at the age of 20 in Vietnam. He looked like dad except for the eyes. Conor had hazel eyes, whereas dad had green eyes like me. They were not identical twins, rather they were fraternal twins. I was suddenly feeling better and asked the only question that I'd had no answer for... "Do you know why they died?" I asked and held my breath.

"Oh, baby girl... it was their time. That is the only reason you need to tell yourself," he said reaching out to hold my hand.

"No... you tell me. Why are you here? You say you have answers. You tell me why," I said sharply.

"I'll tell you a few things, first, that I came here to tell you," Connie said as he shifted over a little more staring directly at me. "The man on your porch... Robert Flannery. He wasn't a good a man. I waited a long time to get to him because he was in prison. When I caught up to him on the porch, I hit him, as you saw in the video. But I just knocked him out, is all. I carried him to your golf cart. Anyway, I sat him in the Moke because I was gonna go get my truck and carry him away... to take care of him."

"Take care of him? As in bring him to the hospital and care for the lump on his head?" I asked.

Connie didn't even stop. He just kept on talking. "He regained consciousness when I put him down in the Moke. But, he took one look at me and started clutching his chest."

"He was an old man," I added.

"He had a heart attack right there in front me. So, you see... I didn't kill him."

"But you were going to kill him, given the chance?" I asked.

"Well... what I was gonna do or not do, I don't know now," Connie put his finger up and wagged it back and forth. "He was a dangerous man. The reason I had to stop him from talking to you is because he was going to tell you something that we didn't want you to hear."

"We? Who is we?" I looked at Aunt Dottie as if there was yet another secret she was keeping. "Are you going to tell me anyway?" I asked, knowing that I had a fifty-fifty chance of getting the truth out of him.

"Turns out he wrote it down in a letter. I'm glad I didn't get to do what I was fixin' to do, because it sounds like from the letter, he found Jesus. He wrote it all to you. His last words were of truth and confession, in the form of this letter." Connie stuck out his thumb and motioned over his shoulder to Aunt Dottie.

Aunt Dottie placed the letter on the coffee table. "You're not going to tell me?" I asked.

"No, Kyra girl. You can read the letter when we are gone," Connie said. "But I will tell you one other thing while I'm here. You keep that letter to yourself. Don't go giving it to the police to get your brother out of jail."

"Uncle Conor, you are a mind reader," I said slyly. "You know that is just what I'm gonna do, because I will not let Killian sit in a jail cell and rot for you for the rest of his precious life."

"Nah... they'll let him go when they can't hold him anymore," he said. "They are just using him to get more information from you. If Flannery died of a heart attack, then there is no real proof of anything other than a little slap to the noggin caught on camera."

Uncle Conor grabbed my hand and placed some folded up paper in it as he held my hand tight. His hands were thick and muscular like a man that had been doing hard labor all his life. "What's this, then?" I asked looking down at my hand.

"This is a second letter I found in Flannery's pocket. It's addressed to your sister Perdi and she is not going to like reading it. He was either giving it to you to find her or he was heading to Perdi next. Either way... the man was fixin' to state his repentance."

"Why are you handing this to me? It belongs to Perdi." My voice trembled, tears welling as the cryptic ring of secrets tightened around me, its hidden truths pulling me into a shadowed pact I wasn't ready to join.

"No. She can't know how you got this, now." Uncle Conor looked over towards Aunt Dottie and then back to me. "Perdi can't know about me. Not now, not ever. It's too dangerous for her."

"What? How am I supposed to explain this letter when I give it to her? I don't like this." I shook my head from side to side.

"Tell her the rest before Kat comes out here wondering what we are all whispering about or God forbid... filming for her channel." Aunt Dottie eagerly tapped Conor on the shoulder.

"Tell me what?" I asked, though a creeping dread warned me I might regret unearthing the truth.

"Now, I'll tell you quick. Your momma found out that Aggie Flannery stole her first-born daughter." Connie started to talk, and my eyes went wide. I hung on every word he said. "She made friends with that old woman, under false pretenses. She was visiting her and having tea with her because Flannery only had half her faculties. Your momma was slippin' arsenic into her tea. Aunt Dottie found out and told your dad that Katherine was poisoning that old woman to put her to her death for taking Perdita away from her. Your Dad went off to stop Katherine. When he arrived at Aggie's home, your momma was coming out the front door and Robert Flannery was going in the back door. Flannery saw his momma passed out at the kitchen table and chased out the front door after your momma."

"How do you know all this, Connie?" I asked with wide-eyed wonder.

"I was pulling up with Aunt Dottie in the car behind your father. Dottie called me and told me everything. I'll tell ya... your mom was shocked to see your father there. She stopped in the middle of the street with the look of fright on her face to see your dad standing there. You know your dad... he put Katherine in his car, and then slapped Flannery around a little in the street. Ken had so much restraint. Your dad got in his car with your momma and drove off. Robert Flannery got up a few seconds later and jumped in his car. That was the last I saw of them."

"Was Aggie Flannery dead?"

"No, she was alive. She was sick and dying slowly. But my guess is, your mom wasn't giving her enough to kill her outright." Unclue Connie, looking away, pushed off the couch and stood up.

"Wait. I was told Aggie Flannery died that same day," I said. "Her death date was the same day as mom and dad's." I grabbed his hand, pulling it into my chest holding it with both my hands in prayer formation. Tears welled up in my eyes and a lump caught in my throat. "Tell me."

"You don't need to know the grim details" Uncle Connie moved his hand to my chin and raised my head. "Keep that mind pure." Aunt Dottie stood up quietly.

"You killed her?" I questioned in a hushed tone. "You killed her and made it look like Robert Flannery did it."

He looked up and closed his eyes as if thinking how to respond or perhaps praying for forgiveness. "Well now... you are smart then, ain't ya?"

"Then how can did you make peace with Robert Flannery?" I asked sincerely.

"Well... at a time I believed violence begets violence." Uncle Conor looked down at me on the couch. "But not anymore. We need to leave the door open... even to those who've wronged us or we thought were our enemy. Especially, to those who were lost and have come back home, so to speak."

"I don't understand."

"The cycle of violence ends with me, Kyra. Read the letter... offer reconciliation from your heart." He kissed the top of my head and waited for Aunt Dottie.

Aunt Dottie kissed me on the head and walked towards the front door. I quickly scurried off the couch and snatched his hand. "Wait... was that you out at the end of my courtyard the other night?

"Yep."

"Where do you live, Uncle Connie? When will I see you again?" I asked eagerly wanting to know my father's brother and hear more about mom and dad.

"I live on Dottie's land in a cabin built a long time ago. We'll see one another again. I'm sure of it." Aunt Dottie was already gone and Connie walked out my front door with me standing there in disbelief. He turned around in the doorway and pointed to the doorbell. "Delete that video of me coming and going on your cameras." Then he headed down the driveway and out of sight into the preserve on the cul-de-sac.

I slowly walked back to the living room and sat back down on the sofa. I looked over at the letter on the table and took a long sip of wine. If I read it, I reasoned, it might tell me something I didn't want to know. I can't un-read that. Mom used to say *'you can't put toothpaste back in the tube now can ya?'*

I was exhausted. This was not the relaxing night I had planned. I found a sister and through the discovery process of how we lost Perdita, sent Perdita emotionally wounded and running from us. My little sister, who I raised and loved, was in a huff. My only living Aunt was a ga-zillionaire and keeping my dead, but not dead, Uncle in hiding within the preserves of Peaceful River Valley. I sipped more wine. The folded letter held my attention like a moth to a flame. Was I ready for the contents within this mysterious letter that was left by the dead guy in my Moke?

I looked over at the candles burning as I picked up the letter and opened the envelope. My brain felt like it was going to explode from the sheer volume of information. This was all too much to handle. I held the letter over the candle flame and tossed the envelope on the table. Lowering the letter towards the flame, I looked up at the photo of Mom and Dad on the bookshelf. I don't want to know anything terrible. At the same time, I wanted to know more than anything what happened to my parents on the Palm Valley Bridge twenty years ago and this letter may reveal that answer. Reading this letter will lead to the vision in my mind forever, good or evil. Is that why Uncle Connor asked me to open my heart to forgiveness? I needed God's grace now more than ever.

I sighed and pulled the letter away from the flame quickly as it burned. I put the flame out between my hands. The letter was a little scorched in the corner but no actual damage. Uncle Connie would not have given it to me if I could not handle it. Perhaps he needs me to know and therefore read it.

It was short and penned in perfect cursive. I read it slowly, consuming every riveting word, as if my body needed it like oxygen. It was a confession, but not the one I expected. After reading the letter, twice, I crawled into my bed and tucked into the fetal position. I cried myself into unconsciousness.

Chapter THIRTY

I woke up the next morning eager to get to the St. Johns County Sheriff's Department and convince them to release Killian. They would have to release him. Especially, if I told them who was on my doorbell camera that night. I didn't know if they were going to believe me. I imagined telling the clerk at the front desk that my long-lost uncle back from Vietnam... and back from the dead, was on my doorbell camera. Yes, that sounded truthful. But would they immediately put me in a straight jacket and padded cell? I couldn't personally afford to tell a story like that, even if it was the truth. No, that was not going to work. How do I explain Uncle Conor?

I would figure it out. Today was going to be a good day. I needed a good day. A day without hearing I have a new sister, or getting frisked, or having the front page of The Ponte Vedra Parrot divulge my family secrets. Today was going to be that good day.

I looked in the mirror and was fully impressed with my effort to put on a dress and sandals. Plus, I did my hair and added make up. This was a real treat. Maximum effort. An effort to look less like a woman on the verge of a nervous breakdown and more like a woman with great opportunity in front of her. That opportunity included a savory quiche.

The house was quiet, as I put the quiche in the oven. It made me wonder if Kat heard anything that transpired last night between me, Aunt Dottie, and Uncle Connie. I enjoyed my coffee on the lanai, holding the letter from Robert Flannery in my hand. I read it again, multiple times. I was still uncertain about what to do with it. Uncle Conor did not want me to reveal what I knew to anyone. I was not sure why but if he had some people looking for him... then perhaps it could be dangerous for me to tell others. I couldn't jeopardize the safety of Kat or Perdi. But I felt compelled to tell them what I knew. Divulging this information would violate the trust between me and Connie. This was quite a quandary.

I needed to get both Kat and Perdi back into my inner circle. The events of last night left us all walking off in different directions. It pained me when Kat turned around and huffed off down the hall towards her room. My little sister, who I wanted to have a sisterly relationship with seemed to be mad at me. I was no longer the caretaker for this little girl. She was all grown up and moving out. Now was the time for me to have a sisterly relationship with her.

Then there was Perdi. How do I explain to Perdi that I know she was taken from Mom at birth and given to her adopted parents. While I still don't know if the Boyle's paid for Perdita illegally, I did know that Aggie Flannery was running some type of unscrupulous operation to deceive young mothers and take their first born babies.

I decided to text Perdi and ask her to meet up with me and Kat. First, I would need to win Kat over and get her to talk to me. There was still more to discuss and to research about Aggie Flannery. Immediately following my text, I received an incoming call from Perdi. I was so excited to hear from her. I was so happy to have a friend who liked to talk on the phone. We both grew up tethered to the wall in the kitchen where the rotary phone, in avocado green, hung. At the same time, I also felt wretched for withhold information from her. If I talked to her, would I accidentally say something I should not? Secrets fester in the shadows, but lies, venomous and unrelenting, carve the deepest wounds in the soul.

"Good morning, Perdi. Thanks for calling me. How are you this morning?"

"Oh Kyra, since I've met you, every day has been a personal soul-searching dramatic adventure. I mean that in the best way."

We both laughed and I knew how she felt. "Okay, fair enough, Perdi."

"What is on your mind today, Kyra?"

"Yes, I've been thinking about your request last night to research Aggie Flannery. I agree and I think it is a good idea," I said, appreciating her idea.

"You do? That's really a relief. So, you will help me with the investigation, then?" Perdi assumed.

"Yes, I will help you with it, and I agree we should find out as much as we possibly can about her life and her death. I wouldn't want to do this without you or Kat," I exclaimed with a sense of relief that we could do this together and that I did not have to bear this alone.

"I'm glad we can do this together, too, Kyra. How about I pick you and Kat up in time to get over to the records storage when they open," Perdi requested.

"We'll be ready. If you want breakfast, come a little earlier," I said offering my quiche breakfast extravaganza to her.

"Thanks, that sounds great! See you soon," Perdi said and hung up.

I got up to get more coffee when I realized Kat was in the kitchen poking around for breakfast. "I made a potato, ham and cheese crust-less quiche, Kat, if you are hungry," I said as I passed her with her head in the fridge. "Do you want me to make you a plate?"

"Yes, please," Was her standard reply when she wanted something. I had no idea what she wanted today, but I'm sure I was about to find out.

I set the Sonos music to my favorite country music and looked over at Kat for an eyeball rolling reaction. To my surprise, she did not quiver with displeasure. Yep, she was for certain going to ask for something. We listened to music while Kat's nose was in her phone at the kitchen island. I two-stepped around the kitchen and Kat's still slumped body on the counter stool while delivering a place setting, then orange juice, and finally napkins and silverware.

After I pulled the savory quiche out of the oven and let it sit for a few minutes, I created several slices, garnished a small ramekin of fresh berries in a maple compote topped with a mint leaf. I added this to the plate and was satisfied with my meal and plating. I delicately delivered the plated brunch in front of Kat from across the island. In hopes that I was forgiven for last night with my efforts to feed and entertain her. I grabbed myself a fork and my plate and joined her.

Kat put her phone down and said, "This looks really good. You make the plate so pretty. What is this a glaze on the dish? You know this is not normal behavior, right?" She glanced over at me with a smile and waited for me to answer.

"Yes, the glaze on the plate is a raspberry maple syrup with a touch of spice. You will love it with the quiche. It's a unique blend. Both savory and sweet," I sampled from my own plate. My eyes closed and my head tilted up and back. I breathed in the maple fragrance complemented by the smoked gouda in the quiche as it wafted towards my nose. A delectable smell. Chewing, I looked back over at Kat. She was still smiling and watching me, almost admiring me. I enjoyed my bite. Once I was done with the swallow, I just had to know what was going on with little sis. "All problems can be fixed with a quiche, not you think?"

"Is it that good... that it can fix the past several days?" Kat quietly ate her quiche and did not go into further detail, although I waited for several minutes.

"Tell me, Kat, why is it not normal behavior to decorate a plate with a sauce or berries." I paused and admired my half eaten plaate. "I do believe I've seen it on the cooking shows."

"Yes, on TV. But no one does this in the real world." Kat emphasized 'this' by pointing to her plate with both hands. "People take photos of their restaurant foods and showcase them on Instagram. But people at home don't cook like that. No one cooks like you do," Kat said, taking a big bite.

"After last night's fury," I paused and playfully bumped into her torso with my shoulder. "I'll take that as a compliment."

Kat burst out in a short laugh followed by "Ok Kyra... ok. I'm sorry I sniped at you last night. I was angry that Perdi was in emotional turmoil. I also had been holding on to the news of moving out for some time. I didn't know how to tell you. But I certainly didn't mean to do it as I did last night. I'm sorry."

I was very impressed with Kat. She was developing into an extraordinary young woman. "Thank you for the apology. I'm sorry too, Kat, that I was not more sensitive to Perdi's feelings. I was thinking only of Mom and Dad. It was unkind."

We both sat quietly and ate a few bites of our food. Kat smeared her savoy quiche into the sweetness of her plate and broke the silence. "But Kyra, you also know you do this a lot. We have a disagreement and then try to smooth it over with goofy music and yummy meals. You never take life seriously."

I stopped eating and placed my fork on the plate. I turned to Kat and placed one arm around the back of her chair and leaned towards her. "That is true, Kat. But I don't want you to think life is doom and gloom after an argument or things don't perfectly go as planned. Life is a challenge but having a sense of humor about my mistakes and tribulations is how I cope. I'm not perfect, Kat. I'm broken. But, I love you. We are sisters. Family. We may hurt one another but we are resilient and forgiving."

"Ok, but the goofy music? You could just be more genuine." Kat stabbed me. I thought I was genuine.

"I'm genuinely showing you not to take life too seriously. Life is a gift."

Kat went quiet, again, and enjoyed another bite. I was still looking at her and said out loud what I was wondering all night. "How long have you been thinking about moving out?" I sat back up and began finishing my meal.

Kat let out a deep sigh and swallowed her bite. "Several months, since before graduation. I think it's time. You can't keep caring for me for the rest of your life... you need to get a life." Kat looked over at me as I stopped chewing, wondering what that meant.

I swallowed hard almost choking on my unchewed food in my mouth. "I need to get a life, Kat?" I turned to look at her face to see if she was joking, as I wanted to deny immediately the accusation. Her face was genuinely serious. "What do you mean? I do have a life."

"No, you don't and if you are not even aware of it... that you don't have a life... then this is more dire a situation than I suspected." Kat continued to eat, looking over at me every few seconds to study my face.

"Kat, I think you need to explain a little more. What do you mean?" I asked perplexed.

"KayKay..." Kat paused and tilted her head and gave me her best come on' smirk. "You don't go out. I've never met a man you were dating. You don't have children. You don't travel. You are home, here, all the time. You spend your free time cooking for me or making sure my clothes are laundered and sorted. Look at your life, KayKay. When you are not caring for me, you are volunteering to care for others. You have been caring for someone or some organization your entire life... instead of caring for yourself."

"Kat, I enjoyed taking care of you. I wanted you to be raised in a loving home, the way Mom and Dad wanted."

"Ok, that is done. Check that off your list. Do you know... the moment I went to college you started cooking for all the sick people in the community." Kat responded quickly and as I assumed she was pointing out my accomplishments in life, I realized she thought my accomplishments were out of duty. "Instead of having some type of life for yourself, you immediately started caring for others as a substitute for me not being as needy.

"Well... maybe. Those were our friends and neighbors. We care for those in our community, Kat."

"I get that. But when was the last time you had a date? Did you ever want your own children? My whole life, I've felt like I saddled you here with a life you didn't want. Then I realized that you were not saddled... you were stuck. It's ok for you to go out and meet people and date and have a life. I will be ok." Kat's words lingered in the air and then hit me in the chest like little daggers.

She was right. I'd spent my life nurturing others. Now, with her moving out to embrace her own path, I could finally rediscover my own. But was it that easy? Where does a fifty-year-old just find a life to slide into like a hand into a purchased glove?

Kat, you don't know my past. I lived a full life before you were five. I love cooking, and I dreamed of building something with that passion, but fate dealt me a different hand. Instead, I climbed the corporate ladder to provide for our family—my siblings, you. It stifled my spirit, but I poured my heart into serving others through my cooking whenever I could.

"So, you do have other dreams in life... dreams you are not pursuing because of me."

"You may not believe this Kat, but it was my honor to raise you and love you and help you develop into a spectacular, smart, witty, beautiful woman. I have no regrets about how I've spent my days caring for you, Kenny, and Killian."

"It was your job. You had to do it. You can't possibly tell me that you enjoyed giving up your life to play Mommy and take care of all of us." Kat expressed and definitely popped a blackberry in her mouth.

"It wasn't my job, Kat. You may not know this, but I volunteered to take on you three when Mom and Dad died. Aunt Dottie was your guardian at the time, per the paperwork."

Kat's eyes grew bigger, and her mouth opened slightly. "Really?"

"Yes. She wanted to take you away from Palm Valley because she was married to her fourth or maybe fifth husband and they lived clear across the state. I didn't want the boys uprooted from school so close to graduating. I didn't want you to not know the love of your sister during your childhood. Aunt Dottie and I agreed that I should raise you all and keep you as long as I could... in Palm Valley," I trailed off quietly recollecting living in our parent's home in Palm Valley for her childhood.

"Aunt Dottie was supposed to raise me?" Kat asked with wonder.

"She did raise you, Kat. She divorced that cranky husband and came back to Palm Valley shortly after Mom and Dad died. She has been here by your side through every major event... with me."

"So, it was your choice to lead a meaningless existence raising your little sister?" Kat burst out in laughter and happy tears as she threw her arms around my neck. She hugged me tight as I squeezed her back.

"I have meaning in my life because I raised you, lil' sis," I whispered in her ear.

Boop-Boop The doorbell chimed when the front door opened. Perdi announced her entrance by saying "Are you kidding me... all y'all left the door unlocked for anyone to walk in here and kidnap you all."

"Perdi's here." I said releasing Kat and wiping the tears from my cheek with my napkin.

"We are in the kitchen, Perdi." I bellowed as Kat composed herself.

"Of course you are." Perdi said as she walked into the kitchen.

Kat, hopped off the counter stool and jumped into Perdi's arms giving her a huge hug before she could even put down her purse and portfolio. "I'm so happy you came back this morning. We were so upset you left last night in an emotional state."

"I was scared you were going to fly to Pennsylvania and leave me to do all this research on my own." I stood up and kissed Perdi's cheek on my way to the sink with the dishes.

"Why do you have syrup on your cheek?" Perdi asked me as she wiped the sticky substance off her cheek.

"Oh... hazards of heart to heart talks over berries." I smiled and fetched another plate for Perdi's breakfast.

"I am sorry I left last night. I was so emotional. I'm so sorry we all fought. Can we not do that again?" Perdi asked as she hoisted herself on the counter stool. Kat poured Perdi a cup of coffee and added just a touch of honey.

"You know me so well already. Thank you," Perdi acknowledged with a head nod to Kat.

"It's difficult not having answers to such important questions in life," Kat said as she provided Perdi with a fork, knife, and napkin.

I placed Perdi's quiche in front of her. "We were all upset and emotional last night. But we can't ever have it come between us. We need to support one another."

Kat and I stood next to one another at the kitchen island across from Perdi sitting and eating her breakfast. I put my head on Kat's shoulder and looked up at her face, then planted a big kiss on her cheek and pulled away before she could complain. She stuck her tongue out at me in rebellion. Ahh... there was the Kat I knew and loved. Perdi smiled at us and sipped her coffee.

Perdi talked about the rest of her evening. I drifted off to my evening and my visit from Uncle Conor and Aunt Dottie. I wanted to tell Perdi and Kat all about my evening last night with Uncle Conor. But I was afraid for their safety. Not from Connie, of course, because I believed he was our protector. Even after meeting him only for a moment, I sensed that Connie was a dangerous man to anyone that messed with his family. But, if someone was after him, the fewer people that knew about Uncle Connie, the better.

I smiled watching Perdi and Kat interact. I wondered how I would tell them what I knew about Robert Flannery and his mother, Aggie Flannery. The past week was an emotional roller coaster for all of us. Despite the chaos of our lives this past week, I felt an odd assurance inside me. I felt, that nothing could break this bond between me and my sisters.

"Are we all ready to go to the records basement again?" I said as Perdi finished her last bite and sipped the last of her coffee. I cleared the dishes, leaving them in the sink.

"Yes, and then we go spring Killian from jail," Perdi added.

"Finally!" Kat raised her arms in victory. "Hooray!"

My phone rang. Perdi and Kat looked at me. "No, I'm not answering it. We need to get to Doris and then the station to get Killian. I'm not getting diverted by anything else today." I said pouring fresh squeezed orange juice for the three of us.

"It could be important or about Killian, Kyra. Please answer it." Perdi made a good point. It could be about Killian.

I rifled through my purse and pulled out the phone as it stopped ringing. I looked at the number. I didn't recognize it.

"Who was it, Kyra?" Kat asked as she downed her orange juice in one gulp.

"I don't know. Let's hope they left a voicemail message." I pressed my voicemail button and put the phone on speaker. As I sipped my orange juice and listened to my message, I choked when I heard Krystal Kelly's voice and name.

'Hello Kyra. This is Krystal Kelly. I know you are probably surprised to hear from me. But... I had a message today from someone who read the article about your family. I think we should talk. This may be a lead for you and your family. He said he knew your mother and about her situation. Please call me.'

My gaze darted from erdi to Kat and back down to the phone on the island in disbelief. "A lead... from Krystal Kelly. I don't believe it." Krystal Kelly had no reason to help me or my family.

"She is just trying to help, Kyra. Don't go savage on her." Kat said with positivity that I was clearly lacking.

"No doubt she is interested in a sequel to the first article." I listened to the message again. 'He knew Mom and about her situation.' "Well, I am curious. Let's call her back."

Chapter
THIRTYONE

W e set out in the Moke to meet Krystal Kelly at Panera. In a slight northern accent, she told us a man contacted her via phone after reading the article. She did not call him back. She apparently gets calls all the time from both fans and enemies of her articles in The Ponte Vedra Parrot. I could relate to those enemies. Krystal appeared kind and genuine. She was not a friend, although she was the same age as Kat and they were classmates at school. I was not thrilled with her exposing my family. She had made me her enemy through her actions. What did Uncle Connie say about our enemies? That I should leave the door open. He didn't say it would be easy, but here I was in the presence of the enemy, with an open door.

Krystal Kelly was not from here originally. She moved to Peaceful River Valley many years ago from the Northeast. She spoke like an Italian, her arms flailing like she was conducting an orchestra of gossip. As she dished out the scoop on this secret reader, I couldn't help but wonder if she'd ever accidentally knocked someone out with those wild gestures. "So, you see he called me and left a message. He said he was the one that left the note on the article. I did not know what a note meant. Then I realized he he meant a comment. There is a place for comments on each article. I checked." Krystal talked so fast it was hard to keep up with her. I sometimes listen to podcasts at 1.5x speed to get through it quicker. This was like listening to a fast speaker at 2X the speed.

I grabbed for her hand. "Krystal this is crazy. What did the comment say."

Picking up her hand like I had imprisoned her she motioned to her heart with both hands, dramatically. "Yes, I was just getting to that. His comment was something like I knew Katherine and I know what happened to Perdita." Once I saw the comment, I listened to the voice mail again. I called him immediately. He confirmed a few details that made me feel like he is speaking the truth."

"Details, what details Krystal?" I couldn't imagine her knowing anything and not publishing it.

"He knew Perdita's adoptive parents' name." Krystal said motioning to Perdi.

"Perdi, do you think you know this man?" Kat asked quietly.

"I don't know. Who is he, Krystal?" Perdi withdrew a pen and paper from her purse and jotted down a few notes.

"Bennie." Krystal said quickly looking for his name in her tablet.

"Bennie what?" I asked.

"No, his handle was Ben Knee."

"That's funny." Kat blurted out, while Perdi and I looked at each other and shrugged.

"B-E-N K-N-E-E." Krystal Kelly spelled it out and Perdi snickered.

"Ok, thank you Ms. Kelly." I said "Thank you."

"Boomers." Kat whispered under her breath and rolled her eyes.

Perdi's phone started ringing. She picked it up and walked away from the table leaving her pad and pen.

"I agree, Krystal. It does sound like he knew something if he was able to give you Perdi's parents' names. Thank you, Krystal. I appreciate you providing this information."

"Yes, well it seemed important. I do wish to go with you to discuss this with him. I would like to do a second story on this as soon as we can. There has been some interest in what happened. We are getting a lot of comments on online."

Oh my gosh. People were talking online about my family. She wanted to come with me while I tried to untangle the biggest secret my parents kept from me. Is she out of her mind? "Oh that is very sweet of you Krystal. I'm going to decline at this time. I think this is a family matter."

"Will you call me if you want to do an exclusive sit-down interview? I'd love to get you all on camera and talk about your story. It would be very tasteful."

Yes, a very tasteful meeting it would be. I imagined thwacking Krystal Kelly over the head with a menu for infiltrating my personal life. She had no idea how erratic a woman could be when in the middle of her own personal mid-life crisis. "Thank you, Krystal. I'll approach the subject with my family should we want to be violated again and smeared all over the front page of The Ponte Vedra Parrot."

"That doesn't sound hopeful. Goodbye King family. I do wish you luck," Krystal said as Kat and I slid out of the booth.

Oh gosh now I was feeling remorse. I went too far, again. What was it about poor little Krystal Kelly that made me so heated, as I began to encounter another hot flash. "You have been very kind Miss Kelly. Thank you for the information. I am a personal person, but I will consider your interview request. I have your number. I will call you with a response soon." I went outside to wait as Perdi hung up her phone call. Kat was inside having words with Krystal again. Probably arranging a date time for that King family interview to go into The Parrot and on Kat's podcast.

I was looking for the comments section on The Parrot website under Krystal's article. "Perdi, here is the comment from Ben." I handed Perdi my phone to read the comment for herself.

"This is the guy that says he knows Mother and about her situation?" She paused as she read the comment. "We need to speak with him immediately."

"I know, here is his contact information." I gave Perdi her note pad back, opened to Ben's contact information. "I'm very eager to hear what he has to say. This sounds like a real lead, Perdi. We may be able to find more pieces of this puzzle.

Perdi heaved a sigh as if she was holding it the entire time I spoke. "What are you going to do? I need to be with you when you confront him."

"Yes, I agree. We should call him and see if he can meet us all at the house." I looked at the time. I was eager to get to the Sherriff's office.

"What about Aunt Dottie?" Perdi motioned to Kat to come here.

"I was just thinking the same thing. She has more history than anyone and might be able to fill in gaps for us. I will reach out to her."

"Now for the really good news." Perdi said and had my attention. "I just spoke with my attorney, and he picked up Killian this morning." Perdi looked back towards Kat and Krystal still talking inside and then down at her watch.

"Oh. That's wonderful. Is he ok? I thought it was going to be a fight... wait... why did they just let him go?" I asked, then realizing I already had the answer to that question from Uncle Connie's visit last night.

"They got the report back... he had a heart attack. Plus, with no scar on the man in the video, they could no longer hold Killian for questioning."

"Oh my gosh that is such a relief. Great news, Perdi. Thank you so much!" I felt a tremendous amount of relief, since I still had not devised a a story for how I knew it was Uncle Conor on my video doorbell. Truth be told, I did not want to tell the police about my Uncle Conor. I've always said family first and protecting Uncle Connie definitely fell under that umbrella. Aunt Dottie and Uncle Conor trusted me with this secret. I had to keep it... for now.

Kat joined us on the patio of the Panera. "I've already tried to reach out to Ben Knee on Facebook. But if he is as old as dirt, he probably doesn't know how to use Facebook Messenger."

Perdi and I both laughed. "I'm sure he will reach back out to you, Kat. He's probably playing Pickleball." Perdi said with great confidence.

"Killian is out of custody." I said to Kat.

"Amazing. We didn't need to go down there and invade the police station after all. They are so lucky."

We all laughed and climbed in the Moke. I read the returned text from Aunt Dottie and she was intrigued at the thought of someone having more information. She was canceling her morning Thai Chi lesson. I shook my head as I threw the Moke in drive and took off out of the golf cart parking spot. "Perdi, can you go pick up Aunt Dottie?"

"Why what's up?" Kat asked.

"We are going to call Ben and I want Aunt Dottie to be there." I connected eyes with Kat in the rear-view mirror as I pulled straight across Crosswater Parkway at the light and turned left on to the golf cart path.

Chapter THIRTYTWO

The four of us gathered around the dining room table to place the call to Ben. Krystal Kelly provided the information but I was not certain he was expecting our call. The phone rang only two times when a man picked up. He had a soft low voice. "Hello?" he said.

"Is this Ben?" I asked in a calm soft tone, assuring I was a friend.

"Yes, yes dear. I'm Ben. How can I help you?"

"Ben, you don't know me. My name is Kyra King. You are on speaker phone and I'm here with my sister, Perdita Ryan. She was recently featured in an article in The Ponte Vedra Parrot."

"Yes, yes, oh my gosh yes. Young Lady, I've been waiting over fifty years for someone to contact me about this situation. I need to tell you about your family."

We were all quiet around the table as Ben relayed his tale, as if it was only yesterday. "I grew up in Jacksonville Beach. My dear Mum, Rachel, worked at Ponte Vedra Inn and Club. She was a staff member there for almost 50 years. She was adored by the wonderful long time clients she served at the club. The same clients wintered there each year. Every winter they traveled a long way to stay in the beautiful Ponte Vedra Inn and Club. She waited on them as their valet. Mum was very popular because she had many talents. She was of course good with the iron, but she was an exemplary seamstress. She was wonderful. She loved it. She hemmed and repaired clothes for all the visitors there at the club. This was of course, back in the day when the clients tipped the staff at the end of the season, before they returned up north."

Kat looked confused already and we had only begun. Aunt Dottie added some context for Kat. "See, Kat, the Ponte Vedra Inn and Club hired people full-time to stay a lifetime. It was one of the most prestigious places to work in all northeast Florida. The selected few were guaranteed a good salary and tips if their service was impeccable. This is back in the day when the Club hosted families for the entire winter and a valet could be working for one or two families the entire winter."

Ben confirmed, "Oh yes, the Ponte Vedra Inn and Club had training for all the employees on how to be the best at each job. How to attend to the guest. Mum, well all the girls for that matter, had to attend etiquette classes. They were very proud to work at such a prestigious association. Mum started there in the late 1940's at the age of 16. You have no idea the stories she told. Mum's family lived in Palm Valley in the 1940's. That was during World War II. Ponte Vedra did see the war up close. Now do you girls know that we used to see the German U-boats patrol off our shores in Ponte Vedra Beach. One of those damn U-Boats even sank the *SS Gulfamerica*. It was an innocent cargo ship, not even a military vessel. It was transporting oil on its maiden voyage. Only 29 of those men were pulled from the drink. But, the most exciting story of World War II was the spies that came ashore. German spies were dropped off and swam ashore at Ponte Vedra Beach there near Ponte Vedra Inn and Club. Those men buried explosives. But they got caught. They were hung as spies, before they could use those explosives for anything nefarious. Yes, girls, this area has an exciting past."

"Ben, sir, did your Mom know our Mom, Katherine King? Well, she would have been Katherine Edwards back then." I said as the Geek Nanny in me guided the conversation back to topic.

"Right, right... now to your Mom, dear. Your Mom was a young girl traveling with her family from way up north in Pennsylvania to Ponte Vedra Inn and Club each year. Mum was their maid first and then later their Valet. So, you see, Mum knew Katherine from a young age."

"Wow that is amazing, Ben. You know all this from your Mum?" Aunt Dottie interrupted to ask.

"Yes, Mum relayed the story to me. Mum found Katherine in the room one afternoon while her Mother was out at an activity. Katherine was not to be in the room at that time, as it was when the staff entered and prepared the clothes for evening supper or events. Mum walked in to find Katherine crying. Katherine was in love with a man. He was leaving for Vietnam. Mum comforted young Katherine. Three months later Mum found Katherine crying in the room again. This time it was for the baby she carried. She did not know how to tell her parents about the baby." Ben's voice seemed to get louder for a moment as he announced "She could not get married because her man was off in Vietnam at war by the time she learned of the pregnancy."

"It was not a favorable thing for a woman to be having a baby before marriage." Aunt Dottie said to Kat.

"Got it." Kat winked.

"Well... the way Mum told the story was that Katherine told her mother she was expecting. There was an argument. Her mother asked Mum for a nurse. Mum, of course, introduced her to a nurse. That nurse lived next door to us in Jax Beach. She was a duplicitous woman with multiple personalities. She befriended Katherine and her mother. Katherine did not return to Pennsylvania with her mother at the end of the season that year. She went to Jax Beach with the nurse. She lived with the nurse for many months and her belly grew."

"Wait... so you and your mum lived next door to a nurse who allowed our mom to stay with her during her pregnancy?" I asked for confirmation.

"Yes, that's right. I was 13 at the time when I met your mom, dear, sweet Katherine."

"You met our Mom?" Kat confirmed.

"Yes, Gosh when I met Katherine, I was smitten." Ben laughed as if he were recalling a sweet memory. "She was a beauty. A big pregnant belly didn't matter, she was a gorgeous girl with the prettiest smile and the softest eyes. She was very smart and read books all the time. She used to wear a handkerchief on her head. She would take the square bandanna and fold it in diagonally into a triangle. She would wrap it tight on her forehead and tie it in the back. Her strawberry blonde hair was naturally curly, and her curls bounced out from the back of the bandanna. Her confidence spoke volumes for her spirit. But the best thing about Katherine was that she was from a super wealthy family, but you would never know it. She was so sweet and down to earth. From March to May, we walked barefoot every day from the house where we lived to the Jax Beach boardwalk. Katherine took me to the A&A Shopping Center every day to buy me a candy or a comic or a taffy or a bubble gum. Then near Easter, she showed me something I never saw before... Peeps. I'd never had them before. I turned to Katherine and smiled, with my hands full of yellow sugar and marshmallow all over my face."

"Hearing about our Mom in your youth..." I paused and reached over to hold Kat's hand as I held back tears. "You have no idea how wonderful it is to hear a story about her in her teenage years. She had not shared this time of her life with us, previously. Thank you, Ben, for bringing her teenage years to life for us."

"What about the nurse. Do you know her name?" Perdi asked and then turned to me and mouthed the words Aggie Flannery.

Aunt Dottie nodded her head and asked, "Yes, can you tell us anything more about the nurse."

"Oh that nurse was a wicked woman. She seemed to only be kind to my Mum and people who could pay her money. The Flannery's, Mrs. Flannery and her son Robbie."

"That confirms it." Perdi said.

Ben continued, "You should know... that Katherine wrote her baby's father every day even though she stopped hearing from him months before then. We walked every day to put a letter in the post box at the Jax Beach post office. She was terrified that her parents would make her give the baby up. Katherine said that her mom was a lovely woman, and she loved her dearly. She told me once that her mom's only flaw was not loving Katherine more than her reputation. She forgave her mother. I never understood how she could, but she did. Katherine was intending to take the baby to Palm Valley. She was planning on living with Kenny's parents until he came home from the war. She was never going back to Pennsylvania. She sat with mum and me the Saturday before the birth asking us for a ride to Palm Valley after the baby was born. Mum said yes, of course. Mum was thrilled that Kenny's parents would take Katherine and the baby into their home until Kenny returned home."

Aunt Dottie shook her head no. "I don't think my parents knew anything about the baby. If they did, they didn't say anything."

"But that's not what happened. When the time came, Katherine didn't go to the hospital. The nurse made her have the baby in the house. The nurse said the baby didn't make it. Still birth. But Katherine swore she heard the baby cry at the birth and then down the hall as Mrs. Flannery took the baby away. Katherine told me she heard nothing for a long time as she laid there waiting for the nurse to return with the baby. Then a screen door slammed. The nurse came back into the room to deliver the news to Katherine and care for her. Katherine cried for more than a month. She didn't go for walks anymore. She just sat all day on the porch crying or looking off into the vast beyond."

Aunt Dottie was crying. I exited the dining room and returned with a box of tissues.

Ben coughed and his voice cracked as he continued. "Then one day right before July 4th, Ken showed up and took her away. He had an old Ford pickup truck. I watched as he put her in the passenger seat and closed the door. The window was down. I ran to the side of the truck. She stretched out her arm and I held her hand. The desperation in her eyes will haunt me until I die. I've never seen a woman in so much pain ever again in all my days. I ran with the truck for a few seconds and said goodbye. I never saw Miss Katherine again. But I never forgot her. This is what I know about your mom Perdita. Now here is what I know about you."

We all looked up from our tissues and stared at the phone wondering what in the world Ben was going to say about Perdi.

"You were not the only lost baby. Katherine was not the first woman to stay with Nurse Flannery." Ben paused, "She was not the first and she certainly was not the last."

Chapter
THIRTY THREE

Every woman at the table was weeping, stunned, and unable to even whisper a word. Tears were being wiped away by tissues. Sniffles were turning into long sobs. There was truly no greater loss in life than the loss of a child. All our lives were changed by Ben's story. But more importantly, all of us ached for the pain Katherine must have felt in those lonely days of May and June 1967. How did she ever recover? Did she ever recover, or was she just forever altered? Katherine was left forever to roam the earth with a hollow compartment of her soul.

I pulled every bit of strength I could muster to compose myself. The lump in my throat prevented me from talking. I hesitated by clearing my throat. "Thank you, Ben for recounting that beautiful and emotional history of our mother as a teenage girl. We were not aware of this time in her life. I do have a couple of questions if you can converse with us just a few more moments?"

"Yes, of course. Take your time. This must be painful for you." Ben said softly.

"The name of the nurse. Was her first name Agnes?" I asked, feeling the lump in my throat return.

"Aggie Flannery, yes. She lived next to us all our lives. I'll never forget that woman. For whatever reason she was lovely to my mum. But she seemed wicked to all others she encountered including me."

"Do you know if she had any family at all?" Perdita said in a whisper.

"I knew Robbie but if there were others, I did not know them." Ben said confidently.

"You said there were others. Are you in contact with other families about Aggie Flannery?" I pushed.

"No, Ma'am. I'm not in contact with the others. But I know there were many girls that stayed with Aggie Flannery after that day. It almost seemed like 1 or even 2 per year for years. At least, for as long as I lived there with mum."

"Ben, thank you for your time and for this little piece of history. It is a big puzzle piece that we were missing. Thank you so much. Would it be too much to ask... can we call you again Ben, if we have any specific questions for you or if new information comes to light?" I asked eagerly.

"Of course. It was real nice talking to you girls. Perdita, you are as beautiful as your mother. When I saw your photo on the front page of The Parrot, it took me back in time. I recalled clearly the season I spent with Katherine. She left a special mark on me, that girl. Looking at you... welp... her memory just came flooding back into my heart. I wish you well ladies." Ben hung up.

Perdita exhaled a heavy, trembling breath, as though she had been carrying a century's worth of grief in her lungs. She began to sob, her head nestled into the palms of her hands. She was crumpled over the table. Aunt Dottie soothing her arm and shoulder from the seat over. It was a short cry but a powerful burst of emotion. She slumped onto the table. Her head on top of her folded arms. I stood up and fetched a second box of tissues from the kitchen pantry. When I placed them in front of Perdi and pulled a few out placing them in her hand, she grabbed my hand and squeezed tight as she looked up at me with those weepy eyes. Mom's eyes. I burst into tears. Perdi stood up and hugged me and we both cried. It was not long before both Aunt Dottie and Kat were glued to us... hugging us. I reached for Aunt Dottie's shoulder. I removed one arm from Perdi and reached around Kat and drew her into us.

"I'm so glad you are here now." Kat said quietly through her tears.

Chapter
THIRTYFOUR

I woke with swollen eyes, exhausted from the stress of the conversations yesterday and all the tears we shared as a family. I called Perdi from the bed. She, too, was weak from yesterday's revealing tale of how she came into this world. Unlike me, she was already showered. She alerted me that I needed to shake a tail feather. She was looking forward to another fancy breakfast. I suddenly felt like a slacker. I hung up and pulled myself together. Even after a hot shower my eyes were still red and swollen. The Irish style drinking was rare, but celebrating Killian's release and sharing Perdi's story to Ken and Killian... well... it was a once in a lifetime family gathering like no other. I will never have whiskey after family drama again. It was true... man, invented whiskey to avoid the Irish from taking over the world.

While I was waiting for Perdita to arrive in the kitchen, I whipped up an egg and sausage casserole with roasted left over potatoes and exotic cheddar cheese. Exotic, in that it was from Wisconsin. I slid it into the oven, hit the timer and realized I had enough time to organize the letters from 1966 between Mom to Dad and from Dad to Mom. I organized them by postdate on the dining room table. Perdita and I agreed last night that she should read the letters exchanged between Mom and Dad while he was away in Vietnam.

As I was organizing the letters, Perdi was upon me. "Oh my gosh you are stealthy. You look fabulous. How did you manage that given the number of drinks last night?"

"Yes, good morning... I need coffee, immediately." Perdi sat at the dining room facing the kitchen looking to see if the coffee pot would magically sail through the air towards her outstretched hand.

"I'll get it. You sit and look through this box. It has the envelope from The Ponte Vedra Beach Inn and Club along with the stationery with the names of potential babies that were taken from their mother's arms at birth. I want you to look through it all. You may see something that I didn't. Or maybe, just maybe we will notice something given we have a new perspective today." I made my way to the kitchen and poured the coffee, black, and in the largest coffee mugs I owned.

"It smells good in here. Are you cooking sausage?" Perdi asked as she removed the top of the box and peered inside.

"Yes, I made a breakfast casserole. It will help. It's not calorie free." I said, placing Perdi's cup of coffee on a coaster on the dining room table. I sipped my coffee expecting relief. The bitter non-alcoholic beverage hit my throat, and I swallowed hard as my face contorted.

"You look like you just swallowed a porcupine. What is wrong with you?" Perdi laughed and filled her coffee with honey.

"I'm not sure. I don't recall my mouth being so full of cotton balls since college." I said taking several more sips trying to quench my dehydrated thirst. Secretly knowing, only water would solve my problem. I headed back to the kitchen, checked the timer on the oven, and poured myself a glass of water. I drank it back one sip at a time. As if I was checking to see if I would dry heave. Slowly, I started to feel better. I resumed the coffee and headed back to the dining room where Perdi was making her way through the papers, notes, envelopes, and mementos.

We each read the letters from Mom to Dad starting in 1966. We found a reference to AF, which we could only assume referred to Aggie Flannery. Dad replied only twice with letters to Mom, while Mom was staying with Aggie Flannery. The rest of the letters were from Dad but at different times throughout his service in 1968 and 1969. The first letter from Dad was how much he missed Katherine. Dad mentioned, briefly, of being stationed with his brother, Conor. He also talked for almost a page about the heat, and the number of illicit drugs being passed around the soldiers. Dad's second letter was after Perdi was born. He wrote Mom that his tour was over, and he was returning to Palm Valley. He would come pick her up as soon as he got back to Palm Valley.

Something didn't seem right. Why wasn't Katherine picked up Grandma Edwards. "Perdi. Do you think that Grandma Edwards paid Aggie Flannery to take the baby away from Mom? Do you think Grandma could have been so evil? So afraid of her reputation being disparaged that she would feign the baby's death?

"Did you know Grandma Edwards?" Perdi inquired.

"No, not really. Just the stories mom would share." I sipped more coffee and selected my next letter.

"Speculation. We need the truth or direct knowledge." Perdi said sounding like a lawyer.

Looking across several letters with the same month's post mark, I knew Perdi was right. We could not assume. "What do we know? We know Mom was told you died. We know Mom was going to keep you and take you to Palm Valley. We know you were provided with a birth certificate by Aggie Flannery with her name on it. But when... when did your parents get your birth certificate? When did they get you? Did your parents ever tell you about the day they brought you home?"

Perdi looked up from her letter. "Not an in-depth story, no. I just recall my Mom saying that it was the happiest day of her life."

"Do you have any letters or memorabilia from momma Susie? Maybe if you looked over photos or documents, you might find something that would fill a gap." I said hopeful.

"I can certainly look. I have all their personal files from both the PA home, and the original beach house. I kept everything in the beach house, after I renovated it." Perdi said with hesitation. "I do have my personal items too..."

"Hmm... a dubious reply. What are you thinking?" I asked, staring at her impatiently waiting.

"Well, I am thinking about Dad's reaction to Mom's death. I was obviously sad and despondent during that time. But Dad was angry." Perdi said looking past me while searching her memory.

I waited for her to follow up that thought with something that would make more sense. I was puzzled but curious. I asked "People grieve differently, Perdi. I'm sure it was not easy for either of you. Why do you think him being angry was out of the ordinary?"

"I don't know. I just recall crying in my room. Dad was on the phone with someone and screaming at them. I stopped crying when I heard him yelling. I went to my bedroom door. The house got quiet. The yelling went to a whisper as if he was concealing something."

"You remember that?" I asked almost fascinated that she could recall that energy and emotion from forty-four years ago.

"Well... I remembered it because I wrote it down in my diary at the time. I read and re-read those pages for weeks after Mom died. I have all my diaries, somewhere." Perdi said as she jotted down a note in her note pad. "I'll need to read those entries as well. I didn't know what they meant at the time. The words that Dad said. I wrote them down. I don't remember them now, but it seems like it was important for me to remember." Her voice trailed off as if she was straining her brain for the memory. I, of course, was familiar with that exact same strain of the brain.

Perdi touched the peach paper with the names on it. "Was there anything to indicate how Katherine got this information on the stationary?" Perdi said looking for anything that would help her understand why she was stolen from her family.

"Nope. No notes and no unfamiliar photos. No photos with a witch in a nurse's uniform, circled in a red lipstick with the word thief on it." I wished the mystery could be solved here among the peach stationery.

"Maybe we will never know what all this means. What is our objective here, actually?" Perdi asked in a deeply sincere and exhausted tone of frustration.

"I know this is frustrating for you. It is absolutely vexing. We lost you for fifty plus years. I desperately want the woman to pay for taking you away from us. I know it is here, and we just need to put the pieces together." I was desperate for her to be inspired by my desire to know and understand what happened all those years ago.

"We do know what happened to Katherine. We know who did it... Aggie Flannery. Even though, I think she died without ever paying for her crimes. I think we are on a fool's errand. We will never be able to punish her. Aggie Flannery, nefariously provided our mother, Katherine, with a home while she was pregnant with me. She, somehow, negotiated with my adoptive parents to purchase me along with a false birth certificate. She told Katherine I was dead. She provided a birth and death certificate for me. Katherine was devastated but went on to live a life with my father and have a family. You all are my family. You connect me to them. They connect me to you. Maybe that is all we are to know."

"So, you want Aggie Flannery to pay for what she did to Mom? Is that why you are searching for answers?" I asked in a harrowing whisper, knowing I could assure her that Aggie Flannery did pay for her sins in pain and death. I could even tell her the murderer and the accomplice. But I could not bring myself to whisper my Mother's name in that retaliation gang.

Perdi looked at me and took off her reading glasses. "No. I'm not seeking vengeance. I'm seeking the truth."

"My grandmother Edwards, Katherine's mother, stayed at The Ponte Vedra Inn & Club. Your adoptive parents, David and Susie Boyle, also stayed at the Ponte Vedra Inn & Club. Aggie Flannery met Grandma Edwards via Ben's mum Rachael at the Ponte Vedra Inn & Club. These are all connection points to the Inn & Club."

"True. I'll have the PI cross check with the guests at the Ponte Vedra Inn & Club. I'm not sure he will be able to get those records, but he sometimes works miracles." Perdi texted the PI.

"I wonder who Aggie Flannery had helping her at the hospital. She had to have help with the birth certificates, right. Don't you think?" I took a sip of my coffee and watched Perdi's face.

"I agree there had to be an accomplice at the hospital records department. Or... perhaps Aggie Flannery had access to the records room. We need to go back to Doris and ask." Perdi said with interest.

"Yes, I agree. But I think we should bring her into the fold on the mystery. Maybe she will be more willing to help us if she knows why we are searching for answers." I stood up with excitement. I bounced over to the kitchen and took the casserole out of the oven. Mmmm... it smelled divine, looked even better and I really needed food to soak up the whisky from last night.

Chapter
THIRTYFIVE

D oris was all smiles when she saw Perdi and I walk through the door of the records room in the basement of the hospital. I imagined Doris did not get many visitors. Doris was, of course, sporting her signature 4 pairs of eyeglasses. One pair on her head, one pair on her eyes, one pair hanging from her neck on a cord and one pair in her right hand. "Well, hey all ya'll. Put on your sittin' britches right 'der." Doris pointed to the table and disappeared through the door in the wall behind the counter. She reappeared through the door we just entered and said "Ladies, when y'all called and told me that story. Well, gesh... I thought you were tellin' tales out of school. But then I started doing what I do. Y'all know what I do, right?"

Perdi and I stared at Doris smiling and nodding our heads. I personally was wondering what did she do? "I dig, ladies. I dig up all kinds of dirt that nobody wants to see the light of day. I dig that's what I do. Look what Doris found." She opened a folder in front of us with a stack of papers. The top paper was the list of names we found on the stationery. Doris had arrows and checked boxes all over the page.

"Here, all these names you gave me." Doris pointed to the piece of stationery with Perdi's name. "These names were like Perdita. Perdita you poor child." Doris turned to Perdi with a genuine mother's sympathy. She reached out to hold Perdi's hand and squeezed. Then she pointed to the top name with her eyeglasses. "Perdita's name was King on both the birth and death certificate. That did not conform to the pattern. All the names had the mother's name. 'Cept you, Perdi. You had your daddy's name." Now she was talking in puzzles.

"I'm not following, Doris. Why does that matter?" I said, completely lost.

"Well, your momma and daddy were already married. Or... Katherine told a lie about her last name."

"Why would momma lie?" I questioned.

"They couldn't have been married yet, right? Momma Katherine would have been only 16 or 17, just a child at that time." I said.

"Well, back then a girl of 16 could marry with parental consent. Didn't need parental consent after 18." Doris educated us.

"Mom was an older looking girl. Maybe she lied about her age to marry Dad before he went off to Vietnam? Because we sure know she didn't have permission from Grandma Ellen Edwards."

Doris moved a folder closer to us. "These names all have three records. One birth record, one death record using the last name of the mother. Then a second birth record, using an alternate name. Each matched the couple's name you gave me for the child. Do you know what this means ladies?" Doris said as if she solved the mystery.

"That there were more babies like me, taken from their mother on the day of the birth?" Perdi solemnly spoke the words and swallowed hard.

"That's exactly right." Doris stated with sadness.

"That is so sad. So sad, Doris." Perdi's eyes were squeezed closed, and tears were cascading down her cheeks. I reached over to console her. She recoiled and searched her hobo bag. When her hand resurfaced it contained a large wad of tissues. I rubbed her back softly, and we sat silently as she regained her composure.

I was pulling a few of the certificates off the top of the pile. Each was paper clipped together with a name. *Aggie Flannery.* "Doris, all these paper clipped notes have Aggie Flannery's name on them. Are you telling us that Aggie Flannery was the nurse overseeing the birth of each of these children?"

"Oh yes, ladies. You said it. Each one of those girls. Each of those births was to underage girls. Each baby born and died the same day. Each one had a second birth certificate. Each one was resurrected with a fake birth certificate into the name of the adoptive parents, yes. Each one of them overseen by Aggie Flannery. But that is not all."

"Not all? You found more children like this with this same scenario?" I said quickly.

"No dear. I have Aggie Flannery's autopsy notes. She was murdered. Someone killed her. Unsolved. Look here." Doris pulled a second folder from the back of the pile. She opened it while Perdi and I waited patiently staring at one another.

"The autopsy notes, right here, says likely cause of death murder. Asphyxia. But look, there is more here on the toxicology report. It says arsenic was found. But what I don't understand is how the coroner could decide she was taken out with a choke and not the actual arsenic poisoning? That is a mystery right there. How'd he know?"

Perdi was perusing the documentation. "Wait, Doris. This autopsy report was signed before the toxicology report came back. The toxicology report came back almost 45 days after this autopsy report was signed. That means the doctor signed the report and maybe just filed the toxicology report when it was returned to him. Maybe he never looked at it."

"Arsenic in her system... so, she was poisoned and suffocated? She was killed twice?" I ran through the recount of the events from Connie. Certainly, seemed that this paper work confirmed what he told me.

"Or two people were trying to kill her and only one succeeded," Doris concluded.

"Perdi... you were not alone. There are more people out there that don't know a crime was committed to them on the day of their birth. You were not the only baby that this happened to at the hands of Aggie Flannery. If there are others out there, we can find them. We can piece together what they know."

"The woman who did this to me was murdered. Should we go to the police and tell them what we know? This is a fresh development into finding out the truth." Perdi looked at me sincerely waiting for an answer.

"Do you think they would re-open her case?" I questioned hesitantly. I truly did not want that to happen. I was so happy to have found Perdi, my older sister. But now she wanted to go to the police and provide crucial information that would find the killer or the poisoner of Aggie Flannery. Re-opening an investigation into a woman who was poisoned by our mother and smothered by our uncle. No, this was not a direction I wanted to pursue.

"Ladies, you can keep these copies. Don't you go tellin' anyone where you got 'em from. But you keep it now." Doris tapped the file folder with her glasses, got up from the table and walked back out the door.

"It's new information, they may re-open it yes." Perdi continued to look through the paperwork Doris left on the table.

"Isn't it enough to know? Do we need to pursue it further?" I said quickly as Perdi's eyes glanced up at me over her reading glasses. "Perdi, you were lost to us and now we know that Aggie Flannery was responsible. But through the grace of God we found you. That is all the answer I need. I'm so thankful for Kat and Mac finding one another. Leading us to you."

Perdi looked perplexed. I, myself, was confused at my behavior and words. I didn't want to lie to Perdi. I wanted to tell her all I knew about Connie, but the fewer people who knew, the better off we all were. I held my best poker face and felt my stomach sour.

I stared at Perdi, my heart pounding, waiting for her to realize this was a good development but we didn't need to take it to the police.

"But now we know there were other children taken, we must go to the police and tell them what we know. These are only the ones we know of, Kyra. What if there are more? Don't we want these people to know what happened? Especially, the mothers who think their babies died and were secretly stolen away."

Oh my gosh, Perdi was right. Katherine was a victim and maybe found out later in life that her child was taken from her. It lead her to poison Aggie Flannery, the murder of Aggie Flannery, and possibly the tragic loss of her own life and that of her husband's life. I couldn't let this investigation go any further. It would jeopardize my entire family learning the painful, ugly truth.

Doris reappeared from a hole in the wall behind the counter of plexi-glass. She was leaning on the counter looking at us. "Ladies, I'm retiring soon. The end of my days here are near. I knew many people both here and at Riverside. Not many of 'em still this side of the dirt, if y'all know what I mean. If you want to know somethin' about the past. Well... you can talk to this guy. You tell him, Doris sent ya. He'll talk to ya on a lucid day." Doris wrote a name and address on a piece of notepaper and pushed it away from her. She smacked it twice with her hand, and disappeared into stacks of records.

"Thank you Doris." I shouted as I got up to grab the piece of paper. I put the paper in the file with the medical examiner's information. I picked the folders up and placed them in my bag.

Perdi got up from the table. She walked out the records room door. I followed. As I walked beside her, I said "At the risk of sounding over-whelmingly optimistic about this situation, I'm disappointed we are not able to answer the question of how this happened. We are left to just assume. But Perdi, we found one another. This is the most important event of my life. I'm so thankful we found you. I'm grateful for the answers we have received, and I do feel closure. I believe that wicked Aggie Flannery got what she deserved. It's done. We don't need to look into it any further."

"Maybe you are right… it is all far too upsetting." Perdi said as she continued to use tissue after tissue from the little travel package I provided her. She stopped, took a heavy sigh, and softened the stray hairs on her head with her hands. Turned, looked at me and said "Kyra, I am beyond thankful for finding you all. You have been a gift to me since this entire soap opera started. I have no words to describe how happy I am that you are my sister and my friend." She grabbed me and pulled me into her for a hug.

We were sisters. What was important was that we had each other.

I hugged Perdi tight. We swayed back and forth holding one another and saying I love you. Then, I whispered in her ear "You're not getting snots on my new shirt are ya, Sis?" as we continued to hug and laugh.

"Maybe" Perdi snorted as she laughed and cried happy tears.

Chapter *THIRTYSIX*

I prepared for my Sunday Supper by crushing fresh boiled tomatoes for homemade Italian gravy. I moved to sauteing hot Italian sausage and ground sirloin for the lasagna. The garlic was roasting in the oven. Once the beef and sausage were done and combined, I drained it and set it to the side in a bowl with a kitchen towel over it. After church, I would simply boil the water for the noodles and pull everything together and bake the lasagna to finish at 3:00 pm precisely. Cooking was a fabulous way to start my day considering the crazed week behind me.

Kat and I scooped up Aunt Dottie from the Starling and met Ken and Killian at church. After church, we all met for brunch for the first time since *The Ponte Vedra Parrot* story was blasted all over Peaceful River Valley. As we breezed into the First Watch, you could almost hear the collective gasp – as if we were a parade of circus elephants waltzing through. Eyes bugged out, whispers flew faster than gossip at a bingo night. "Look, it's Killian, the 'killer'," they murmured, as if he hadn't been just another Ponte Vedra dude, surfing his life away here. The only thing Killian ever killed was time at the beach, and maybe the occasional brain cell with one too many surf boards to the head. Everyone knew he was more protector than predator, unless you counted his vigilant defense of the last slice of bacon at brunch.

"Killian, what types of questions did they ask you at the police station?" I asked once we slipped into the largest booth in the restaurant.

"Yea, they were all over the map. At first it seemed like they didn't know who died and questioned me about who it was in your garage. Of course, I didn't know, so I wasn't helpful." Killian looked around to find a few lingering stares coming from the nearby tables.

"Well, it's over now and we can put it behind us," Aunt Dottie pulled down her reading glasses from on top of her head and opened the menu.

"It may be over, but will anyone around here forget?" Kat added, looking over her shoulder at the tables behind her for only a moment.

"No harm, no foul," Ken threw his menu on the pile at the end of the table. Clearly, he knew what he wanted.

"Ken, you are amazing. How do you forgive so quickly? It's like a male trait in this family." Quickly realizing I referred to Uncle Connie, who no one at the table knew about except me and Aunt Dottie. My fingers fumbled with the menu as I quickly opened it, my cheeks burning, and tried to hide my face. I felt Aunt Dottie's leg kick my ankle under the table.

"Ya know what is weird..." Killian paused waiting for anyone to react.

"Hmm... what?" I replied quickly, still hiding behind my menu. I waited for the family to pepper me with questions about what I meant. I can't lie to them. I'm terrible at this secret stuff. I'm gonna break or it will fester inside my soul.

"They had more questions for me about the fires in the Peaceful River Valley Town Center area, then they did about the dead guy. Almost like they knew I did not have anything to do with the murder, or heart attack as it would turn out."

This was a curious turn. Before I could pull my menu down and react, Kat said, "Interesting... do you think they knew you were innocent the entire time?"

"What did they want to know about the fires?" I asked, putting my menu down. I was relieved we were moving off the subject of my omissions.

"Just if I knew the various families. Where I was on the days of the fires."
Killian laughed, "like I could recall where I was on all those dates without
a calendar."

Aunt Dottie turned over her coffee mug waiting for the pretty, young
waitress to fill it with the smooth nectar, her eyes keenly on Killian who was
smiling way south of the waitress's face as her cross necklace dangled on her
apron. "Killian, it's too early in the day for you to be acting like that."

Still mesmerized, without even moving his eyes Killian asked "Like what
now?"

"As Pastor Joby would say... a wretched, self-indulgent, depraved sinner.
Now... I just won't tolerate that behavior... before noon." Aunt Dottie
playfully scowled and nailed his knuckle with her coffee spoon.

"Owe... yes, ma'am." Killian shook his right hand and downed his eyes at
his mug and then back up to the girl's face and dazzled her with his gleaming
smile. Her flushed apple cheeks raised as her lips smirked to one side and
she winked at Killian. Killian's hand secured the cup steady, as she filled his
cup of coffee as she held her hand on his.

Killian's mouth opened and I knew they would be couple before the day
was out, if not before the end of brunch. I should probably add another
place setting to the table tonight, just in case. Thank goodness, all eyes on
Killian and not me.

"That is weird, Killian. Do the police suspect you?" Aunt Dottie asked
without looking up from the menu.

"Nah, I don't think so." Killian sipped his coffee, still watching the
waitress walk away.

"Oh please, Aunt Dottie. The only thing Killian ever lit on fire was me,
and that was mostly my fault for wearing a bell sleeve while cooking."

Killian's jaw dropped, a look of stunned disbelief etched on his face as
he desperately searched my eyes and expression for answers. "How do you
do that? How do you know me so well? You're like a soul surfer... riding
the waves of my spirit." Killian waxed poetic, his words flowing like a river,
painting vivid images with his eloquent speech.

We all blinked at Killian, half-expecting a "dude" to tumble out. Aunt Dottie finally broke the silence. "What do you mean?"

"That was exactly what I told the police... that the only thing I ever torched was KayKay and that wasn't even my fault anyway. It's like she saw the transcripts or was chilling in my brain." Killian leaned back, grinning. "KayKay, you're freaking me out—you know me so well, it's like God hit 'shuffle' on my soul and you've been jamming to my playlist since the '70s!"

The table erupted with laughter and the curious stares from around the restaurant tripled towards our direction. I was relieved the conversation never came back to my comment, as I had no way to explain myself.

After brunch, I let Aunt Dottie drive the Moke back home to The Ranch. As we pulled across the brick pavers at the entrance of The Ranch, I realized we only had a few more weeks of Sunday Supper before Kat moved out and I was an empty nester. A little over a week ago, my world was so small and simple. I was a pseudo-mom to my two brothers and one younger sister. Between then and now, I found an older sister, stolen at birth, discovered my Aunt Dottie was heir to most of the land in St Johns County, a previously thought dead Uncle was still alive, and the mystery of my parents' accident was solved, at least for me. I now held the secret of my parents' death in my heart and head. I decided I should write down all I knew and leave it in a safety deposit box for my family upon my death. Along with the letters from Robert Flannery. If I could keep the secret that long.

Kat was moving out. That sounded so sad. How would I survive without caring for someone or something. Maybe I should get a dog? Or maybe I should start one of the many side businesses I dreamed of the past twenty years. Perhaps one of them would make enough money to support myself and be more fun than working the grind. I guess I didn't need to make as much money now that Kat is through college and moving out. It's just me and my potential new dog. I could do anything else now and follow my entrepreneur's dreams. Heck, if I could make as much money clipping toenails, I would do it rather than work in IT for the next ten years.

The Moke jolted from side to side as we leapt over the curb on my side. I watched as Aunt Dottie pulled into the driveway at maximum speed, and I was afraid she may crash into the porch. I was suddenly aware that I was in a trance. "Aunt Dottie." She was not slowing down. "Aunt Dottie." I said louder and she turned to me.

"What dear?" she smiled at me.

I pulled the emergency break up and we bounced off the hibiscus plant that Killian had just planted for me at the beginning of spring. Kat bounced off the back of my seat, undoubtedly looking at her phone and not even aware of our impending doom.

"Oh goodness. Stop touching the controls while I'm driving, dear. You know how I hate when you interfere." Aunt Dottie said as I unhooked my seat belt and pulled a beautiful, big, pink flower out of my lap.

"Ok Aunt Dottie. Thanks for getting us home safely. I appreciate you." I gave her a kiss on the cheek. I waited for her to make her way into the house, then moved the vehicle out of the flower bed. I decided I would not let this gorgeous flower go to waste. I grabbed my shears and cut five more just like it. I pulled the little arrangement together and went inside on a quest for a small vase.

I arranged my flowers in the vase and added water. They would make a lovely center piece arrangement for the dining room table. I smiled at how lovely it looked in the center of the place-setting arrangements for eight today, instead of five.

Kat went straight to her room. Aunt Dottie sat on the couch with her book and started reading. "Let me know if you need any help there, KayKay."

"Thanks Aunt Dottie, I got it. You rest."

Ken and Killian walked into the kitchen from the garage and the door-bell rang. Killian looked over at me at the stove and said, "I'll get the door, KayKay."

"That's either Jess or Perdi and Mac," I yelled over my shoulder as he walked towards the front door.

I greeted Perdi and Mac with a hug. Mac immediately went to work in the kitchen prepping the lasagna noodles in the pan and making layers.

"What is wrong, Kat? You look absolutely mad." Perdi said as she kissed Kat on the forehead.

"I'm moving out and Kyra won't let me take my furniture in my bedroom or podcast study. Ken refuses to co-sign a loan for me for a new house, so I will need to rent a place instead of buy a place. Plus, I lost out on great content on my channel with this secret because it was first exposed via The Parrot. Personally, I'm having a rough week." Kat said as she crossed her arms and gave me evil eye.

Perdi laughed at Kat and hugged her, saying "But you gained an older sister that will donate some furniture to you, if you would like.""Really, Perdi? That would be great!"

"Kat, Ken and I are not going to co-sign loans for you. You went to law school. You took the bar exam and passed on the first try without hardly studying. Please get a steady job to supplement your so called influencer career." I internally cringed at the thought of influencing being a career and continued handing Mac firm noodles while he placed them meticulously in the pan.

"I want to do this full time. I don't think you understand." Kat whined.

"You are right, Kat. I don't understand. You said you wanted to be a lawyer, you spent so much time and energy on getting here. Now you accomplished your goal but you don't want to get a job," I tried to convey my displeasure in the softest tone possible.

"That podcast is not a money maker, Kat. Plus... it's a sporadic stream of income," Aunt Dottie added wisely. Although I don't know how Aunt Dottie knew more about Kat and her podcast than I did. It felt like we were ganging up on Kat. But I wasn't her mother anymore. She had to defend herself and make her own decisions.

"It feels like you should try a steadier career for constant, consistent income. Then you can save and buy that house you want... all on your own," Ken guided her.

In an upbeat voice I added, "you can still create content part-time and on weekends."

Perdi was witnessing all the family guide Kat. We didn't want her to get distracted by the next shinny thing before she at least tried a career in law after all that work. "I need an assistant at the law firm. Do you want to apply for a job with my firm? I would love to try to get you started with the law. I tried to get Mac involved but he prefers the culinary route, as apparently so does KayKay.".

Perdi was saving the day. Kat's eyes grew big. "Really? That would be fantastic. Could you really help me get started in law?" Kat hugged Perdi and that was all it took was a big sister stepping into the rescue. A big sister, that was not me.

Killian served everyone a beverage. I glared over at Perdi in utter amazement at her powers over Kat. "Perdi, you have a superpower. With one sentence, you willed what Kat needed most in her world... a chance." I hoisted my wooden spoon in the air with a victorious arms up in celebration. Mac quickly cleaned the tomato sauce from the white cabinets behind me.

As Mac mixed up a ricotta concoction that smelled like garlic, I went back to spooning sauce on my noodles. The aroma was pleasing and would flavorfully moisten the meat sauce in the lasagna. The conversations were now around Perdi and the mystery of Aggie Flannery. Perdi was filling in the gaps for Aunt Dottie, Jess, Ken, and Killian. They hung on to her every word and stared in awe.

For at least the moment, I've circumvented a continued investigation into Aggie Flannery that could expose our Mom as the poisoner and our uncle as the murderer. Did this make me a faithful member of the family? Or was I now keeping secrets and betraying the trust of everyone at this table? I just needed more time to think through how to tell them all I know... without exposing Uncle Connie. I was confident I would find a way.

I leaned up against the counter, sipped my Scotch, and watched my best friend, my Aunt, my new family, and my siblings converse in my home. We were having cocktails and cooking pasta just the way a Sunday afternoon should be with the ones you love. It was a good feeling to be surrounded by the most important people in my life. In that moment, I was not merely blessed; I was awakened to the eternal truth that life's deepest meaning is found in the shared moments of joy and the unspoken bonds of friends and family. Also known as 'framily'.

Epilogue

K^{yra,}

    You don't know me but we are connected. First you should know, I am not guilty of the crime that incarcerated me, but I am guilty of getting away with murder. I was paid, to run down and kill Susie Boyle, your sister's adoptive mother. Then our paths crossed again when I chased down your parents as they fled Mother's home on the day she died. They tried to hide under the Palm Valley Bridge, but the mud gave out and their car slid down the ravine, hit a barrier of rocks, flipped over and submerged. It is important for me to remember the person I used to be because now I look towards the cross. I did not live a good life, but in here, I found God. I do have Jesus in my heart and through His grace I am saved through my faith. He got me and now I'm right before God.

    In reconciliation.

    Undeserving,

    Robert Flannery

The End

Love this book?
Leave a Review!

E very review is incredibly valuable to authors like me! If you've enjoyed
this book, please take a moment to share your thoughts on Amazon
or wherever you bought it. Your feedback not only helps me grow as an author but also guides other readers to discover this story. I am deeply grateful
for your support and time. Your readership has touched me profoundly,
thank you.

Health & Happiness,

Suzanne

Xoxo

Read More!

Unlock the Secrets of Peaceful River Valley Before Anyone Else!
Are you eager to dive deeper into the world of Peaceful River Valley? Here's your exclusive chance:

- **Be the First to Know**: Straight to your inbox, get insider information on the release of my next book in The Ponte Vedra Series.

- **Exclusive Content**: Receive sneak peeks, deleted scenes, and behind-the-scenes stories that you won't find anywhere else.

- **Special Offers**: Enjoy early bird discounts, signed copies, and maybe even a chance to win a personalized shout-out in the book!

- **Connect with Me**: Join a community of readers who love what you love. Engage directly with me through Q&A sessions, live events, or book discussions.

All you need to do is:

Sign Up Here

SuzanneSinclairAuthor.com

Your journey into Peaceful River Valley awaits. Join now to never miss out on the latest and greatest from my writing desk to your heart.

Author Bio

S uzanne spins yarns from her own life's misadventures, set in the quaint yet quirky town of Peaceful River Valley. She self-publishes these tales for anyone craving an escape into a world where characters live, laugh, and sometimes get a bit tortured (but in a loving way, of course).

Suzanne's stories are a wild dance between the dark and the light, promising to play mind games with your sense of reality. Will you survive the journey? Only one way to find out...

Dive into Suzanne's world at SuzanneSinclairAuthor.com or join the fun on social media @SuzSinc on Instagram and X. Beware: following might lead to sudden bursts of laughter, deep existential pondering, or both.